Ice Rose

A Young Adult Spy Novel

by

Alison Neuman

FIRESIDE PUBLICATIONS
LADY LAKE, FLORIDA

Fireside Publications
1004 San Felipe Lane
Lady Lake, Florida 32159
www.firesidepubs.com

Printed in the United States of America

All Rights Reserved. No part of this book may be reproduced, stored in a retrieval system, scanned, photocopied or distributed in any printed or electronic form without permission of the author or publisher.

This is a work of fiction. Names, characters, places and incidents are either the product of the author's imagination or are used fictitiously, and any resemblance to actual persons living or dead, events, or locales is entirely fictitious

Copyright © 2010 by Alison Neuman

ISBN: 978-1-935517-11-5

First Edition: September 2010

For additional copies of *ICE ROSE,* please visit:
www.firesidepubs.com

or contact publisher at:

Fireside Publications
1004 San Felipe Lane
Lady Lake, Florida 32159
USA

Ice Rose

Acknowledgements

Thanks to:
My fellow students in PROW Publishing Prose (2004-2005) for providing both me and Elissa with a nourishing environment while we found our style and voice,

All the instructors and support staff in Grant MacEwan, especially for the Bachelor of Applied Communications in Professional Writing Degree (2001-2006), for giving me a foundation on which to build my writing career,

Nicole Badorek for chauffeuring, taking pictures, and confidence, Shelley Reichelt for leaping into Elissa's world and helping her to jump off the page, Jaclyn Kshyk for untangling the meaning sometimes lost in the semantics, BD Wilson for making my passage onto the Internet highway a stress free transition, Cheryl Kaye Tardif for opportunities, coaching, advice, and inspiration, Jeff Rivera for providing me the road map to travel the publishing world. Stephanie Frazer and Nora Pelizzari for the editorial enthusiasm that added color and clarity to subsequent drafts of Ice Rose,

Our family, friends, and neighbors for patience in waiting for the opportunity to read Ice Rose, Linda Robinson for being my fan and supporter, Ashley Griffin for the advice, Ted Bretzer for decoding the world of computers,

Special thanks to:
Lois Bennett for her believing, her passion, editing, and shaping Ice Rose with a passport to explore the world,

Fireside Publications for providing the Ice Rose characters an unlimited ticket to explore the world and make this adventure possible,

Each character in Ice Rose, thank you for being great friends and allowing me to ride along with all your adventures.

Dedication

This book is dedicated to my mom, Vi, for exploring the world by my side; to my dad, Bill, for giving me a refuge; to my brother, Cliff, for providing me an inspiring example; to my sister-in-law, Sandy, for exceeding my every expectation; and to Uncle Ingmar for bestowing me an unspoken understanding.

Ice Rose

TORONTO, CANADA. February 11. On Monday, January 31, an explosion rocked the Treble Time studios. Christopher Morris, his wife and daughter, were believed to be inside at the time of the explosion. John Marks, chief investigator in the Treble case, said at a press conference Saturday that "the debris at Treble Time studio has been examined and Christopher Morris was not found."

Marks continued, "Evidence found indicates Christopher was alive and removed from the scene by force. The CIA and the FBI have joined our search."

Mr. Morris' wife Stephanie has bruises and a broken wrist. His fifteen-year-old daughter Elissa sustained serious injuries and is now unable to walk. Both are in stable condition at Mount Sinai Hospital.

Christopher Morris is best known for his 2004 song "Better Be Good," which stayed on top of the Billboard charts for twelve weeks. He was in Canada recording his new album that was to be released November 11 of this year. Joan Fairchild, an Upbeat Records spokesperson, said, "We have set up a twenty thousand dollar reward for information leading to Christopher's safe return." The police are not releasing the names of any suspects or details of their leads at this time.

Ice Rose

One

Baggage

June 28

Elissa was searching for an identity to the voice she had heard after the explosion. There was a voice that had threatened to come after Stephanie and Lissy, and it had stayed in her head, in her nightmares, since the accident. She kept feeling like she and Stephanie were not getting the full truth, with all the missing pieces from the agency's investigating. If she could get into the Agent Links Network, finding the information would be simple. But access, to a separate Agent Links Network non-public server, along with the hard copy mission file, was stored on the Ocean-Alias Campus of Madisyn Academy. And the campus was in an undisclosed location, at most times of the year. It was on a cruise ship, where she could only gain access if she were a student attending the program.

After staying at their Ontario cabin for a month, both Elissa and Stephanie knew they needed to face life and the cruel reality of Christopher's disappearance. A reality that every independence gadget and tool did not address. A reality even her custom climbing and lowering wheelchair would not fix.

The first room she drove into at home was the dance studio Christopher built to rehearse his stage show. This was her favorite room, which she was allowed to share with him so she could also practice. Half the room was decorated with dancing posters and articles, while in the far corner stood a clothes rack with all her costumes hanging and waiting for the upcoming performances. Her heart fell a bit when she realized they would never, ever be worn again, at least not by her. She took small comfort in the fact that they would be donated. Christopher's half full bottle of water, covered with dust, still rested on the floor next to his towel. A black baby grand piano, crowded into the corner, still held his sheet music and the last edition of *Flying* magazine he had been reading reading.

Elissa looked at the wall calendar, still showing the month of January, before the accident. Her contemporary jazz and ballet classes, three hours each weekday evening and six on Saturdays, and monthly shows were marked in pink. Christopher's weekday eight-hour recording sessions, personal training sessions, and weekend stage rehearsing time was marked in blue. Stephanie had meetings every Monday, Wednesday and Friday mornings, marked in green. Still, she was always home to have supper with Elissa and drive her to her dance classes or recitals. Sundays had family day pencilled in red ink. Only when her father was recording in one stationary place, could the idea of family Sundays even be a faint possibility.

Elissa's practice dance shoes were waiting in the corner where she had last left them. She flicked the power on and the projector started to play tape of a dance recital from when she was a kid. She and Christopher watched old performances to try to improve them. Elissa wanted to look away from the video but couldn't stop watching the girl dancing and smiling. She found herself smiling as she remembered being on the stage, in that moment, and letting the music move her around. It was hard for her to remember her body gliding effortlessly and seamlessly across the dance floor. Before the accident, the movement had come so naturally.

She turned off the projector and drove to the barres, putting on the wheelchair brakes and attempting to pull herself up. Her muscles tightened and pain shot down her legs. With a deep breath, she tried to lift her right leg up onto the barre, but it wouldn't reach. Cursing, she pushed away from her chair and fought to step along holding onto the barre. Staring into the full-length mirror, she let go and attempted sliding her foot towards the wall, then pulled it towards her left leg. Intense pain shot into her hip and knee in her left leg as it folded and she crashed onto the floor mat. Tears ran down her face. She ripped off her ballerina watch and threw it across the room at one of her dad's framed gold records. How did this happen? Who had stolen her legs from her, not to mention her father?

Madisyn Academy. That's where the answers are. That's where I need to be. She smiled ruefully. Would Dad hate that? Would they even let her attend being in a wheelchair? The regular world was a challenge enough and the world of secret agents would surely have additional regulations, but attending was something she needed to do.

The door swung open. Stephanie ran over and sat down next to her.

"It's all over," Elissa said softly. "My dancing. My friends. I'm ready. I want to go to Madisyn Academy."

"To be a pilot?" Stephanie looked at her. "That's a good idea."

"To be a CSIS, or FBI agent – to fly planes – to be in the Edmonton Ridge residence like you and Dad."

"Your father wouldn't approve. It's too dangerous."

"Dad lost his vote when he put his job as a field agent above us." Elissa grabbed Stephanie's hand. "You chose to work in technology and science and not be a dangerous field op. Please, I need to find a place for myself."

"But honey," Stephanie said, brushing the bangs out of Elissa's face. "You've never shown any interest in intelligence programs before."

Elissa thought about the two days before she left the rehabilitation hospital. On one of their regular evening walks, in the warmth of the spring sunshine, Stephanie had taken her to a park area behind the hospital. They'd sat at a picnic table and Stephanie had set down a portable radio.

Each time Elissa asked, Stephanie had avoided her questions about Christopher's disappearance. Stephanie reached into her purse to pull out her BlackBerry. This time changing the topic or using an urgent telephone call or message to return was not going to stand in the way. Elissa's cheeks flushed. She leaned over, grabbed the phone from Stephanie and held it in her lap.

"Ugh. I want the truth. What really happened? Now!"

Stephanie took a deep breath, exhaled and stared past Elissa towards the trees.

"I'm involved whether you like it or not. I have a right to know." Elissa moved her wheelchair in Stephanie's view until they made eye contact.

Stephanie looked around, turned up the volume on the radio and leaned in towards her.

"You're right," she'd said. "You deserve to know. While your dad was a singer he was also a…" She lowered her voice even more, "secret agent."

Elissa had laughed, looking around her, thinking this was another diversion on Stephanie's behalf. Stephanie's face was serious. Elissa's mind had never considered a secret agent – maybe an officer working undercover – maybe he was a witness to a crime, but never a secret agent. Agents were just in the movies, books and on television and not anyone's Dad. She shifted in her wheelchair as she processed the information, while not giving Stephanie any indication of the thoughts swirling in her head.

"Your dad and I are both agents – both members of COOL (Central Organization Operative League). Christopher was working on a clandestine operation. This aftermath is related to an incident at the studio. Not that I can prove my hypothesis. Stupid Agent Links red tape and their security have led me to many dead ends."

Elissa's heart sunk in her chest and she felt her stomach churn. Despite the occasional argument, she always considered herself close to her parents. Well, as close as a fifteen-year-old could be with their parents. Christopher had an honesty policy in which, if she needed either of them, she could call and they would come get her, no questions asked. How hypocritical had they been to expect her to be honest when both of them were keeping the biggest secret ever from her?

"Why'd you keep this from me? Didn't you trust me?"

"We were trying to protect you."

"Great job Dad did of that." Tears rolled down Elissa's cheeks and she hid her face with her hands. Stephanie leaned over and hugged her.

"There's still no official cause for the accident but it's presumed the studio had been rigged. They think the explosive device was on one of the support beams."

"Did they find Dad's …um," Elissa quietly sobbed. Elissa noticed one man in a suit hiding behind a tree and wondered who was following them. She turned her head to see if anyone else was watching them.

"No."

"Are those men watching us from the agency?"

"Honey, they insisted we have security."

"Haven't they done enough?" Elissa scowled at the partially hidden suit and then looked at Stephanie. "So was anything about you true?"

"Everything we told you was true, even about Madisyn Academy."

August 31: Day One

Elissa sat on her bed and put on her required Madisyn Academy uniform – a boring blue dress shirt and her ironed black dress pants knowing that now was not a time for individuality; rather she should try to blend in. Still deep inside her heart was a negative voice undermining her confidence and making her wonder if she could even manage by herself. She sang along to a dance compilation jamming from her Runlink phone, which had all the features of an iPhone but included satellite range, required for her classes, but instead it was filled with her own music, photos and pieces of her life she'd miss. A phone that warned it only worked four floors below ground and 20 feet under water. Somehow the thought that she might need to call underwater did nothing to make her feel more secure about the tasks they would ask of the students at Madisyn.

As she put her orthopedic insoles in her runners, a small piece of paper fell out. She reached, over-balanced, and landed on the floor with her comforter balled up next to her.

Her legs ached and burned against the hard wood. Bending her knees was painful and took some time before she could brace herself enough to move them. Elissa rolled onto her stomach and, arm by arm, went back over to the bed. When she turned to put the piece of paper on the sheets, her dad's framed photo, with his brown-streaked bangs obstructing his green eyes tipped off the nightstand. He held a huge pair of scissors and was cutting a ribbon for his funded elementary bridge school in Namibia, She picked it up. Her heart ached when she thought how he wouldn't be there to teach her how to drive, to scare away her first boyfriend and have another game of basketball with her.

"You promised you'd always be here, but you were only here when it fit your schedule. You did this to me and left us to pick up the pieces."

She threw the picture into her bean bag chair. For a minute she sat on the floor against the bed, tears streaming down her face, while she waited for the throbbing in her knees and hips to subside. *Stupid knees. Stupid hips.*

Elissa suppressed the frustration and the anger and for just a moment her heart felt empty, aware that she'd thrown away the photo of a dad she missed more with each day. A dad, who understood her at a level no one else could and who appreciated her passion for music and dancing and animals and Original Glazed Krispy Kreme donuts.

She used her hands to pull herself over and up onto the bed. Her heart raced as she looked at the paper. It said:

> THANK YOU FOR CHOOSING ESFR PRODUCTS. PLEASE SEE THE BACK OF THIS SHEET FOR INSTRUCTIONS FOR THE SECRET COMPARTMENT LOCATED IN YOUR RIGHT SHOE.

She pulled out the insole and tapped on the sole. Sure enough a small door slid down to reveal a rectangular compartment big enough to hold a deck of playing cards and a toothbrush, which she knew could come in handy. She reached into her bedside table, pulled out a nail file and placed it in the compartment before she put her insole in and her shoes on. Then she picked up her vests. The formal vests were a light, silky fabric that contrasted with the rough canvas material of the everyday vests. The design was brutal and she wondered who had created such functional but boring attire.

She sifted through her vest pockets and pulled out the tiny individual instructions. Each vest was ESFR certified, which stood for **E**mergency **S**ecured **F**ormulated

Regulators. Each ESFR certified item had a special feature. One pocket had a pull tab like a beach ball to allow the user to inflate the vest. Two pockets had secured carabineer harness hooks.

Wall climbing had been one of Christopher's chosen Sunday afternoon physical activities for the family. Elissa and Christopher had raced to the top of the climbing wall, with Christopher winning, as usual. When Stephanie went, Christopher was right next to her, encouraging her to climb up to the top, while Elissa stood at the bottom screaming and cheering her along.

Physical exercise of any kind was not Stephanie's idea of a good time, but she made it to the top and beamed as she looked at Elissa. The Sunday before the accident, the activity was Stephanie's choice: the science centre.

While Christopher and Elissa would never admit it to Stephanie, they actually looked forward to her educational choices. She missed the weekly activities that ended when Christopher went missing, but physical activities would now prove challenging if not impossible.

One narrow side pocket was designed to hold a miniature oxygen tank when provided. She put her Runlink into one pocket then grabbed her mirrored wrap around silver Academy-approved prescription sunglasses and read the instructions: **Press the left arm button for low grade night vision.** *Can't wait to try that out*, Elissa thought as she slid on her vest.

Some of the supplies for Academy purchased online weeks ago would surely get her into trouble. She had taken the code breaker one afternoon and sat outside their garage, trying to get the rolling code to gain entry. Christopher had purchased the best door remote opener with the biggest amount of rolling codes for the garage where he stored his Harley Davidson Motorcycle collection. It took Elissa about ten minutes with the code breaker to get into the garage. Stephanie was not at all pleased that she was able to gain entry by finding the code.

Rummaging through her black messenger bag with the logo for Madisyn Academy, Elissa pulled out her list and double checked to make sure she had everything. The night before, she had packed her bag with all the required items she could order online, including the electronic textbooks, which were loaded into her new Eliminator Seven laptop. It was the size of a paperback book, but with many features, including voice dictation software, but it had no games installed. It had definite possibilities, being so small and portable, but needed desperately to have some games downloaded. After making a disk with a hacking program which she was going to load onto it, she wished she could have had Christopher and Jon's *Ice Rose* program. The program, she was convinced, either contained information about Christopher's last mission, perhaps indicating his current location or who might have kidnapped him, if he was kidnapped at all.

Christopher and Jon were always challenging her knowledge of computers with new security and websites to access. Sometimes she did wonder why they were into breaking into secure sites but she presumed that it was to improve security. When the truth came out about them being agents, the hacking took on more of a purpose for her.

She remembered borrowing Jon's laptop to work on school projects during breaks in rehearsal when she was under deadline. Once, while she was supposed to be working, she found an installed program called *Ice Rose*. Three hours later, her curiosity had guided her past the entry virus, which began if the fingerprints and passwords were not entered in a specific amount of time. Jon had his fingerprint saved on the system and his passwords were easy to figure out, so gaining access before the virus kicked in was easy. She then decided to add Christopher's fingerprint and her password and fingerprint, thinking Jon needed a greater challenge. So while Jon was at a conference with Christopher, she'd borrowed his laptop and put those items in place. When he discovered she had been into the program, he refused to let her borrow the computer again. Christopher had also given her a lecture about using his personal information and identity, which he changed immediately. It was weird behaviour for both of them, but they refused to discuss it with her further. She let it go, but getting into the network was something she could not let go of.

She finished all the changes and ran the *Ice Rose* program, stunned by the black screen and white codes that came up for just a second before a prompt screen appeared asking the user to enter the website it wished to explore. She entered the COOL website, Central Organization Operative League, of which Christopher and Stephanie were members. The program allowed her to hack into the website and open invisible doors which allowed access into whatever she wanted to review and change. At the time, she couldn't understand why either Christopher or Jon would require a program to hack into secure sites but that changed when the truth about them being secret agents was revealed.

Electronic Textbooks:
Gadgets and Gizmos – T.V. Fessenden
The Giant Book of Codes and Signals – M. C. Dash
Introductory Computing for Agents – S. W. Bytes.
Speed Reading and Memorization – T. A. Synapsis
Introductory Aviation – Amelia Wright
Technology, uniform and gadgets
1 Runlink phone (Color of choice)
1 Hyperlink beeper (Color of choice)

1 Climbing kit (Color of choice)
1 Codebreaker
1 lock-pick kit
1 portable scanner

Optional Supplies*:*
New Student Kit (Included)
Identi-cover (privacy protection)
Secret Diary (enabled with a fingerprint identification system)
1 Madisyn Academy Key Shaped USB drive
Meltaway Paper with activation liquid
Invisible/Visible pens
Speckles Chews (smoke for cover)

When Elissa's school items came to the house, Stephanie went through the items with her. Elissa thought the gum sounded stupid.

"Elissa, it smokes and gives you time to run for cover." Stephanie pulled out a piece, chewed on it and set it on the ground. It gave off smoke.

"Isn't the smoke dangerous?" Elissa leaned down and took a small whiff, which made her cough.

"No, but it tastes awful. Don't ask."

Those words stayed with her as Elissa took one last look around her bedroom – one last look at everything arranged neatly in its place, just like her life. A crystal vase and a trophy resting on the windowsill created shadows where they met the sunlight. Christopher had given Elissa the vase, and every time he departed on tours he filled it with fresh flowers. Now the carnations were dry and brittle, very unlike what they were a few months ago, similar to her feelings towards him. After the explosion, Stephanie gave Elissa the Academy Courage trophy she'd won for overcoming her intense fear of heights.

Maybe one day I'll figure out what's going on with my parents, once and for all. I'm going to miss Mom. Heck, I might even miss getting grounded.

Down the long hallway, past the cabinets filled with her dancing trophies and Stephanie's and Christopher's various awards, Elissa headed to the lift. Christopher insisted Stephanie's trophies be displayed, but she was never impressed with awards or accolades.

When she passed Stephanie's room, she noticed a large pile of clothes on the floor waiting to be laundered. The chore board had the tasks divided for each person. Her parents owned numerous houses, condos and two cabins, but didn't believe in having a maid, cook and gardener when they could do the tasks themselves when they were home. A smile spread across her face as she remembered Christopher, wearing a white hazardous material jumpsuit, gas mask, and rubber gloves, entering her room to pick up her clothes and place them in the plastic garbage bag he used to collect the laundry to take downstairs.

"Come on, they don't smell that bad," Elissa had commented.

"Lissy, protect your father." He imitated Darth Vader from "Star Wars."

"Yeah, that never gets old." He did have his moments of acting like he was seven years old. She grabbed a handful of her clothes and put them in his bag. Now everything and everyone waited for him to return.

The aroma of burning bacon joined her on the lift, making her wonder if she was stuck in some kind of time warp. Each year, on the first day of school, Christopher made the bacon since Stephanie always burned it. Obviously it wasn't a time warp, and Christopher wasn't here since this continued as a bad tradition without him.

She rolled off the lift, past the living room, and into the bright kitchen, past the island covered in Stephanie's secret pancake mix, which Lissy was sure came in a box from the grocery store. The pancakes smelled good and she was trying to enjoy the last breakfast she would have with Stephanie, for awhile at least. A guitar solo blasted from the radio on the counter next to Stephanie's mushroom and frog canisters.

"Elissa, excited about the journey to Madisyn?"

She was excited to gain access to her true past, the truth about what Christopher was really up to and the life she had been kept out of. But she wasn't sharing those details.

"No pressure. I just need to excel past the conditional acceptance week of challenges to the Ocean-Alias ship campus. Then there's my wheelchair and navigating..."

Stephanie winked one of her blue eyes at Elissa. Stephanie Morris's face was oval, her long eyelashes were curly and her skin free from blemishes, which Elissa wished they had in common. A white apron with the saying *Chef in Training* had remnants of egg, flour and butter smeared across it. The Millennium Friend Bot, Stephanie's latest invention that looked like a metallic dog, drove over to Elissa, barked and waited to be petted. Elissa understood that it was a sensor she would touch that the dog reacted to, and really when she asked for a dog, that wasn't what she had in mind. *Crash*. The waffle pan crashed to the floor.

Here Mom goes again.

The Millennium Friend Bot drove over the floor where the waffle dough was spilled, vacuuming and washing the area before it returned to the back door to keep an eye for potential intruders.

"Agent Larsson has assured me a few adjustments have been made to provide you access to the full Madisyn Academy academic experience. If you're not on the Ocean-Alias campus, it's Madisyn's loss. There's always next year."

Elissa nodded but reminded herself, *By next year the trail will be cold.*

She thought about the night at the park, many months back, at the rehabilitation hospital when Stephanie told her the truth about them being agents. When the tall man belonging to the black shoes had walked over from the bushes, Elissa recognized him but only vaguely. Once he pulled off his mirrored sunglasses, she recognized Christopher's best friend and her godfather, Mr. Larsson.

"Helmer, it's so good to see you." Stephanie had stood and hugged him when he approached.

Mr. Larsson walked over to Elissa and gave her a big hug before taking a seat across the table.

"I told her," Stephanie said as she looked at Elissa.

Those words echoed in her head but felt empty. This secret about her parents being agents had been known to so many other people, but not to her. And she had thought they shared everything. Did she even know the people she had called family? It made her heart ache. If it were possible for it to break further, after learning about Christopher and her legs, she knew for sure her heart would be shattered into pieces by now.

"Mr. Larsson, you're one of them, too." Elissa realized she'd been lied to by everyone in her life. A sickness sat in her stomach. Mr. Larsson and Christopher had visited each other every other month, even when Dad was on tour. They were as close as family.

"We went to Madisyn Academy together," Mr. Larsson began. "Your dad is…was…my best friend."

"What happened to him? Is he dead?" For a second she wondered if she really wanted to hear the truth but she needed answers to be able to piece together this puzzle for herself. "Even if you knew, you wouldn't tell us would you? Stupid security rules right? But we're his family."

Elissa needed to get away, to have time to process all that was being told to her. She flicked her wheelchair to high speed and drove away. She stopped by the farthest picnic table. Mr. Larsson followed behind her. She could not understand how he could look her in the eyes and be hiding a secret – a secret that he didn't appear to feel at all guilty about withholding.

"Here's your debrief." He shoved a photo of a bald man wearing shades in front of her. "We believe Christopher was captured by this NERD-One operative, a.k.a. Mr. Russel."

A million questions swirled in her mind as she tried to absorb the news that for most of her childhood, Christopher had kept a part of himself from her. He'd managed to live a secret life without her even noticing.

How stupid could I be?

"Wait…no... All those extensions – different clothes – and his leaving in disguise. All this time Dad lived two lives. His fame was a cover for his travelling."

Who is he anyway? she wondered.

Elissa stared at her feet as she waited for the lump in her stomach to settle. All this time he was keeping this big secret from her and now these people were expecting her to trust them. Just how was she supposed to trust anyone? She couldn't let them know how this was eating her up inside or they would use the standard adult excuse she was being a typical teenager. Elissa was sure they would be riding the wave of emotions she was if the situation were reversed and the secret agent news that their family had kept from them was just being revealed.

"Christopher has been our extrication specialist and has brought many operatives home to their families. NERD-One is aware of his real identity but there is an unspoken rule between agencies, good and bad, that such information never be leaked to the outside world. Other than the four of us, you, your mom, your dad and I, this information must stay confidential. Understand, young lady?"

She understood. She'd hated it. But she understood. While she'd keep that information to herself, she needed answers – answers that came from other sources, rather than trusting Agent Larsson, and to a lesser extent, Stephanie – answers she was going to find for herself no matter how anyone felt about it.

Her Runlink beeped, bringing her attention back to the kitchen, to signal an incoming text. Elissa finished eating her waffles and bacon. Stephanie was eating her last bite. The kitchen and all the smells and sounds gave her comfort which she soaked in to take with her on her journey.

"Meet you at the entry in fifteen minutes?" Stephanie carried their plates to the sink and turned to face her.

"Absolutely."

"I'll grab my purse, put on some lipstick and get the van warmed up. It's chilly. We almost beat the sun up today." Stephanie left the room.

Elissa pulled her Runlink out of her pocket and clicked to read her two new texts. One was from Jon. He'd gone back home to Windhoek, Africa, while he waited to hear news of Christopher's location. Despite the warnings of everyone involved, he continued to investigate what had really happened to her dad and what he was working on. Jon was trying to help her get the answers she needed that were tied up in the security and privacy protocols of the Agent Links Network.

When she had found out that Jon was also a secret agent completing his training with her dad, she freaked. They were like brother and sister, and she felt betrayed. Jon kept contacting her until she caved and started emailing and texting him back. He had helped her achieve some of the requirements for Madisyn Academy, as he was about to graduate from the Academy himself, so he had a good idea on how to improve her chances of acceptance.

The text said "Good luck. If you need anything let me know. We can be a team again. Took that tech position on the Ocean-Alias. Maybe I'll see you. - Jon"

The second text didn't have a name or address she had seen before.

"Elissa. Can't remember my voice. Soon, I'll help you. Share the message, or track message and answers, or locations, and Christopher's real connections will be leaked worldwide via the media. Stephanie will also be staying with us. - The Voice."

How could this person leak the information? Mr. Larsson said there was an unspoken code. Obviously this person has no scruples.

An eerie feeling swept over her, like when the paparazzi were staked out in the bushes, taking their photographs. She turned and looked out the window but couldn't see anyone. She stared at the screen. Her mind raced. *How did they get my number? How am I supposed to keep this from Stephanie?*

Her hands shook as she tried to save the message but accidentally deleted it instead.

Two

Ghosts

August 31

Elissa slid her phone into her vest pocket and drove out of the kitchen. The living room held several burgundy pieces of furniture and was where the family watched movies on their massive plasma television. On the very rare occasions when Christopher was home, Stephanie made popcorn and his responsibility was the beverages.

He could sing, play four instruments, and write chart-topping songs but, despite his flare for bacon, to microwave popcorn was a challenge he had yet to master. Usually they watched a romantic comedy, and usually Stephanie and Christopher would give each other that look – a look which grossed Elissa out and made her wonder if they were aware she was still in the room. Sometimes Christopher picked his action flicks then she and Stephanie exchanged looks as Christopher repeated the lines. The couch was worn where she and Stephanie spent so many nights watching movies together.

The memories broke her heart. *How can I leave Stephanie*, she wondered. *Who will take care of her?*

After taking a deep breath, Elissa aimed for the front door and put on her black vinyl jacket. She looked at the entry mirror, brushed her long blonde hair and placed it in a pink ponytail holder to cover up the thinning spots from her arthritic medication. Her face used to be slim, like Stephanie's but now it was round from the medication. Prominently, in the middle of her face sat her long nose so like Christopher's. Every time she sneezed, Stephanie teased about the small sneeze coming out of such a big bugle. She looked at her blue eyes through her small framed glasses and smiled at the opportunity ahead of her.

As the front door opened, a cool fall wind brushed against her face, and sent nervous shivers through her. Every year, on the first day of school, she wondered what challenges would await her. In some small way, it comforted her that her feelings about Madisyn were the same.

Stephanie already had the lift down, on the side of their metallic blue Hybrid mini-van. She was wearing a floor length skirt, *as usual*, and her favourite baby blue angora cardigan that Christopher brought back from Paris. He'd told her it made her eyes a brighter blue.

"In a few hours you'll be on your journey. Excited?"

"Nervous, actually." Elissa forced a smile as she wheeled herself onto the lift. "New surroundings; new people; and new subjects. What if I don't fit in?"

"No *what ifs*. You'll do fine," Stephanie assured her as she leaned over.

Once Elissa had driven into the passenger's side, where the seat was removed to accommodate tracks to lock in her wheelchair and Stephanie secured the wheelchair to the floor, they pulled away. Elissa took one more look at the house and the safety she'd miss.

"So, why is Mike's comic book place close to the airport anyways?"

"The property is a cover for Madisyn Academy. You'll see how convenient it is."

"Mom, remember when Dad would take us camping and he'd barbeque?" Elissa eyed the state park pass stuck on the dashboard.

"He'd bring his acoustic guitar…" A faint smile appeared on Stephanie's face.

"And sing around the campfire."

"Elissa, those were good times." Elissa's mother adjusted the rear view mirror for a distraction from the tears that had sprung to her eyes.

Seizing the moment, Elissa tried to ask, "Why did he …?"

Stephanie turned to face Elissa. "Honey, he believed he was making the world a better place."

"I know, but…how selfish," Elissa trailed off.

"I'm mad too, honey."

"Really?" Elissa looked at her and smiled. She was glad that she was not the only one who was angry.

She nodded as they drove onto the front street. The old elm trees cast shadows on the houses and hinted at the truth about each neighbour's story. There was Mr. Jenkins, who always came over when her dad worked in the front yard. He came and went at odd hours, and he had a new car every few weeks. Maybe she was being snoopy, but it never hurt any of the detectives in the movies her family watched.

She looked out the window at Mr. Jenkins' house, keeping her eyes on his front yard as the car rolled past. He had a photograph of his wife and daughter but said he was divorced and had lost custody to his bitter wife. He kept his curly blonde hair short, and always wore a tweed jacket, black dress pants and a crisp white shirt.

The basement light was often on late at night, but by day the house was quiet. Elissa regularly walked past his house and front driveway. Once, in the middle of the night, she'd thought she heard muffled yelling. She stumbled to the window half asleep, and saw a man entering his house but never saw him leave, so she kept an eye out every time there was a noise.

One day, as she strolled by Mr. Jenkins' driveway, the garage door opened and he sped out in an orange sports car. At the edge of the trunk lid, material that looked like a piece of a red jacket stuck out against the orange paint. She was sure it had to be the coat belonging to the visitor who had never left – but now the car was coming at her and wasn't going to stop. She processed the information but couldn't move in time. He screeched to a stop just as he nudged her with his back bumper. Elissa fell to the cool driveway. Looking up at the car, she saw that his back left brake light had been knocked out.

"Elissa, I didn't see you there!" Mr. Jenkins, ran to her, blocking her view of the trunk. "Need an ambulance?" He asked as he bent down, his hazel eyes temporarily distracting her.

"No. I think I'm okay…" Elissa was numb, in shock and didn't feel any pain or bruising. She was too preoccupied by what he was hiding.

"I'll get your dad." Mr. Jenkins dialed his cell.

Elissa sat up and rubbed her right leg where bruises were starting to form. She heard voices behind her. As she grabbed onto the bumper to pull herself up, she looked into the trunk through the missing brake light. If she could just find out where the visitor went from the other night without being obvious, then maybe she could get the lingering doubts that Mr. Jenkins was up to no good out of her head. Mr. Jenkins leaned against the trunk, in a very intimidating manner, keeping her from answering her own questions.

Christopher ran up to Elissa.

"Lissy, are you all right?"

She continued to stand, knowing Christopher was there now, and that would be the end of her investigation.

"I'm fine."

"Let's get you home, clumsy," Christopher said. He picked her up and turned towards their house. When they returned home, she told Christopher about the jacket and the man. She told him about her feeling and the weird hours and visitors she had witnessed. All she wanted was for someone to go over to the house, check the car, and find out if she was making something out of nothing.

"Your curiosity and imagination will indubitably get you into trouble, young lady."

She forgot about it for awhile, until late one summer evening when she was playing basketball in her backyard. The ball bounced across the fence and into Mr. Jenkins' yard. This wasn't the first time a ball had ended up there, and Mr. Jenkins had never objected to Elissa or her friends retrieving their things. So Elissa ran next door, as usual. When she bent down to pick up the basketball, she caught a glimpse of a silhouette through a piece of cardboard falling off the basement window. As she grabbed the ball, she tried to focus on the shadow. It almost looked like a person tied to a chair, like in a spy movie.

Footsteps came down the back stairs. She ran back over to her yard as fast as she could. Later that night, she talked to Christopher before he went to help Mr. Jenkins build a deck. By the time he'd gone to the house, the cardboard was off the windows and the basement had been freshly painted and hung with orange and brown wall paper. Christopher tried to reassure her that she just had an active imagination. She knew it was more than that.

She overheard Christopher and Stephanie discussing how odd it was that Mr. Jenkins had wallpapered the basement in a brown and orange flower paper overnight, as if he was trying to hide something. Elissa hadn't thought much about Mr. Jenkins lately. Now that she was leaving, she didn't feel like she'd miss him exactly, but maybe would miss having a reason to think about him at all. Besides, right after Christopher went missing, he was transferred, for his job, whatever that was, to New York, so someone else was leasing his house.

Elissa and Stephanie waited for the light to change and then merged into the main lane of traffic. A swarm of cars raced past them. The last time they drove Christopher to the airport there had been banks of white snow. Now the leaves were painted various shades of green. Life was so much simpler then. Simpler at a time when the world, people and future seemed to be safe and sprawled out in front of her.

"Today I was supposed to be on Dad's Paris tour."

"He'd be proud of you," Stephanie said, turning to face her. "Proud you're moving past what might have been."

Elissa wasn't sure in that moment if she needed Christopher to be proud. Inside she knew she was going for selfish reasons. She wasn't moving on at all, rather still dredging up the past to find the answers she needed. She was glad her mom couldn't read her thoughts.

"Even going to Madisyn?"

She briefly glanced away from the road and to Elissa.

"He'd understand your passion for flying. The intelligence part would be an issue."

"When he comes home alive…right?"

Elissa studied Stephanie to gather some hope that he really was going to come home. Stephanie's face became serious, and she turned her head to check the rear view mirror as she changed lanes.

"He needs to come back. He's got unfinished business. You know how he is about tying up loose ends. I keep expecting him to walk in the door."

"Ditto." Elissa nodded, reached into her bag and pulled out her worn acceptance letter and read it.

Dear Elissa,

Madisyn Academy is internationally certified, field accredited and acclaimed for real world training. Our instructors are Madisyn Academy alumni, field and intelligence agents, military, aviation, law enforcement and wilderness survival experts. Madisyn Academy takes an active role in ensuring our students learn communication, cooperation and conscience.

At Madisyn Academy, we only accept students with advanced knowledge and enormous potential. Every year Madisyn receives 5,000 applications for 500 places. For the first week, all students are on conditional acceptance and must compete in the Academy Games, through a series of mission challenges. At the end of the week, pending the results from the games and academic challenges, 200 students will begin their first year at Camp Summit to bring them up to Madisyn standards or for the lucky 300 who excel, they will be sent directly to the Ocean-Alias Campus to began advanced training.

Our students, for year one, are divided between two campuses; the Ocean-Alias, on board a cruise ship, and Camp Summit, a land-based campus. On the Ocean-Alias, our advanced students travel to exciting destinations while taking advantage of our training in world-wide locations, science and recreation facilities. At Camp Summit, students take advantage of one-on-one training and state of the art facilities. After completing a year at Camp Summit, if the students, pending approval of assessment, are ready they will join the other students on the Ocean-Alias to complete the remaining two years of the program.

Each Ocean-Alias student is placed in a team based on their achievement and lifestyle goals while attending Madisyn Academy. Edmonton Ridge focuses on academic excellence and prowess in field ops and technology. London Yard cultivates confidence and security with achievements in science and preventative planning. Sydney Arch promotes public relations through social interaction and surveillance skills.

Ninety-eight percent of Madisyn Academy graduates are currently working in their fields of specialization. Our graduates have invented field operative devices that *provide intelligence that is a step above our enemies. Our agents blend into society, collecting intelligence and infiltrating and destroying active terrorist cells. They work in law enforcement and the military to keep us safe, aviation to keep us moving, and complement their skills in search and rescue to bring the lost home all the while keeping their true identities of being a secret agent under the radar.*

"Can I hold that? We'll need it at Mike's Compound."

Elissa handed Stephanie the letter which she slid into her sweater pocket.

"He'd be glad our attendance and your grandparents' attendance and chosen fields have opened up your future. All potential students must have one relative, no less than three generations prior, who attended Madisyn Academy."

"Mom, will you be okay on your own? What're you going to do?"

Stephanie smirked and patted Elissa on her left shoulder.

"You're so sweet. I'll sure miss you. I'm going to Los Angeles to work on the Tsunami early warning system. Maybe the sun will do me good." Stephanie tilted her head left and right as she looked in the rear view mirror at her pale face.

"So you were both in Edmonton Ridge?"

"The technology program gave me the skills to invent new items like your custom secret agent wheelchair, and to improve everyday items."

Yeah, or to make them dangerous. Yet, Elissa was sitting a bit taller in her seat, proud of both her parents.

"Your dad excelled in field ops. My marks were failing and I was on academic probation. He saved me in our mandatory classes."

"Like which classes?" Elissa sat forward waiting to hear little pieces of a past that could help her future.

"Lock picking; computers; anything involving escaping. From submerged cars, buildings, ropes, you name it. I'd still be in those predicaments if he hadn't shown me his tricks."

Stephanie checked and merged into the right hand lane.

"Hold on. You had to get out of a submerged vehicle?"

No way. Elissa gulped.

Panic settled in her stomach as she flashed back to swimming at the lake and the current pulling her underwater. Doubt began to wash away all the confidence that had built up inside her. She couldn't do this! She was going to let everyone down! Taking a deep breath and letting it out slowly, she gradually pushed away the doubts. She was going to bring Christopher home – by whatever means necessary.

"Not in the first year. You'll be ready when the task comes. I just had a fear of everything – of everything until Christopher."

"He was good at that – got me over my fear of performing – dragged me onstage over and over till it didn't freak me out. I'm going to get into those files and find us the truth."

"Breaking into those files could cost you your future at Madisyn Academy. I can't encourage such plans, but I won't stop you from attending. Is that what's been bothering you?"

"Yes." Elissa turned her head away from Stephanie. She didn't want to show any trace that someone claiming to be The Voice was contacting her.

Stephanie pulled up to a red light, grabbed her wallet and handed Elissa an old worn photograph of her and Christopher at 15 in formal wear with their arms around each other. Her wavy, wispy hair hung to her waist. His was long, too. On the back of the photograph, Stephanie had handwritten "reception dance" in girly script.

"What was I thinking with that hair?" Stephanie turned her attention to the green light and drove into the intersection.

"I won't report you to the fashion police." Elissa giggled, quickly covering her mouth with her hand. "Mom, don't leave me hanging," she begged, dying for more details. She loved stories about their past.

"I didn't talk to him until we were both at Madisyn. He asked me to the reception dance. We've been together… well, were together…ever since."

"There's Mike's Compound." Stephanie let out a deep sigh as she pointed to a building straight ahead.

Three

Requirements

August 31

Several bright comic book characters decorated the huge sign next to the parking areas. Stephanie pulled into the full warehouse lot adjacent to the airport parking. An ancient rusty station wagon sped up and beat her to the last physically-challenged space. A slim woman in a grey suit with matching shoes and handbag rushed out of the rust bucket and ran across the parking lot. She wore blue eye shadow and pink blush caked so thick on her face, a house painter could have applied it. Her long brown hair was pulled back into a ponytail.

"What's up with that?" Elissa stretched out her arm to point at her; she was truly annoyed that someone who was so able bodied was being lazy and not wanting to walk the extra few steps.

Stephanie found one parking spot on the side street, in between a small coupe and a dusty truck. As Stephanie came around the van to open the door for the lift, Elissa took a deep breath and reminded herself that leaving to find the answers and draw 'The Voice' away from her mother was the best course of action. Smiling to herself, she wondered if she was now thinking like a secret agent.

As soon as Stephanie released the wheelchair, Elissa proceeded to the lift. Stephanie pulled the silver metal suitcase that matched Elissa's wheelchair out of the back of the van and set it next to where the lift would rest, in the parking lot. Elissa eyed it suspiciously and wondered if had been improved by Stephanie, as it appeared so innocent.

Just to be safe, Elissa stayed on the lift as she didn't want to be attacked by the suitcase if all the bugs weren't fixed yet.

Stephanie set the suitcase on the ground then pulled a remote the size of a video camera tape out of her pocket. She pressed some buttons and the suitcase growled like their fridge as it charged back at her. Stephanie ran in the opposite direction towards the grass curb but the suitcase cut her off and tripped her, so she ended up on the ground. They both looked at each other and broke out laughing.

"Maybe there are still a few glitches." Stephanie stood up and gained control of the suitcase. Once the suitcase was going straight, Elissa rode down the lift, and butterflies beat their wings in her stomach. Men and women with the logo of the Academy on their uniforms were mowing lawns and trimming the bushes while others pruned the boulevard trees or washed the benches by the bus stop, overall trying to look intimidating.

Elissa and Stephanie made their way across the parking lot, weaving through the vehicles, towards the bus stop. The sun was shining between the fluffy cumulus clouds. Elissa grew excited just thinking about being up in the sky flying once again. She hadn't been up for any flying lessons since the accident, but their airplane was supposed to be getting fitted so she could fly it without having to use her feet. It was yet another thing that both she and Stephanie had discussed but hadn't gotten around to doing. Green grass with dead brown sections lined the boulevard along the sidewalk.

"Ahh, a gardener using my techniques," Stephanie remarked, and pointed to the brown spots.

Elissa smiled and prepared for every jolt as they passed each crack in the pavement but kept looking at the uniformed men and women. She wondered who they were trying to look intimidating for, the students, or for anyone uninvited trying to get into this world. After a look around, she decided everyone who was there at that time more likely had a Madisyn Academy connection so it had to be for the students benefit.

"Mom, what's with all the security?"

"Madisyn is serious about keeping their students safe."

In the center of the parking lot sat a car wash with black mirrored glass over where the cars entered. A procession of cars weaved, around the donut shop, and to the car wash. Elissa followed Stephanie, in the parking lot, over to the bus stop. The woman who beat them to the parking spot climbed into a vehicle with a driver.

That car drove off, over to the back of the donut shop, past the four cars that waited in the donut drive-through lane, and joined the car wash line. A black, extended-roof transport van parked in front of the bench and blocked Elissa's view. Stephanie took Elissa's letter and walked over to the passenger side window of the van. The side door of the van opened to reveal a lift.

"Come on," Stephanie motioned for Elissa to join her. A man, in a black business suit with greased black hair and Nike running shoes walked over to Elissa and squatted down. He reached out his hand to shake hers and although she didn't react by wincing, she was grossed out by his sweaty palms. Elissa shook his hand and casually wiped her hands on her shirt. Running shoes with a suit or a dress was a look Elissa enjoyed as it seemed to break the rules of fashion – rules that were overrated and too soon outdated.

"I'm Agent Day. Let's get you secured and we'll be on our way."

He secured Elissa in the second seating row by one passenger seat. Behind the seat row was a table and a booth seating area that encircled the table. Having a team meeting in a van en-route to some exciting location was just the activity they must have purchased the van for, which made sense to Elissa. He closed the van door. Once Stephanie had put the suitcase in the back and Agent Day attached a luggage tag, giving her the stub to collect it, they joined the car wash line up. Stephanie handed the letter back to Elissa and she put it in her vest. She had to admit that this undercover world seemed to have potential to be cool, but just as easily could be lame. After all, when Stephanie and Christopher went, the world, technology and she was sure, even buildings were different. Hopefully this world had been updated.

On the car wash's concrete entrance boulevard was a signal light attached to a pole. When the light turned green, cars pulled up one at a time. Then the metal bay door opened and the cars drove in. Elissa watched the clock on the van. Each vehicle took five minutes. Five long minutes in which she looked around and wondered what could possibly be taking so long and why a clean car was important to the Madisyn experience. If this was so important, why couldn't they use their own van?

Agent Day put on the radio and the DJs were taking requests.

"Could you please play *Better with You* by Morris?" an older woman asked.

Although it was only 6:00 a.m. when she entered the kitchen, Christopher was standing on a chair and taping up a banner with Stephanie's help. The homemade sign read Happy 10th Birthday, Lissy. Stephanie stood at the door to watch and looked at the banner and Christopher as a large smile spread across her face. Elissa didn't know what he was doing there. He was supposed to be on tour for the entire month, but nevertheless she was going to take full advantage of having him home.

"Daddy! How'd you...?" *Elissa ran to him. He jumped off the chair, picked her up and swung her around. Stephanie left the room.*

"I couldn't miss my Lissy's birthday. Well, the morning anyway. For you, my girl, I'll always be here."

Stephanie came in from the living room carrying a cake in the shape of pink ballet shoes. Elissa's parents sang "Happy Birthday." For just a moment the world outside and all the expectations on her, Stephanie and Christopher, couldn't penetrate their family. Then as Stephanie cut the cake, her dad picked up his acoustic guitar.

"I wrote you this song called "Better with You." Every time you hear it, remember our life is better with you. Everything is better with you."

The memory ended there. Tears gathered in her eyes.

"I'll turn that off." Agent Day reached toward the button on the radio.

"No, please leave it on." Elissa casually wiped off her eyes and examined her shoes while the wave of loss retreated. It had been months, and while her heart still felt the emptiness for all the things Christopher had missed, it also was filled with waves of anger for the betrayal of trust and making decisions that had cost them so much. She would not let her emotions become a weakness; instead they would be used to focus her to get to the truth.

Agent Day became quiet as they listened to the song. Stephanie squeezed Elissa's hand. Elissa didn't let go. She wanted to hang onto Stephanie for just a bit longer. When the song was over, Stephanie wiped a tear off Elissa's face, coughed and asked, "Donald, how's Mary?"

Agent Day's face brightened. He grabbed his wallet and passed a few photographs back to Stephanie.

"Mary's getting into everything. Last night she rearranged the cupboard and rolled cans of baby formula around on the floor."

Stephanie held the photographs so Elissa could see them. A chubby, brown-haired girl was wearing a pair of pink overalls, cowboy boots, a pink cowboy hat and was petting a kitten.

"Elissa was more of a pots and pans girl. With the most wicked drum solos."

Redness flooded into her cheeks as Elissa asked the universe, *Where's a distraction when I need one?* In response, Stephanie rubbed Elissa's leg and smiled.

"She's beautiful." Stephanie handed Agent Day back his photos. The van was finally at the front of the line and the light was green. Agent Day ran his identification card into a square card reader and typed in a six-digit code. A large metal door opened. He drove into the average brushless car wash bay, except the car wash windows were mirrored, keeping the secrets of this place hidden from the outside world, ensured his tires were on the correlator and killed the engine. With the van turned off, Agent Day took the keys out of the ignition and the van moved to the roll bar assembly to direct the van over a yellow platform. A boom came down from the ceiling and aimed the hose and nozzle at the van shooting water droplets. Elissa was waiting, to be amazed, awed, but where were all the neat advancements she had seen in the secret agent movies?

After a jolt and the hissing sound of the hydraulic lift, Elissa realized the van was being lowered down beneath the floor, so she turned her head and watched the bottom of the van sink below the thick concrete floor.

Cool.

The change in lighting, from sunshine to underground lighting, required her eyes a few minutes to adjust as the van was lowered, down an entire floor, into a room made of concrete – a room with no windows and only one door, a red door, along the far wall. Her hands began to sweat as she looked for any other exit to the room. The excitement bubbling up inside her was suffocated by the confinement of this small room.

"I'll help you out of the van then you can proceed through the red door," Agent Day said as the van touched down on the floor. Elissa looked out the van's windows to see the open vehicle lift door above her, which sat open, as drops of water dripped from the car wash floor above into the room. Being a secret place, the fact that the water dripped to the lower floor made her consider how old this place really was and why it had not been fixed.

"Thanks, Donald." Stephanie stepped out of the van and waited by the red door.

Agent Day saw Elissa looking up at the water and the car wash lift platform door. He came into the back and got her wheelchair free and on the lift.

"The water is set so it automatically goes off after a few drops. I guarantee there's no danger. You're safe here."

The damp musty smell of chlorine and warmth combined with the half lit room made Elissa wish she was back up in the parking lot, in the fresh air. She drove around the small puddles that had collected on the ground and joined her mom by the door. There was a green light on the gray concrete wall next to the red door. Stephanie pressed a doorbell under the green light and the door made a bell sound, like the ones in a store to alert them of shoppers, while the red door opened to a small room about the size of Stephanie's walk-in closet.

Stephanie closed the door behind them and it made a beeping sound and some lights flashed on a small box against the door frame. Nothing decorated the white painted concrete walls, except for three lights, recessed into each wall, and there were no furnishings. So far Elissa was not very impressed with this place and hoped that Madisyn Academy wouldn't be so old fashioned. A painted blue line, leading to and away from a Madisyn Academy logo located on the floor and a reinforced silver metal door at the far wall were the only things to look at.

"Someone needs an interior designer in here." Elissa looked around the room and at Stephanie wondering what kind of weird place this was.

"Practicality isn't always pretty."

The enclosed room and the pungent smell of cleaning solution made Elissa's palms sweat. It reminded her of her hospital room and being trapped in-between the metal railings of her bed. Her mom took a few steps, waved for Elissa to join her, and stopped in the middle of the room. After taking a moment to remind herself that this was not the hospital, she could leave any time, she joined Stephanie on the logo.

Sudden darkness descended as beams of magenta light shone out of where the lights were positioned on the walls, changing the entire room to a muted shade of magenta. Elissa jumped and her heart raced. Beams passed over them. Then the magenta lights went off. The room returned to normal lighting, and the reinforced metal door creaked as it slid open and fresh, cool air entered the room to her relief. Elissa wasn't sure if she should be laughing at this strange area, but as Stephanie was serious, she kept her comments to herself.

Long, narrow tunnels, just like the England air raid shelters Elissa had seen on a history show Christopher was watching, awaited them on the other side. The tunnels were made of cream-painted concrete for the ceiling and walls, but the floor was a light painted grey. A neon orange ceiling height clearance sign hung from two chains just a few inches above her mom's head. An aroma of perfumes, candies, and what she thought was frying oil greeted them.

The smooth concrete floor was easy for Elissa to drive on. She silently begged the lights not to go out. Her nerves were raw enough without adding darkness to the equation. Along the rounded walls, picture frames resembling windows with three-dimensional panoramic views of a mountain top provided the area a less intimidating appearance. Voices echoed from a short distance down the tunnel where parents and teens were opening and closing doors. The excitement filled her again as she saw the other students laughing and talking.

When Elissa tried to turn to the right, the dip in the floor made her chair veer towards an old fashioned signpost with three arrows that indicated different tunnels: Entertainment Avenue, Mercantile Avenue, Medical and Requirement Street. Elissa followed her mom into the first on Medical and Requirement Street.

Inside parents and students were lined up in front of seven machines resembling the cheesy photo booths in the mall, only with advanced computers and identification equipment, all of which Elissa snuck a look at when students left the booths. The wall by the door had a plaque on either side for all the men and women who died in the line of duty, including their photographs. Her heart sank as she looked at each face, each secret agent who had a family who waited in vain for them to return. Elissa scanned the wall and there was Christopher's picture, with a date for the explosion. Elissa swallowed deep and took a deep breath to clear her head and vowed to get him off that plaque.

Elissa and Stephanie joined the long new student identification queue, delineated by two blue velvet ropes on either side. For a moment she was worried she would knock over the rope and would cause everyone to fall over like dominos and be the laughing stock of the Academy. Holding on to her wheelchair joystick tightly, Elissa just barely manoeuvred her wheelchair in between the ropes without running over the silver bases of the poles holding them. The only place she was used to seeing ropes like that was along the press line, keeping the media away from Christopher.

Elissa scanned the room. Behind her was a medium height, tanned girl with long black hair who pointed at Elissa and whispered to a short, slim girl with long red hair. Both girls were wearing Stella McCartney, short dresses, and handbags that gave them the runway effect, despite the required vests. Elissa owned a few designer pieces of clothing, and could recognize various designers thanks to Stephanie's large clothing collection, but Roots or the Gap were her stores of choice.

In front, a girl with espresso-colored curly hair pulled up into a ponytail with two faded cinnamon-dyed strips that stood out against her honey-colored skin was chewing her lip. A tiny rhinestone nose stud looked out of place with her boring dress pants and shirt that were both worn thin but perfectly ironed and creased. With the second-hand clothing and the hair needing a new coloring, she wondered if this girl was a bit short on cash or going for a look, but calling someone on the fact they look poor was not acceptable.

"Malina's nothin' but trouble."

The girl in front of her casually pointed and referred to the girl behind Elissa,

"I'm Katherine. What should I call you?" Her blue-green eyes twinkled as she reached out to shake Elissa's hand.

"Elissa. This is my…"

"Personal assistant Stephanie," her mom interrupted.

"Pleasure to meet ya." Katherine shook her hand.

Elissa looked at Stephanie and wondered why she was so quick to say that.

"Next!" the Agent called from the head of the line.

"Oh, I'm up. See you later." Katherine walked to the machine.

She's probably cool, Elissa thought with relief. The knots in her stomach disappeared and she finally felt a little excited at the possibility there were nice students at Madisyn.

"Hanging with your mom is not what a teenager wants. Are personal assistants cool?" Stephanie winked at her.

"Yeah, but so's my mom. If you embarrassed me I wouldn't have you with me." Elissa nodded at her and smiled.

They watched as Katherine received her orientation from the agent standing next to the tall, mall-type booths.

He opened the metal door to show her the stool inside.

She entered, sat on the stool, and closed the door to the booth.

Stephanie pulled out her BlackBerry, which Elissa was sure she couldn't live without since she took it everywhere, to check for messages.

Elissa pulled out her RunLink to check to see if the person who had contacted her had sent further instructions. No luck. Out of the corner of her eye, she saw the girls behind her sitting on the floor playing a game on their laptops.

A boy with short brown hair that shifted in the breeze as people walked past, winked at Elissa and sat down with the girls.

Elissa shyly kept her head down but couldn't help but smile. Her RunLink beeped and showed a message: *You've been invited for a network challenge.*

She pulled out her laptop and joined Malina in playing Mission Five, a secret agent game with a head-to-head match-up where each player collected cards by exploring rooms and answering questions. Jon had Mission Five on his computer but, while she was familiar with it, she had only played a couple of rounds. She noticed Stephanie glancing at her computer screen several times.

"Just messages from my office but I'll deal with it later. Anything exciting?" Stephanie asked, looking at Elissa.

Despite her best effort, Malina won. As Malina stood up, she formed the letter 'L' with her fingers, held it in front of her forehead and smiled. Resolved to not slouch or give Malina any satisfaction, Elissa hit reply and sent her a congrats message.

"Not yet but..." she looked towards where the boy was standing with Malina, "perhaps later."

The boy swatted Malina's arm. Turning to face him, she grabbed his sleeve and dragged him out of the line-up.

If I'm lucky, Elissa thought, *I might bump into him again. It's too bad he seems to be taken.*

Soon they were at the front of the line.

"Next! Follow me," the agent looked at Elissa and moved the ropes to give her more room to get into the booth area. They followed him over to a machine with a wheelchair symbol on the front. This agent wore a black suit and had a Mohawk of green hair and a pierced eyebrow. His blue eyes sparkled when he smiled. All the other agents were totally generic, but this man had a keen eye for fashion.

"I'll pull out the stool and we can get your wheelchair parked in that spot. Follow the instructions on the screen."

She pulled into the spot, glad that the process of transferring off the wheelchair and onto the stool would not have to be witnessed by the new students. The agent walked over behind the counter and realigned the camera to her position.

"You'll need to type in the code on your letter to start."

Stephanie closed the door and Elissa turned her attention to the screen. Inside the booth, all the voices from outside were just a quiet hum. Instructions prompted her to type her identification number. She pulled out the letter and looked around. A keyboard sat above her lap and a vinyl blue background hung behind her. Below the screen were several different slots like computer compact disk drives.

Once the ID number was entered, she checked to see if her identification information was correct, before she returned the letter to her pocket. Then the computer prompted a countdown to snap her photo. Elissa sat straight and flashed the smile, the one she had practiced in the mirror, the one she gave when the newspapers and television shows came to do a story on Christopher. A humming sound came from inside the machine. She looked around to see a wad of pink chewing gum in the far corner of the booth and made sure she was nowhere near it.

Next, she was prompted to provide her fingerprints. One of the small slots opened and a clear glass pad popped out. She placed her hands on the glass, and the glass sensed the warmth emanating from them. The screen counted down the start of the scan and then a light glided under her hand. It was really anti-climatic as it looked like a fancy version of their scanner at home.

The screen explained she was required to pass a security clearance and provide a DNA sample. A sheet of questions about her life, including whether she had ever been arrested and her criminal history required her to answer and then hit confirm. While the security clearance analysed the data, she read the screen instructions for the DNA sample. Simple, just run the swab that came out of an additional slot along her right cheek and place back in the tube and in the slot. After Elissa had completed a retinal scan, her clearance for security was approved, and she was prompted to stay in the booth while it printed her identification.

A photo of Christopher flashed on the screen. She turned around and tried to figure how someone was able to hack into the system and send this message, unnoticed into her booth, but of course there were no answers while she was still inside.

The caption read: *Elissa bring me home. We'll contact you.*

Excitement filled the emptiness in her heart as the message confirmed Christopher was alive. A question came to her mind: *Why is he still in his disguise when the people who have him know his identity*? Elissa aimed her wheelchair towards the door, to be ready the moment the door opened so she could tell Stephanie all about the message, as the secret was bursting to be told.

She looked at the door and as she was about to open it the machine beeped and her card slid out of the slot. The photo vanished and the following message appeared in red letters:

"Tell anyone and you'll never see him again."

She swallowed hard, held her identification for a minute then peeked her head outside the door. Elissa shared almost everything with Stephanie for two reasons; one, she was a terrible liar and two, she believed in the truth despite everything being kept from her. The weight of having to keep this to herself then find the truth, and perhaps bring Christopher home all on her own, settled in her body like weights from the gym. The agent helped Elissa negotiate her chair out of the booth.

"What year are you?" Elissa asked him. She saw his identification was different from those of the agents at the door. A distraction to keep her mind off her racing thoughts was what she needed at that moment. Casually she looked around for anyone who could be carrying a laptop and sending a signal to her booth, but no one looked suspicious or out of place.

"I'll be entering the mentoring program tomorrow. I can't wait to be in the field working."

"Good luck."

"Thanks. Totally in need of it."

They returned to the main tunnel where they had entered from the car wash. Instead of going back into the entrance, they followed down another long tunnel. The tunnel had painted cream walls like the others but was insulated from the noises and happiness of the previous tunnels. Instead of being friendly, this hall had an air of authority as along the walls were framed prints of the policies of COOL, and the punishments associated with breaking any of them.

Elissa tried to swallow despite the dryness in her mouth and throat. She still was not sure this organization was one she wanted to be a member of. In a small alcove towards the end of the hallway, two doors were unmarked. The miniature round lights above them were dark and no light escaped at the floor.

"Mom, what's in those rooms?"

Stephanie looked at her with new seriousness in her face.

"Those are the interrogation rooms. No one ever wants to visit them." She hurried Elissa along the main hallway.

The deeper Elissa became immersed in the world of secret agents, the more determined she was to get Christopher free.

At the end of the hallway they found a guarded elevator.

"Allow me," the guard said as Elissa and Stephanie approached. He pressed the call button, held the door open, and stepped away. After a short ride, the doors opened to reveal a pretty standard big-box store entrance to Mike's.

Inside, the store looked like a warehouse. There were tables covered with bagged comic books. The large counter display cases held baseballs, footballs, and other types of collectables. At the back wall of the store, stacks and stacks of boxes and autographed jerseys stretched across the walls. Elissa searched for a face, a person that seemed out of place, convinced the message sender should be around but there was no one.

"Welcome. I'm Agent Dancer. You must be Elissa. ID?" A tall agent wearing a clear wire in her ear looked at them, and the wheelchair, as they entered.

Elissa handed her new card to Agent Dancer, who looked at it and handed it back.

"Well, Stephanie Morris. How are you? Your mom and I were in the same section at Madisyn Academy," the agent explained as she looked at her identification and then at Stephanie.

"Proud of your daughter?"

"Sure am," Stephanie smiled at Elissa and rubbed her head.

"Those were some fun times." Stephanie and Agent Dancer looked at each other and shook their shoulders. Elissa tried to hide her face. They danced in a circle and clapped.

Elissa glanced around her, hoping no one was watching, but none of the shoppers, who were all students and parents today, paid any attention. Stephanie and her dance buddy completed an improvised hand jive before an intricate handshake. Then they acted casual as if they didn't just put on a public show of crazy. Other friends told her how 'cool' her parents were because they listened to rock music, talked about pop culture and didn't embarrass her too much. It was true they were recycled teenagers, but not the kind she always wanted to be around, especially when they were goofing around in public.

"Steph, we should go for coffee," the agent said. "Elissa, once you go inside they'll get you ready to board."

Stephanie smiled at her old friend. "Call me. We'll get caught up."

Elissa and Stephanie passed the entry doors and proceeded into a large hanger, via a door indicating hanger access, with bright lights hanging from the ceiling. Joining the rest of the crowd, they moved to the boarding area sectioned off with red velvet ropes spaced apart so Elissa navigated more easily.

"Once you are checked in we have to say goodbye," Stephanie explained, squeezed Elissa's hand.

Elissa looked at the big clock on the back wall. Time seemed to be speeding up. *Slow down,* she silently begged as they approached the counter. A customer service representative, wearing a black tailored jacket, skirt and pink blouse, smiled at Elissa with her overly whitened teeth. For just a moment, the thought of leaving home and Stephanie took her breath away, and she needed to remind herself that luring the man away from Stephanie was the best choice.

"Miss Morris, we'll be pre-boarding you onto the aircraft. I'm sorry, but FAA regulations require electric wheelchairs, because of the batteries, to be stowed in the baggage compartment."

Quickly she passed the counter towards Elissa and put a purple and white tag on her wheelchair.

"Your suitcase that you left with your transportation agent will go straight to Madisyn Academy. Your wheelchair will be waiting at the airport when you arrive."

With that, she pulled an ancient wheelchair from behind the counter and unfolded it.

"Can you transfer into this wheelchair?"

Commercial airlines have special wheelchairs made to go between the aisles of seats, but this one seemed like a joke. Nothing about the low-tech chair looked comfortable, but Stephanie helped Elissa transfer into it. The tires were solid rubber instead of the air-filled bike tires she was used to, and the seat was a cold crisp leather rather than soft canvas.

"There you go," Stephanie said, helping her get the seatbelt secured.

"You are good to go. One of our flight attendants will escort you to the aircraft." The customer service representative handed Elissa the paperwork.

Stephanie started to push her towards the security area.

"This is good bye, sweetie." Stephanie stooped to give her a hug.

Elissa didn't care if hugging her mother made her uncool. She grabbed on tightly and looked at Stephanie's face. Both of their eyes were filled with tears despite their smiles.

"You promised no tears," Elissa said.

"My goofer."

Elissa burst out laughing.

"What?" Stephanie wiped a tear off Elissa's cheek.

Elissa rolled her eyes. "It's *my bad*, Mom. That expression's so yesterday now."

"Oh." A smile spread across Stephanie's face. "Well, go ahead Miss Know-It-All."

Elissa gave Stephanie a final hug and pushed herself over to the security scan. When she turned around, Stephanie waved. Elissa raised her hand then turned back around, wondering how she felt so very alone in a room filled with people. She wiped a tear off her face before she continued towards security. Then she stopped in her tracks; a shiver ran up her back as she thought she saw the NERD-One operative, the man in the sunglasses, from the photo Mr. Larsson showed her. She abruptly turned around, and almost knocked over a student passing her.

By the time she dodged the student in front of her, the man in the sunglasses, a leather jacket, blue jeans and baseball cap was gone. His smirk seemed unnervingly familiar but the baseball cap stopped her from a 100% positive identification. She glanced back at Stephanie, who was still smiling at her. She returned the smile, turned around and sped up to get to security.

"I'm going to run the scanner over you and the wheelchair," an elderly man explained. He had gray curly hair, small gold-rimmed glasses and was dressed in uniform. The small wand beeped and buzzed when it reached her wheelchair.

"Can I push you to the lobby?" he asked.

"No thanks, I'm good."

Her mind was racing as the manual wheelchair pushed heavily on the thick carpet. Finally, she pushed herself through a blue curtain and into the waiting area. Black leather sofas and several glass tables were filled with excited students. Madisyn Academy security waited by the gate. Elissa was glad to see them, as she wasn't sure the man meant her no harm.

Elissa looked around at all the strangers' faces and everyone sitting with someone else. She was the only one alone. Instead of focussing on her loneliness, she looked at the back wall gate. Outside the large window, airplanes were taxiing to take off. The planes were larger than her family's private one.

She felt eyes staring at her. From the corner, Katherine and a boy she was seated with waved. Elissa waved back, relieved to know someone.

"Now we'll commence pre-boarding for Flight 000," a voice announced.

Four

Introductions

On the airplane, Elissa noticed no rows of seats like standard jumbo jets. Instead, the long narrow hallway reminded her of the horror movie she and Stephanie watched last week; it seemed to grow as the camera panned backwards and they'd both screamed and laughed when the creature finally jumped out. Seated in front of Ashley, the flight attendant, as they made their way down the hall, Elissa waited for something to jump out at her, but nothing appeared.

Numbered metal doors resembling bank vaults lined the hallway. The comforting hum of the air system reminded Elissa of happier times on her family's private plane.

"Six," Ashley said as they proceeded on. She opened the sixth door on the left.

Four small round windows stretched along one wall, giving Elissa one last reminder of the landscape of home. A tall, wide table was illuminated by the window's light. Elissa smiled, thinking about how the table would look out of place anywhere but a spy movie. Two soft leather airplane seats sat against the wall. Ashley pushed her over to silver, ski-like tracks built into the carpeted floor.

"This cabin is adapted for special-needs passengers and is equipped with a washroom," Ashley explained, pointing to the tracks. "I promise they'll work better than the chair alone. I'll let you wheel your tires onto them."

As Elissa approached, the pressure of looking like an idiot using a new invention tensed up her arms, her front tires sunk into the lush carpet and stubbornly veered right.

After several tries, which sucked completely, she correctly placed the wheels over the tracks. Ashley stood next to a panel and demonstrated.

"Next to you, on the side panel, are two buttons. Red puts the clamps on, green releases them. Give it a try."

Elissa pressed the red button. A motor ran. Several round silver clamps sprang around her large back tires and her small front tires. Sure enough, the green button did the opposite.

"The same rules that apply to seat belts apply to you. If the 'Fasten Seatbelts' light is off, you may move around. Secure the chair during take off, if there is turbulence, and when we land. Another student will join you shortly." Ashley walked out of the compartment, grabbed the doorframe and stuck her head back in. "Oh, by the way, you'll de-plane last, and access to the upper level is next to the staircase at the end of the hallway."

Unable to focus on the portfolio in her lap while she was alone, Elissa decided to explore the room. First she checked out the washroom. It was double the regular airplane size and decorated in a lavender and sea shell theme. There were support bars next to the toilet. The color reminded her of hiding out in the seashell-themed girls' bathroom at her last school.

It was a performing arts school, full of musicians, artists, dancers and athletes. The main clique, a group of mean girls, made life unbearable for their selected targets. Proving their blame for the stunts, such as loosening a stage board so the lead dancer twisted her ankle, tampering with the soloist's water resulting in laryngitis, covering instruments in glue, and placing evidence to link their targets to smaller pranks was impossible.

One day, the cliques set up Elissa to take the fall for a nasty screen saver that showed up on all the computer monitors in the building. The incident landed her two months of Saturday detention. That was when Elissa met Megan, with her thrift shop style and sarcastic sense of humour, who spent every second Saturday in detention because she regularly stood up to the clique. Together, Megan and Elissa had plenty of time to plan how to take the clique down. A few properly placed hidden cameras, proof of the clique's next chosen plan to fry the lead's guitar, his baby, the thing he wouldn't perform without, and a live feed to the principal, and soon the clique couldn't get away with anything.

Regular classes were easy for Elissa. She used to break into Christopher's highly secure websites to challenge herself. When the school realized her misuse of school computers, they decided to reward her talent as a punishment and assigned her to make their computer network ultra safe. She didn't particularly like being the lame tech girl and constantly being called on to clean a hard drive or patch a firewall.

Elissa left the lavender bathroom and returned to the main cabin, rolled over to the tracks, and pulled out her portfolio again. But instead of opening it, she looked out the window. A large black conveyer belt moved suitcases of every shape and size into the aircraft. Two baggage handlers lifted the baggage into the airplane's hold. Elissa imagined who each bag belonged to. The plain black ones probably belong to plain, boring people. Afterall, hers was very plain as well. A black suitcase covered in grey tape probably belonged to some kid who couldn't afford to replace it. A guitar case went either way cool, or way, way not and made Elissa wish she would have brought her guitar from home. Playing the guitar helped her sort out her thoughts. A bag with a lock attached to every opening that was also sealed in plastic wrap probably had a security freak as an owner.

Elissa's custom wheelchair was the last item to be stored and relief washed across her. That said, it was good to have the wheelchair disengaged or it might have made a break for it down the runway. Now that would have been a sight.

Two weeks ago, in Stephanie's garage workshop, Elissa lifted the tarp slowly. There it was – a new wheelchair, far less bulky and taller than the one she was sitting in. It had a blue and silver flecked frame and black canvas seating. A smile spread across her face as she looked at her new independence.

Stephanie smiled as Elissa ran a hand along the seat. "This is the new secret agent issue wheelchair – The Ability 07. It's one of a kind."

Stephanie plopped into the chair and drove out onto the tennis court. Elissa followed behind her. Once on the court, Stephanie motioned Elissa closer and helped secure her into the new chair. The thick cushion melted underneath her.

"Well, try it out."

She bounced on her heels, beaming with pride.

Nine buttons surrounded the joystick control. The D button moved the wheelchair down, U moved it up and C allowed her to climb steps, but she was interested in the others. She hit K and spikes shot out of the foot rests and back which made her think lines shouldn't be a problem anymore.

"Kickin," Elissa said with an approving nod. The F button sped her up enough to feel the wind blowing her hair; T allowed her to navigate a sharp circle. There was a smoke function, a button that sent powdered beads shooting out the back, a winch beneath the left armrest and a slide-out extra passenger seat. While she was ready to use a wheelchair, as it got her off the couch and back out in the world, she hadn't realized it could be so cool – that it would be like a James Bond car, only make the world a much more accessible place for her to explore.

"Look out for me."

Stephanie wiped out on the small powder beads she left in her wake. Stephanie laughed. "It's slippery." She fought to get up, but couldn't get a solid grip on the ground. "Honey, don't hit the E."

But she was too late. The wheelchair hummed and shot her five feet into the air. Elissa looked down at the ground and enjoyed the sensation of being free. She hadn't felt that way since her last dance recital. The seat inflated around her, creating a nice, cushy inner tube before she fell onto the tennis court. Stephanie ran over, concerned.

"Are you okay?" she asked.

"Woo hoo," Elissa squealed in response.

They both sat on the court laughing.

"The Academy is a place for secret agents to become their best," Stephanie explained, patting Elissa on the knee. "And it's a lifestyle choice. Is this life really for you?"

Elissa stopped laughing and looked her mother in the eyes. "If attending Madisyn will help make sure that other agents' families don't have to lose their father too, I'll never regret my decision."

Elissa breathed a sigh of relief knowing her own wheelchair was securely on the plane. Distracting her from her thoughts, she noticed one of the baggage handlers was wearing sunglasses. Familiar sunglasses. This time his baseball cap was off and the sun reflected off his bald head. He turned towards the airplane as her phone beeped. When she listened to the waiting message, a gruff male voice said, "Congratulations, Lissy. We'll talk at Madisyn about Christopher's potential release. Keep this between us to ensure aliases stay private." When the voice stopped, her phone beeped again and flashed, "Message erased." Elissa's heart raced, knowing she had not hit erase.

She looked outside, but the man in sunglasses was gone. It's the NERD operative, Mr. Russel, from Agent Larsson's photo, she confirmed to herself.

She jumped when the cabin door opened.

"Hey, Elissa."

Katherine placed her small plastic garbage bag, with a few carry on items, on the floor. A small oval locket dangled off a gold chain around her neck. Elissa glanced back at the now empty tarmac. The handlers were both gone. An uncomfortable silence filled the cabin.

Elissa turned her attention back to Katherine. "Nice locket. Who's in it?" she asked, forcing herself to be interested.

"My family," Katherine replied, tucking the locket in her shirt, then turned around and checked out the washroom.

"First time on your own?" Elissa asked.

Katherine grinned. "Took long enough."

"Absolutely." Elissa tried to convince herself that she was just as excited to be independent as her cabin-mate.

"**This is your co-pilot Mark Powers.**" The male voice blared over the intercom. "**Prepare for taxi and take off. Please fasten your seatbelts and remember to review your briefing portfolios.**"

Katherine fastened her seatbelt. She glanced out the window then tightened the seatbelt more as she watched Elissa secure her chair.

"Easier than having to rely on someone else." Elissa said, looking up at her.

Distracting them, a thin monitor slid down from the ceiling to rest in-between the seats. A video instructed them about the location of the seatbelt lights and exits. Then the lights went out, the cabin door opened and the lights glowed throughout the cabin and the hallway. When the cabin returned to the normal lighting, the monitor slid back into the roof and a small panel in the ceiling closed behind it. A flight attendant shut their cabin door as she passed.

"So, do you like flying?" Katherine asked. She took a deep breath and tightened her seatbelt.

Every forth Tuesday, whether her dad was on tour or not, he took Elissa up in his plane. Little by little, he encouraged her to take the controls. One day he brought a camera along.

When they were through the pre-flight check and seated in the plane, he'd turned to her. "Today's a good day to solo, unofficially," he announced.

"Now. You sure?"

"Of course, just let me taxi out to the runway. Then she's all yours."

At the end of the runway, he took his hands away from the controller and put them in his lap. Elissa smiled at Christopher and gave the airplane power. Adrenaline pumped through her body as it raced down the runway and she urged the plane to lift off. Once she was up to her cruising altitude, Christopher snapped a photo of her holding the controls with low-hanging clouds outside the window.

"It'll be our reminder of your accomplishment."

Although she was officially too young to get her license, he and her flying lessons had trained her well enough to take off, fly and land by herself. At the end of that day she wasn't sure who was more excited, but she for one couldn't wait to see the picture.

Elissa looked out the window as the airplane turned and lined up with the runway.

"More than anything. You?" Elissa asked Katherine.

"Freaks me right out." Katherine's knuckles were white from gripping her armrest.

The airplane jerked forward. They traveled faster and faster and the airplane rattled and shook. Adrenaline pumped through Elissa's legs and temporarily relieved the aching. Take offs and landings always gave her a rush. The ground vanished and they quickly entered the cloud cover. For some time, the girls sat in silence, reading their briefing. Elissa looked at the information but was stuck on the statement that there would be an in-flight mission. She didn't feel ready yet.

"I'm freaking out more," Katherine admitted. "A mission on the plane?"

"Extremely premature," Elissa agreed.

There was a knock on the door.

"Entree," Katherine called. Elissa noticed the seatbelt light was off, so she released the chair. At least not being strapped down made her feel slightly more mobile, despite the crappy old wheelchair.

The door opened to reveal a boy of medium height with a bright Hawaiian shirt that highlighted his short spiked blonde hair.

"Hey Kat," he said. He looked at Elissa, raised his eyebrows and then looked back at Katherine.

"Jacks...Elissa. Elissa…Jack."

Jack reached out his hand. "I'm Jack Dancer. Sorry about the look. There's just never been anyone with… Well in a … Using a…How come you're in a..." Katherine interrupted him before he kept stammering.

"Jacks. Stop. Maybe she doesn't want to discuss it!" Katherine hit his arm to get his attention.

Elissa jumped in. "Accident. How do you know each other?"

Katherine and Jack looked at each other before Katherine turned her attention back to Elissa. "My brother and I live in his family's garage apartment when my parents have work trips."

He seemed nice and Elissa enjoyed having the company to pass the time. To keep her from obsessing what would await her at Madisyn and wondering if Mr. Russel would be there. They studied their portfolios filled with briefing information and geography and technology updates. When they finished, they pulled out magazines: Jack had hockey, Katherine's was teen gossip, and Elissa read about computers.

"Elissa, we so have to take this quiz later." Katherine flashed a page with the title "Is your guy hot or not?"

Elissa nodded, but realized that she wouldn't know as her family had a no dating until age fifteen rule, and as she turned fifteen shortly after the accident, she hadn't had time.

"Wicked threads," Katherine continued pleasantly. She showed Elissa a model who wore a tight dress complimented with tall black boots.

"Wish the body came with it," Elissa said.

"Please. Like those are natural."

The girls looked at each other and laughed.

"I'm clueless to our intended location. Sure hope it's worth missing hockey," Jack declared, looking out the window at the landscape. It had changed from green trees and lakes to open flat prairies and parks with trees.

Curious, the girls glanced up to see what had grabbed Jack's attention. The trees reminded Elissa of the tree house Christopher built in their old maple tree at their cabin in Canada. The memory relieved her homesickness for a moment. In that tree house, she always felt safe from the world. It was a good feeling to have.

"Please Jacks. Like the hockey academy was as important as my gymnastic academy."

Jack shoved Katherine and looked at Elissa, who was hoping the question about what she was missing would not come up.

"How about you?"

"I was entertaining the idea of backing up a family project." That was the truth, but that was all she was willing to share at that time.

"We all sacrificed so much. This so better be worth it," Katherine said.

The answers and the truth better be on that ship, so Christopher can come back to our family, Elissa thought as she nodded in agreement to Katherine's statement. A flat monitor hummed and slid down from the ceiling. Computer monitors rotated up out of the table top while keyboards moved up level with the table. Mr. Larsson came up on the screen.

"I'm Agent Helmer Larsson. Please open the residence envelopes that have been placed under your cabin doors and follow the instructions."

Katherine ran over, picked up the envelopes and handed Jack and Elissa theirs.

"Maybe we'll all be in the same ship section," Katherine said excitedly.

"Here's hoping."

Elissa swallowed deep, opened the envelope and a letter, a new identification card, and a residence pin fell out. She examined the silver pin with a snow-covered mountain logo. Elissa read the letter and tried to clear the lump that formed in her throat. Her palms began to sweat and her eyes blinked several times to clear the view. She was absolutely convinced if she didn't get into Edmonton Ridge, she'd die.

Elissa opened the portfolio to see the welcome letter:

Dear Miss Morris:

Welcome to Madisyn Academy. We look forward to having you as a student.

Congratulations and good luck in Edmonton Ridge – Section 7.

Head Agent & Principal,

Agent Larsson

When Elissa turned her attention back to Katherine, Katherine's eyes sparkled and a smile illuminated her face. They high fived each other.

"Well Jacks. Give us an update," Katherine said as they turned their attention to Jack.

"Ridge material. No doubts here." Jack stuck out his chest and brushed his hand off.

As per the instructions, all of them placed their old ID cards in a small metal bowl sitting on the table. Jack picked up the sheet and read:

"**Cover the bowl with plastic wrap and stand back**."

The bowl contents smoked. Suddenly, the cards were gone and only ashes remained. Somehow the results were expected and less than impressive. Finally, though, this place seemed to have potential to be everything Stephanie had told Elissa about. She hadn't been entirely convinced after the car wash and Mike's.

"So television reruns," Jack said.

On the screen, Agent Larsson looked at the camera giving each student the feel that he was staring them down. That was an expression Elissa had seen him give his son when he wanted his attention.

"**The challenge begins in three minutes. Look around as the students in your cabin are your teammates for this challenge.**"

Jack shook his head and scowled from Elissa to Katherine.

"Oh man – my luck! I'm stuck with two girls. Two…" Jack looked down his nose at Katherine.

Elissa's jaw dropped as she tried to absorb what he had said and if he was joking or really meant it.

"No you didn't just say what I think you said?" Katherine crossed her arms tightly across her chest. Elissa looked at Jacks sure he must be joking.

"So what if I did?" Jack sat back.

"Jacks, you'll live to regret it. If I *let* you live."

"Team, can we focus?" Elissa asked. She tried to ignore the daggers Katherine shot at Jack.

Katherine looked to Elissa and put out her hand, "Are we a team to beat?"

Elissa put her hand on top of Katherine's, "Most definitely."

Jack looked at them, crossed his arms and smirked.

"Sure you want us to kick your butt, Jacks?" Katherine looked at him and he looked at her and laughed. Katherine winked at Elissa.

Jack placed his hand on top. "Just bugging you squirts. Bring on the challenge."

Five

Ability

Jack, Katherine and Elissa were settled back in their seats when Agent Larsson's face appeared on the screen once again.

"**Your first mission as agents will require you to participate as a team, to answer three questions, retrieve puzzle pieces, complete the puzzle and discover the location of a hidden aluminum briefcase. Then you must break the code to gain entry to the case. Good luck.**"

Elissa tried to stop the doubts and nervousness entering her head. She had come all this way to find the truth and answers; one silly challenge was not going to get the best of her.

The ceiling monitor returned and they went to their computers. Instructions flashed: "**Answer two questions and figure out how they are related. With the correct answer, go to the numbered cabin identified to receive the next clue and puzzle pieces**."

The first set of questions appeared.

> *Until 2004, which city had the largest mall in the world? The Atlantic Bottlenose nose is a what? What did these two items share in common?*
>
> ***Go to Cabin 21***

"Been there. Edmonton, Alberta. Watched the dolphin show." Katherine stood up and bowed.

"Great, let's go," Jack said.

Katherine raced Elissa down the hallway toward the winding staircase. The narrow hallway was challenging, even with the students flattening themselves against the wall as they passed.

"Those students are cramping our cruising style," Katherine whispered as she slowed down to avoid running over random classmates.

A metal grate covered a glass and metal door which sat next to the stairs. Elissa gulped and wondered how safe it was. Jack pulled the door open and Katherine and Elissa went into the small enclosure.

"Race you upstairs," Jack grinned before he secured the lift door and headed up the stairs.

Katherine hit the button and they jolted up slowly. Without a solid elevator door blocking their view, the upper floor carpet and Jack's shoes was the first thing they saw above the floor. Once the elevator stopped, Jack opened the door and they proceeded down a hallway identical to the lower level.

Jack opened the door to cabin number 21. Inside, mean-girl Malina and her friend stood, shifting from leg to leg like small children waiting for the washroom. Waiting behind them was the same boy who was with Malina in the line up. He glanced at Elissa and smiled slightly, his green eyes twinkling. Elissa shyly bowed her head, desperately trying to keep her cheeks from blushing. Self-consciously, she looked away, attempting to free her front wheelchair tires which stuck between the bump along the door and the carpet.

Both Jack and Katherine grabbed a wheelchair handle, stuck their legs out behind and pushed as hard as they could. Abruptly the wheelchair raced over the carpet and doorframe toward the waiting students. The two girls dove onto the floor. The boy ran toward the back of Elissa's chair and pulled her to a stop. Elissa was pretty sure that if one could die of embarrassment, this would be the moment.

Jack and Katherine fell into the room, and onto the floor.

"Body check," Jack said.

"Drive much?" Malina asked.

"Malina, have a good trip?" Jack asked. He smiled. Malina's face flushed red, and she got up and brushed invisible wrinkles out of her clothes.

"Thought I'd come down to your level."

Jack smirked and sat up, still on the floor. "Shouldn't be anything new for you."

Elissa drove over to where Katherine and Jack were on the floor and by now laughing. She offered Katherine a hand to get up.

"You're a better door than a window. Move," Malina said. She tried to trip Jack as he was getting up.

"Do they know each other?" Elissa asked.

"She's our …"

Katherine stopped when Jack leaned over, covered her mouth and loudly said, "Bully."

Katherine shot a look at Jack.

"I wasn't about to say…"

"Let's get the clue," Jack interrupted.

"Are you okay?" The boy rushed to Elissa's side. She looked up at his face and her palms started to sweat.

"Perfect. Thanks for stopping…I mean…."

"I'm Benjamin, and you are?"

"Elissa."

"Pleased to meet you." Benjamin's smile lit up the room. Her cheeks flushed.

"Come on, Benji." Malina grabbed Benjamin's arm, the clue and pulled him towards the hallway. Benjamin turned, his short honey brown bangs covering his eyes and smiled at Elissa as Malina dragged him away. Elissa wished he could stay longer but looked forward to seeing him at Madisyn.

Elissa joined Katherine and Jack by the instructor. Her Madisyn Academy name tag indicated she was Agent Sullivan, the woman who took the last physically challenged parking spot back at Mike's. A frown on her face indicated her feelings towards Elissa.

"Congratulations, team." Agent Sullivan handed a disc to Jack and turned her attention to Elissa. "Perhaps it would be faster, if not safer, for you to remain in the cabin and send your team to retrieve the clue."

Elissa bit her bottom lip to stop from saying something she'd regret.

"Time's a wasting. My turn on the lift," Jack said, rushing Elissa out of the room and to the lift. He opened the gate and bounced on his feet before the lift began to move. Elissa could do without the shaking.

"Electric. Has potential," Jack declared. Elissa was going to ask potential for what but was distracted by the shaking. Katherine waited for them and cleared a path through the other students.

Back in their cabin, Jack put the disk in his computer and the girls huddled around him.

> ***Jobs and Wozniak invented the first personal what? Nemertea is one of a group of what? What do these have in common? Type in the correct answer before it is too late, and get the location.***

"Nemertea ... worms. Gross," Katherine said. She squished up her nose.

"Jobs and Wozniak...the first personal computer," Elissa said.

"I'll check the puzzle pieces," Jack said.

Jack emptied small puzzle pieces from the plastic bag he'd been given and the last disk onto the table. Elissa tried to differentiate the edge and middle pieces and fit them together. The image resembled an airplane blueprint. She joined Katherine by the computer.

"It's a type of ribbon worm. Worms infect," Jack said. He walked over to the computer where Elissa and Katherine were gathered.

"Jacks, I'll type it." Katherine cracked her fingers and then typed in the keyboard. They crowded around her monitor and saw a graphic of a worm attacking and eating through the system.

"I, I just..." she said.

"Software," Elissa said.

"Yeah, but will it load?" Jack handed Elissa the disk from his bag.

"With a mode change. Possibly," Elissa said.

She inserted the disk and it wouldn't successfully load. Elissa typed some codes and the monitor went black. Then the disk loaded and she programmed it to destroy the worm. Jack rubbed her shoulder.

"You rock," Katherine said.

Soon the worm was terminated and a room location popped up on the screen.

"You two go ahead. I'll wait here." Elissa returned to the table and started to look at the puzzle. Katherine stopped by the door and looked at Elissa.

"You sure? That instructor was a jerk."

"It'll be quicker," Elissa assured her. She returned her attention to the puzzle pieces and thought about why this agent, whom she never met before, would dislike her so much.

Even with several pieces linked, the exact image remained elusive. Elissa pulled out her phone from her vest to check for a message from Mr. Russel, but put it back disappointedly when there were no messages. Jack and Katherine burst into the room and opened the next clue.

They are in low-orbit around the earth. This paper item is used to guide your journey's path. What portable advancement included in some vehicles and cell phones do these two items have in common?
Bring the answer to cabin 8.

"Satellites are low orbit. Aren't they?" Elissa asked.
"Map," Katherine excitedly yelled.
"Maps…satellites…cars…GPS," Jack said.

They ran out of the room and Elissa returned to the puzzle. It was an airplane. One cabin had an unidentifiable mark. Once back in the room, Jack emptied the puzzle pieces and placed the blue briefcase, which looked like a change box from an office store, on the table.

"There's something there." Elissa pointed to cabin eleven.

Katherine placed the last puzzle piece to reveal the letter X. Elissa took out her beeper and refreshed her memory about how to use the lock combination breaker, so they could use it on the blue case. She plugged the main cord into the device and connected it to the computer.

"Know how to use this?" Jack asked. They watched as she worked.

"Ask me something difficult," Katherine said.

Jack turned to attach the suction cups on the device. In the process he tripped over his feet, pulled the cord out of the computer and he stayed on the floor.

"Such a goon. Twice in one day," he mumbled.

"And you thought girls were clumsy." Katherine stopped and looked at him, "You okay?"

"Do I look okay?"

Jack hit the ground with his fist, got up and fiddled to ensure the device was securely connected at both ends. Immediately, the computer prompted the user to fill in the lock type, size and model. One by one the combination numbers were revealed. The lock made a clicking sound and a time was displayed on the screen. Jack opened the case and pulled out an envelope. He sliced it open, cleared his throat and read the letter.

"Congratulations, team. You have solved your first mission. Listen for an announcement as to which cabins came in first, second, and third."

They gave each other high fives and Katherine looked at Jack.

"For your info, girls rule."

"**This is your co-pilot Mark Powers. The first place cabin is eight. Congratulations.**" he listed off the team's names, of which Elissa knew one, Malina, that sent her heart crashing, "**and second place is six…**" She was kinda hoping Malina wouldn't be competition academically as well.

Katherine stood up and began a clumsy Krumping-style version of chest pops, stomps and arm swings. Jack and Elissa laughed and missed the third place cabin. At least Malina hadn't managed to knock Elissa, Katherine and Jack out of the top five. Elissa would take second place any day but wondered how many other things Malina might challenge Elissa to.

"**We will be approaching our destination soon. Please return to your cabins and fasten your seatbelts. Flight attendants prepare for descent and landing,**" the co-pilot announced.

"Kicking power play, ladies. See you." Jack walked to the door.

"Later," Katherine said.

Once Elissa's chair was locked in the tracks, Katherine joined her by the window. There were snow-covered mountains in the distance. Elissa swallowed the big lump in her throat as she looked at their destination. As the ocean and the airport runway got closer and closer, she was suddenly very aware that there was no going back.

"**Please remain seated until the seatbelt light is off**," the co-pilot requested after the wheels touched down.

"Getting off first?" Katherine asked.

"Last, actually. They're escorting me to my electric wheelchair."

"Want company? I'm in no hurry," Katherine said.

"That'd be great." Elissa was more grateful than she let on. Maybe if she was with Katherine, her special treatment wouldn't be quite so noticeable.

When the seatbelt light went off, Elissa anxiously pressed the green button to release her wheelchair. Students were laughing and rushing out of the airplane. Her legs ached more intensely due to the air pressure change. She and Katherine watched out the window as the conveyer belt let the suitcases escape the airplane. Elissa looked in vain for Mr. Russel, the man she desperately needed to question.

When the door opened, Elissa jumped.

"Miss Morris, let's find your wheelchair," the flight attendant said.

With a quick check to ensure they had everything, the attendant pushed Elissa through the airplane and into the main carpeted skyway. Through the glass walls they saw the runway and the surrounding area.

"Madisyn Academy is over the farthest mountain," the attendant explained. Above the green trees, large green towers blended into the landscape. Elissa hoped she could blend in, too.

They walked into the main airport, which had a pyramid-style glass ceiling with grey clouds hanging above. Anyone flying overhead wouldn't have any idea this place existed.

"I hope my return flight won't be delayed," the flight attendant said.

"Too bad the weather doesn't take requests," Elissa quipped.

Various flags hung along the walls. Agents moved like sheep dogs attempting to collect the students in groups and lead them in the right direction.

In the corner, an attendant waited with Elissa's chair. Once she transferred over, she sunk into the comfort of her familiar soft foam cushions. They proceeded through the glass doors. The cool crisp mountain air brushed against her face and revived her tired body and wavering spirit.

"Here's your transportation. The other students are travelling on buses, but you two can take this van," the attendant said, pointing to a black extended roof van with a lift ready and waiting.

Elissa rode up and Katherine climbed in.

"Nice," Elissa said, securing her wheelchair.

"Howdy, Miss Morris. Miss Bennison. I'm Sam," the driver said with a Georgia accent. He tipped his cowboy hat. "Please fasten your seatbelts and we'll be on our way."

As they pulled out of the parking lot, a black sports car followed behind their van. Elissa could see the person in the driver's seat. It was Mr. Russel.

Six

Assembly

Elissa watched the car until it continued along the main highway when their van turned off the main artery onto a spruce and cedar tree-lined dirt road. She wished Mr. Russel would stay behind them so she could keep the answers and the truth in sight. As long as he was in her sight, she knew Stephanie would be safer. As they entered the forest, they passed an old white fence with a large **No Trespassing** sign dangling on it. The van bumped along old rocks residing on the forest floor. Elissa braced herself with each bump and tried to anticipate the jolts.

The trees opened up to reveal the ocean and rocky mossy beach before them. As they approached the ocean, the girls saw the ocean roll up onto the sand.

In the distance, the trees ended at an intersecting road. As they neared the intersection, the traffic light turned red and the never-ending stream of buses drove off in the opposite direction.

"More students. More competition," Katherine said. The two of them gulped and cleared their throats. Elissa was trying to ignore the fact that some of these people wouldn't make it on the Ocean-Alias for the year-one training. She tried to ignore the niggling doubts telling her she couldn't complete her mission to find the information and bring Christopher home.

They leaned back as the van drove up an incline, away from the ocean and onto a narrow gravel road. At the top of the incline, a large blue cruise ship with the Madisyn Academy logo tastefully painted on the smoke stack and a round glass building surrounded by green pillars came into view.

Sam opened the van door and the fresh mountain air caressed Elissa's face and ignited her excitement. She was ready to explore the world in front of her. Students walked through large glass double doors. Above the doors, a large banner read:

"Welcome All New And Returning Students."

"Two ramps will get you up to the main landing. Your identification and pin will get you into the residence. I reckon you should never mosey without them or you'll be stuck worse than a hound dog after a rainstorm," Sam said with a twang.

"Will do," Elissa said. Sam escorted them over to the first ramp where they vanished behind the blue metallic fence surrounding the ramps and completed the steep climb. A long red carpet lay sprawled out before Madisyn Academy's double doors.

Katherine ran up the carpet, turned to face Elissa and cradled her imaginary award.

"Thanks to my crew and the fans. You rock." She wiped an imaginary tear off her cheek.

Elissa laughed so hard she had to stop driving her wheelchair. Once inside, they followed a long hallway decorated with cases of gold and silver trophies and framed photographs of past graduating classes.

"Let's check out our parents' nerdy pictures," Katherine said.

"Those clothes and hairstyles are so nasty."

"Pure embarrassment. Maybe I should transfer now," Katherine pointed to a photograph on the wall.

Katherine's dad wore the Madisyn Academy vest with a bright tie-dyed dress shirt, matching pants, and a brown leather headband. The peace sign he was making completed his look. Her mom wore a flowery lime green pantsuit with a bright pink collar and cuffs, her Academy vest barely visible under her jacket. A pink hat decorated with green flowery fabric sat on her head, setting off the brightest green eyes Elissa had ever seen. Really, for the time when Katherine's parents attended, Elissa thought they should have been in style.

"My mom's here." Elissa pointed her out.

Stephanie's long blonde hair rested on a red polyester jacket but Elissa thought her new shorter hair suited her better. She was wearing a Madisyn vest, a red, orange, and blue striped fabric belt, and a matching tie in her hair.

"Hello...he's a total hottie," Katherine pointed.

"Ew! That's my dad," Elissa groaned.

"My bad." Katherine kept walking but Elissa lingered and wondered what other secrets about his life he kept from her.

In the photo, Christopher had long wavy hair and a goatee and was wearing the plain vest with a green shirt highlighting his green eyes. Elissa took a deep breath and reminded herself why she was here: to find out the truth and to bring Christopher home where he belonged. She followed Katherine and the other students into a large room.

"First years, join your respective tables," a tall woman in Madisyn attire announced.

"Already being ordered around," Katherine whispered.

The modern room was filled with dinner theatre-type riser levels with many large round silver tables with matching chairs. Instead of steps, there was a zigzag pathway gradually weaving its way past the tables and down to the front of the room. Most of the tables had students sitting around them. Other students were standing around talking. The big windows provided a view of a bay and the large cruise ship.

At the lower end of the room, next to the largest window, was a long table. Several adults were seated and watching the students. Unfortunately, Elissa recognized Agent Sullivan and knew she might make this entire experience more difficult than it needed to be, but then again, finding out why she felt that way could prove interesting. There was one unoccupied chair at the end of the table. As Elissa scanned the room, she saw Agent Larsson walk behind the seated adults. She wanted to be glad to see a familiar face, but wondered if he would get in the way of finding Christopher.

He walked over, stopped by the podium, and then shuffled some green note cards around. His blue eyes sparkled as he looked up at all the students.

"May I please have your attention?" he asked.

The room fell silent. All the new students sat at attention in the corner of the room. Returning students were preoccupied with their computers.

"I'm Helmer Larsson. Welcome new and returning students. All your fellow students eagerly await your arrival. Please be seated."

All the residence tables were covered in streamers and balloons: silver for Edmonton Ridge, navy for London Yard, and purple for Sydney Arch. The London Yard table was full of conservative-looking students wearing designer glasses. The Sydney Arch table had students with the latest haircuts and seemed tired, with dark circles under their eyes. The Edmonton Ridge table looked the most low-key.

Elissa's wheelchair glided easily along the black and white tiled pathway as she drove over to the table. A short girl with long black hair, flawless mocha skin and a yellow dress shirt, slid out a chair from the table.

"Welcome. I'm Rachel – third year student."

"Thanks. I'm Elissa. This is Katherine."

For the first time in a long time, it felt good to be with other students her age instead of only seeing Stephanie and various doctors all day. Several other students welcomed them to the table. Sitting a short distance down was Benjamin, and when he saw Elissa he winked at her. She searched the room and found Malina seated at the Sydney Arch table.

Jack raced over, gave them both a high five and grabbed the last empty chair next to Katherine. The room was filled with a mesh of voices. An aroma of Italian tomato wafted through a green door on the side of the room.

"Students, will you direct your attention here?" Agent Larsson asked. "After eating, you are encouraged to get settled in your residences."

Formally-dressed waiters waltzed around the room, placing plates in front of each student. Each plate had a miniature pizza on it. All the toppings were on lazy susans in the middle of the table. Once the toppings were on the pizza, a large heat station rose up from the middle of the table. The pizzas were quickly heated, cheese melted and crusts crisped.

The new students sat quietly, listening to horror stories about various instructors and assignments. Elissa noticed that she was not the only one who seemed to be growing more apprehensive about the week ahead. By the rings around several other students' eyes, she knew too that she was not the only one waiting to go to bed. Once they were done eating, the waiters returned to collect the plates and deliver ice cream sundaes.

"Please watch the ship safety video," Agent Larsson said as a video screen lowered from the ceiling. Once the lifeboat video was done, Agent Larsson returned to the podium.

"A note on our new academic policy: Miss one assignment or get a grade below 80% and within 24 hours, you will be taken via helicopter to our land campus, Camp Summit, where you will complete a year of studies before being considered to return here to the Ocean-Alias ship campus next year. No exceptions. Also ship curfew, on weekdays, is at 9:30 p.m. At 9:35 all students must be in their cabins, as we complete a cabin check and an advisor will be in a cabin in the hallway. We will also be monitoring any doors that are accessed. Friday, Saturdays and Sundays curfew is 11:30 p.m."

Elissa swallowed as the reality that she was not an A student anymore, and that her inability to concentrate might stop her mission before it even began. She needed to stay on the Ocean-Alias to get Christopher's files. Having to keep such high standards with the assignments and tests was going to make getting into the files and bringing Christopher home even more of a challenge – a challenge that Elissa was ready to take on.

"Have a good night. Your class schedules will be on your desks. Classes begin tomorrow. Team selections for the Madisyn Academy Challenge will be posted soon and the first round will begin on Thursday. The first round will be completed prior to us selecting which students will be accepted to train on the Ocean-Alias or Camp Summit campus. The first three teams from each residence will receive an invitation to join us on the Ocean-Alias.

"Remember, the first round for the Academy Games is only for new students. *Lykke til*," Agent Larsson said. Katherine and Elissa looked at each other, confused.

"'Good luck.' It's Norwegian. Always testing our vocab," Rachel explained.

Agent Larsson returned to his table and sat down. The stakes were laid out for Elissa. If she wanted to be on the Ocean-Alias campus, she needed to take all the challenges seriously. She needed to try and keep her mind on more than just bringing Christopher home. The thought after the long day just seemed to exhaust her further, but a little tiredness wasn't going to stop her.

"I'll take you to your ship escort, Agent Larsson's location. Said he wanted to talk to Elissa and Katherine. He'll get you access to the elevator towers." Rachel pushed her chair up to the table.

Elissa did not want to be treated any differently. She just wanted a chance, like every other student, to explore Madisyn Academy, but she knew there would be mobility challenges.

"Rachel, what's your specialization?" Katherine asked as they followed her into the hallway.

"Technology development. My parents own a gadget company," Rachel said. She pulled out her sunglasses, pressed a button on the right arm and handed them to Elissa.

Elissa put them on. The notice on the outside bulletin board became clear as the glasses focused on it.

"It's a prototype. With the magnifier and night vision, it has serious potential." She lifted up her bag in Elissa's eye line.

Elissa clearly saw the bag's contents: pens, computer, telephone, MP3 player and a bottle of water.

"You must've had the coolest toys," Elissa said with a grin.

Rachel looked at Elissa, smirked and nodded. Elissa handed her back the glasses. Malina and Benjamin were sitting on the steps talking and pointing at Elissa and Katherine. Elissa tried her best not to notice but wished she knew why Malina acted that way.

"X-ray glasses are so back-of-comic-books. Privacy is essential – these can't scan anything emitting a heat signal." Rachel smiled.

Katherine tried the glasses on and Rachel said, "Look up and blink twice. You'll see a connection to the Internet and can retrieve info by looking at the keys displayed in the lens."

"Wicked," Katherine said.

"Try squinting, blink once and look at my face," Rachel put her hair behind her ear and looked at Katherine.

"All your personal file info is displayed. These are essential." Katherine handed the glasses back to Rachel.

"Can I check that out?" Elissa asked as she looked in Malina's direction.

Rachel handed Elissa the glasses.

She put them on then tried to casually look at Malina to get access to her information.

Malina Jenkins
Parents: (Divorced)
Mr. Scott Jenkins – Secret Agent
Mrs. Reilly Jenkins – Pediatrician
Siblings:
 Breanna - deceased age 7 – cancer
 Jacey – Doctor program at Harvard

That explained why Mr. Jenkins was always coming and going. The information made Elissa sad. It reminded Elissa of Mr. Jenkins' photograph in the living room of an older girl in her high school graduation attire and a younger girl standing alongside her. He never shared their names, but his eyes always had an aura of emptiness when he spoke of them. The more Elissa looked at her, the more she thought Malina was the pre-teen girl. Elissa wondered if she missed her dad. Maybe that's why she was so mad at the world.

As they headed out of range, Elissa stopped, took off the glasses and handed them back to Rachel. After she caught up with Katherine, they followed Rachel outside the building. The air was crisp and fresh compared to all the pollution Elissa was used to. Fall was starting to change the landscape, just as Elissa was sure the next two weeks would change her.

Seven

Acclimate

Elissa first noticed the lack of noise: no sirens, no traffic and no aircraft flying overhead. There was no smog, only pine trees and wild flowers filling the air and reminding her of the potpourri Stephanie kept in her bedroom. Now there was no way Elissa could secretly wonder if a forest really smelled that way.

"It's sure quiet here." The silence reminded Elissa of her uncomfortable hospital room. Of their house since Christopher was gone. When he was at home, he always had the radio or the television on as the quiet made him nervous.

"After you've been here awhile, the brutal noise back at home takes some major adjustments," Rachel said.

They followed Rachel toward two pillars connecting the stairs to the gangplank that led out to the ship. Several students pointed at Elissa and whispered and she wondered why her wheelchair made her any different.

"Ignore them. You're the first student with her own wheels."

"Really?" Elissa asked.

"I wish I could be the first at something. Breaking 'em in good." Rachel patted Elissa on the arm.

Elissa waved at the gawking girls as if they were good friends. The girls exchanged looks and then waved back. For a moment, Elissa felt a bit less self-conscious.

"If you two need to talk about anything, anytime, feel free," Rachel handed both Elissa and Katherine a business card with her contact information on it.

"Miss Morris," a deep voice said. Elissa looked up to see Agent Larsson. "I'm here to escort you and Miss Bennison to the vessel. Follow me. Thank you, Miss Abbot." Rachel nodded to Agent Larsson and walked back towards the building.

"This elevator tower is your entry to the ship. When you embark or debark, your access will be identical at every port." He led them behind the tall round mirrored pillar to the darkest area in back of the structure. Hidden under the shade of the gangplank, elevator doors stood flush, blending into the pillar.

"For security purposes, only physically challenged students are allowed to access the gangplank elevator. Miss Bennison is prohibited from using the elevator without you. You are required to run your identification into this port."

Once in the elevator, they climbed toward the sky, higher and higher away from the safety of the ground. The doors opened slowly and they entered the gangplank. Elissa looked down and saw the waves below, took a deep breath and raced towards the ship, with Agent Larsson and Katherine in tow.

Jack was standing directly ahead of them with a group of other students.

"We're here," Agent Larsson announced. "You excited?"

"I, well… yes."

"It can be overwhelming at first. But you'll acclimate quickly. Before you know it, it'll be like your second home."

"I suppose so," Elissa said as she smiled at Jack.

"Hey Kat, do you have your cabin assignment?" Jack asked, startled by Agent Larsson's presence.

Katherine pulled her sheet out of her pocket, which she'd had no time to refer to yet, and waved it in the air as they walked past Jack and his crowd.

"That reminds me. You two will be roommates. Would you like me to escort you to your cabin?" Agent Larsson asked.

"Please," Elissa said as she eyed the large ship and felt lost in such an unfamiliar place.

Katherine and Elissa followed him along the rich wooden top deck crowded with students. All the while, Elissa scanned the crowd for a bald man wearing sunglasses. Mr. Russel was on the ship somewhere, of that she was sure, but finding him could prove challenging.

"This ship is, and I say this scientifically, humongous," Katherine declared.

Agent Larsson laughed. They passed a large swimming pool with a small deep pool at the far end with a hoist and chains above it. Elissa swallowed and hoped if that was where they held the submersion classes, she wouldn't have any soon.

"This is the bow of the ship. The other end is the stern. Students are welcome to swim during supervised spares and weekends. Miss Morris, we have assistance if you wish to go swimming. Just contact me."

"I'll remember that."

They passed through sliding glass patio doors into a hallway and past several wooden doors before entering a green door leading to the stairwell and elevator.

"Here we are. Your room is on the Edmonton Ridge deck."

In the elevator, Elissa turned to Agent Larsson. "If we need to evacuate the ship, or a fire alarm goes off, will the elevator work?"

"I was just about to mention that. If you are in the elevator, it will return to the observation deck for exit. In a fire, the elevator will shut down, but we'll come get you."

"No worries. My chair can climb steps."

Katherine looked at Elissa as if she were crazy.

Elissa experienced a moment of déjà vu as they exited into a silver lobby decorated with a dark floral carpet and doors labeled **Girls Only**, **Edmonton Ridge Club Room**, and **Boys Only**. It reminded her of every hotel she'd ever stayed in, all over the world. Bad taste in carpet was universal. The dark colors and patterns made it difficult to see any stains – any secrets.

"Here we are." Agent Larsson walked to the **Girls Only** door, slid in his keycard and opened the door to reveal another long silver hallway. He used his keycard again to get them access to the first room on the right.

"We designed this cabin larger to accommodate all your special equipment. Miss Bennison and Miss Morris, your presence is required in the field ops room at seven am, before breakfast. I'll leave you to acclimate to your new surroundings." Turning away from Katherine, he said, "Elissa, meet me in a half hour on the observation deck, stern side, in Morocco's room."

Their escort closed the door behind him and left her to wonder who Morocco was.

"Elissa you know Agent Larsson?" Katherine looked at her for an answer.

"He's a family friend."

Katherine examined the room. "Excellent. Private washroom." Katherine pulled her arm into her chest and twirled around. "Come look. Come look."

Elissa raced over. There was a large tub in the corner of the bathroom.

"Jets. We have jets," Katherine squealed.

"Great." Elissa drove into the main room. She couldn't remember the last time she was as excited about anything as Katherine was about their bathtub. Maybe it was just because it had been such long day that the bed looked so inviting. All she wanted to do was stretch out and sleep.

In the main room, silver bedspreads with Edmonton Ridge logo covered two queen-size, metal-framed beds. There was a table along the wall next to the door and two separate work tables against the other wall. A full-length window gave an endless view of ocean waves glowing in the moon and starlight, a view that made Elissa feel small and insignificant.

"Awesome view. What's over there?" Elissa pointed to an open door leading to a dark room.

"Don't know." Katherine walked into the room.

Another squeal sparked Elissa's curiosity. She drove into the room. There was a patio door leading to a small veranda. In the right corner was exercise equipment and in the left, Katherine was on a red couch watching TV with her feet on a coffee table. Some things looked familiar, like her iPod and speakers. Atlases, grammar, science, and fiction books and a Wii filled the wall-length shelves. Alongside was a guitar and keyboard. Having some items from home made this new place and new room feel a bit more like home.

"Ours is unquestionably the presidential suite," Kat said, sighing as she closed her eyes dreamily.

"Maybe we shouldn't advertise," Elissa suggested.

"Totally hush-hush," Katherine agreed.

Elissa drove back into the main room where she noticed a spiral-bound notebook resting on one workstation by the window. It contained student maps and ship floor plans – an entire world Elissa couldn't wait to explore. She groaned when she saw all the stern, bow and other ship terms that at this moment just made her more confused.

"Found the student guidebook." Elissa stuck her head into the other room.

Katherine nodded, but her eyes remained glued to the television.

Elissa eased up to the workstation by the window and pulled out her computer to check access to the Agent Links network.

Good connection, she thought. *Wish I had more time to hack my way into the ship's blueprints. Need to find the exact room where the files are housed.*

Before putting away her computer, Elissa checked her email. The empty inbox reminded her how much she hated waiting on other people to get a job done. *Still, I'm here and closer to the truth about finding Christopher than I was a few hours ago.*

"I'm off to meet Agent Larsson," Elissa said. "See you later."

Eight

Confidence

Elissa drove to the elevator and proceeded to the observation deck, stern end. *Astonishing! I've just arrived and already I'm summoned to the principal's office.*

The elevator doors silently slid open, revealing a quiet, dimly lit hallway. The tires of her wheelchair made a squishing noise on the dark wood flooring, making it hard to sneak up unannounced. Photos of cars and inventions adorned the plain white walls, adding a bit of character to the surroundings.

A door suddenly opened in an alcove, off in another hallway, where Agent Larsson appeared.

Elissa sighed heavily, happy to see a familiar face.

"Glad you came. Welcome to Morocco's room." He opened the door and backed away to give her space.

Elissa drove into the large room, surprised at its size and park-themed decoration. The walls were covered in a mural of a fenced forest; green potted trees rose up from the grass and brick pathway along the floor. A dog-sized dog feeder with food and water sat in the corner. On a shelf above was a red bubble gum dispenser filled with colorful dog treats.

Over in the far left corner, a light brown Labrador retriever wearing a black vest rested its head on its paws. When the lab saw Elissa, she lifted up her head and looked at the man sitting next to her. He whispered something and the dog returned its head to its paws but kept moving its eyes towards the new trespassers in the room.

Elissa fought her initial reaction to go over and pet the dog.

"Elissa, this is Ryan and Morocco," Agent Larsson explained.

The man stood up and came walking over to them, but the dog remained in place. He motioned for the dog to come but she stubbornly covered her head with her paws.

Elissa smiled as she looked at the dog who had so much personality.

"Morocco is annoyed with me," Ryan said. "You call her."

"Come on, girl." Elissa reached out her hands and clapped her hand on her leg.

Morocco again lifted up her head, stood up and ran over. She stopped just before Elissa, sniffed her, and then lifted her paw up on Elissa's lap. Elissa delightedly shook it.

"The reason we asked you to join us was to introduce you to your new partner. Morocco will be with you at all times." Agent Larsson stood proud.

"No... really? You mean it? Morocco is mine?" Elissa petted her and for a brief moment felt a joy like she hadn't felt since before the accident.

"Totally..." Ryan said.

Agent Larsson cleared his throat and shot Ryan a look that seemed like a reminder that he's not actually a teenager.

"Morocco will stay with you on the ship and return home with you. I'll let Ryan explain the rest."

"Thanks, Agent Larsson."

Turning to Elissa, Ryan said, "Gotta warn ya, even when she's working in her vest, she stubbornly insists on playing with her Frisbee. Morocco is specially trained to assist you."

He paused a moment to gauge Elissa's reaction, then continued. "Even though you're not going into field ops, with your physical limitations, sometimes unexpected things happen. With your limited mobility, we wanted to even your odds a bit. Morocco understands more than cute tricks. We'll show you." Glancing quickly at the furry animal, he grinned and added, "Well… if she'll forgive me."

Morocco looked up at Ryan, lifted up her head and walked off. Ryan followed, petted her and whispered something before he returned to Elissa.

"May I set you on the ground?" Ryan asked.

She frantically searched for something in the room she could pull herself up onto to get up off the floor. Being on the floor, without her chair took away her mobility and reliability to take care of herself.

"We'll be right here," Ryan said.

Elissa unclipped her seatbelt.

He gently picked her up, set her down on the hard ground then left her alone while he joined Agent Larsson in the corner.

Her wheelchair was behind her. *Gotta stay calm – I'm not really trapped,* Elissa reminded herself. *There's two other people in the room with me.* She eyed Morocco, who came running over and licked her face then barked.

"I can't, girl," Elissa said, doing her best to hold back the panic forming in her chest.

Morocco lay down flat on the floor next to her, butted her nose under Elissa's back and got behind her.

"Ryan, I'm too heavy."

"I'm twice as heavy and she lifted me. Follow her lead. Sit on her shoulders. Tell her 'brace'."

"Brace," Elissa said, haltingly, and gently pulled herself up onto Morocco's shoulders. Morocco slowly stood up, and waited while Elissa transferred into her chair. The tight feeling in her chest lifted, replaced with a feeling of freedom and relief that she wouldn't be stranded again with her new friend. This gave Elissa back a degree of independence that she had been missing.

"Sure she's okay?"

Ryan nodded.

"Elissa, come over here," Ryan said, as he walked over to the light switch. "Point to it and tell Morocco, 'off'."

On command, Morocco reached up and flicked the light switch off. With a second command, she flipped it back on. Then showing her excitement, she ran down the length of the room, flicked her legs out and barked at her audience.

It took Ryan a few minutes to regain her attention. Finally, he tossed a paper bag on the floor where Morocco retrieved it and promptly took the sack to Elissa.

"That's awesome," Elissa said.

"Play dead," he said. Morocco plopped down on the floor. "She will stay there until you tell her to get up." Ryan walked away and then returned to where Morocco was.

"Morocco. Up."

The dog stood and looked at them, waiting expectantly.

"Should you feel insecure, if you want to draw attention, despite her being non-aggressive, if you click your tongue she will bark loudly."

Morocco stuck her head between them trying to hear what they were saying.

Elissa smiled and petted her head. She enjoyed Morocco's sense of curiosity and fun as they seemed to be a lot alike.

Agent Larsson said, "We'll give you a few minutes to get acquainted." He and Ryan walked out of the room.

Morocco stood still. She and Elissa surveyed each other for some time.

"Hey, girl."

Morocco walked over and put her head on Elissa's lap. Elissa petted her. Then Morocco ran to the corner, picked up a Frisbee, ran to Elissa and placed it on her lap.

Elissa tossed the Frisbee to the other side of the room. Morocco jumped and ran towards it.

Elissa laughed.

Morocco turned, looked at her and then increased her speed. Then she dropped the Frisbee back on Elissa's lap.

"You okee dokee with Morocco?" Ryan said.

"Definitely," Elissa nodded.

"This will be Morocco's area, where she can stretch her legs. There is more room up here than could be provided on the residence floor. That said, she will stay in your room with you. This room is a special place for the two of you. Just bring her food dishes with you when you go to eat," Agent Larsson said.

"Is she house or…ship broken?" Elissa asked.

"There's a doggie door in your cabin leading to an adjoining private room, and for when she has to go. When you're off the ship, she'll let you know when she needs to go. Here's my card. Anything, anytime, give me a shout," Ryan said.

"Thanks so much. She's just beautiful," Elissa said.

"You're welcome. Your keycard will provide you access to this room," Agent Larsson said.

Ryan handed Elissa Morocco's bag with her bowls, toys, treats and a small book titled, "About Your Trained Dog."

Morocco followed Elissa to the elevator, ran in front of her and waited by the elevator button. With Elissa's instruction, Morocco stood up, lifted her front paw and pressed the down button.

"Good girl." Elissa patted her. Inside the elevator Morocco waited for further instructions. The elevator stopped and a man wearing a ship employee's uniform raced to get into the elevator before the doors closed. He pulled a remote out his pocket and clicked it up towards the camera in the corner of the elevator to provide privacy.

Morocco placed herself between them. Elissa looked up and recognized him, despite the really bad blonde wig, clip-on earring and padding to give him the impression of having a belly. She sucked in her breath, stunned. The fact he was on The Ocean-Alias, working on the staff, made her wonder how he got past security. Her mind raced; before she could clear her thoughts, she made eye contact. She stiffled a scream. *This is the man who has my dad, the man who took away the use of my legs.* She leaned back and took a deep breath. She wanted to run but the elevator wasn't on a floor.

"Don't know why animals don't like me. Remember me?" He offered his hand to shake hers.

Elissa refused, and started to scream.

Mr. Russel pulled a gun out of his pocket and pointed it at Morocco.

"I suggest you keep quiet and keep that dog under control if you want her to leave this elevator alive. I thought you were more mature than this."

Elissa's mind raced, realizing the camera was most likely playing a video loop and she was alone with Mr. Russel. Yet she thought that when she looked at the camera, it had moved and the light had blinked.

Morocco barked, growled and showed her teeth.

Anger heated up Elissa's cheeks as she stared into the cold hazel eyes of the man who had taken Christopher and the use of her legs away from her.

"At least I'm not hiding, playing dress up under a disguise, Mr. Russel."

His face flushed red then he calmly leaned back, crossed his arms and looked at her.

Morocco bared her sharp teeth and posed in a protective stance.

"Christopher is safe for now. I need your assistance with the Ice Rose program. The program requires Christopher's password, which he needs some motivation to share, and your password. We have secured his fingerprint. If you secure what I need, I'll return him."

"Why isn't he helping you?" She searched his face for answers.

He squatted down so she could clearly see his face.

"Christopher has not broken during our questioning. I thought perhaps you might want to save him from another questioning session."

"What makes you think I know it?"

"My dear, I have seen your work. Only you would add another level to a program entry," Russel said.

Elissa felt like a mouse caught in a trap as she stared into his eyes but she held her fear back. Then, thinking about all he had taken from her and her family, she let a wave of anger and adrenaline fuel her courage.

"A simple exchange, Miss Morris – your services for Daddy – your choice. Contact the authorities, leave this ship other than for Madisyn-sanctioned field trips, and this offer will not be the only thing that expires."

Elissa leaned back in her wheelchair, drove closer to him and enjoyed his obvious discomfort as he attempted to shift his legs so she didn't pin him against the wall.

Morocco closed in, the hair on her back bristling. She silently bared her teeth and moved closer to him.

"Bring me real proof. Then we'll talk," Elissa stayed against him for a moment even though his garlic breath repulsed her.

The elevator beeped.

Confidently, she unpinned him, turned and pressed the elevator button to rush it to the floor.

Elissa said, "This is my stop. I need proof he's alive and a promise that you won't hurt any more members of my family."

She reached out her hand to shake his.

The doors began to open.

He shook her hand just as the doors opened.

"I'll contact you."

Elissa let go of his hand, flicked her electric wheelchair to high and drove out to the safety of the busy hallway.

Morocco stayed between her and Mr. Russel until she was clear of the elevator. Then she took her place, once again, by Elissa's side.

The elevator doors closed with Mr. Russel still inside.

Nine

Judgment
Day Two

Elissa awoke occasionally after drifting off from time to time, in a dark cabin in a place that, as of yet, lacked any real comfort. Before bed, they did a cabin check to ensure everyone was present. Elissa also heard the hallway being checked several times during the night as she was awake so often.

She missed the familiarity of her own room. She missed being able to go downstairs and sneak a snack from the fridge, or on the nights when her nightmares woke her, curling up on her bedroom sofa and watching something from her massive DVR television collection.

The ship had debarked at midnight, and she was sure Mr. Russel couldn't take the risk of being trapped on it so he surely had gotten off. A cold comfort, as he left her powerless until he contacted her. The best she could do was to get into the instructor's schedules to know when the traffic on the floor would be limited and to find the power system for the doorknob security.

The ship gently swayed, reminding her how far she was from her house – and dry land. An enormous moon cast ominous shadows on the floor and the wall behind her. Out of the comer of her eye, she glimpsed a tall silhouette. Slowly, she turned her head to see Katherine's man-sized teddy bear in its stand. It took her a minute to re-orient herself to her location, in a new room and bed. Katherine's rooster alarm clock blared.

Katherine groaned. She swung at the clock and knocked it to the floor, but the rooster crowed persistently.

"Sorry," she mumbled.

Morocco pawed Elissa's arm.

"Morning, girl."

While Katherine took her shower and got dressed, Elissa completed her tricep and bicep repetitions. Morocco disappeared behind the doggie door, returned and chased a ball around the room, but all the while she kept an eye on Elissa. Her routine gave her time to think of a plan. She knew she needed to find and talk to Mr. Russel, even if she was terrified. She also needed time to find the file room and gain access.

The never-ending ocean view reminded Elissa of her limitations: *she was sinking and treading water in a sea of physical expectations.* Her heart raced, tears gathered in her eyes and her palms began to sweat as she drove over to the veranda door. Once outside, with the cool breeze blowing on her cheeks, her feeling of confinement floated away with the seagulls. A knock on the cabin door jolted her back to reality. With a sniffle, she turned to go back inside.

"I'll get it." Katherine skipped to the door. Elissa heard a mumbled female voice-and then Katherine closed the door. "For your info: Rachel, breakfast, main dining room, after meeting."

"Almost good to go," Elissa said as she kept her head down so any trace of red or her temporary discomfort wouldn't be witnessed, or even worse, questioned. She rushed into the washroom and tried to wash away her discomfort. Composed, she checked her face one last time in the mirror.

When she exited the washroom, Katherine was tossing Morocco's disk. Morocco's tail wagged happily as she returned it. As Elissa put her bag on the back of her wheelchair, Morocco grabbed her sleeve and gently pulled her towards the play area. For a few minutes, Elissa felt happy – like they were the only three living things on the entire ship. But they were running late.

"Let's go, Morocco," Elissa called. Morocco waited for her to slide on her work vest. Katherine led the trio into the hallway.

"Excited?" Katherine asked.

"Kind of, but tight places freak me out."

"Space is essential. We'll explore the ship when the walls close in around us. This place is huge!"

In the field ops room, a group of students milled around. Elissa and Katherine spotted Jack. A whiteboard had diagrams and step-by-step instructions on how to gain access to various locks. There were rows and rows of tables; each had two sections with what looked like game show dividers sticking out of them. Resting on each table was an oak box with a gold door knob. When she found the room that housed the files, Elissa knew a lock and some kind of security would stand in her way. Maybe this would help her gain access. Not to mention this skill, the ability to open various locks, was sure to come up during the Academy Games.

The large room had ladders built into two walls. Along the ceiling were large pipes and a climbing harness track. Blue mats were piled up in the corner. One wall had a chain link fence, complete with barbed wire, pushed to the side. Several lasers and motion detectors were set up, but all looked disengaged. A small bookshelf sat in the back corner filled with hard cover crime books and had a citrus air freshener that made the room smell of the produce area at a grocery store. Looking at all of the equipment, Elissa was relieved not to be a field ops student.

Agent Sullivan strutted to the front of the room in her high heels but didn't scuff up the tile floor. Her dark hair was pulled up in a tight bun with a black crocheted snood that secured any hairs that might try to escape. Her strong perfume caused the students close to the front to clear their throats and rub their eyes.

"Hello, first years. I'm Agent Sullivan. Everyone find a desk. We'll be administering another test today, but this one is pass or fail. Read the instructions on the board."

Elissa and Katherine stayed next to each other. Morocco sat at Elissa's side.

"Take out your lock pick kits. You have five minutes to open the lock in front of you. When you're done, sit on the floor."

Elissa set her lock pick kit on her lap and hoped no one heard her stomach growl.

Agent Sullivan's heels clicked as she walked up behind Elissa and spoke just loud enough so both girls could hear. She placed her hand on one hip and leaned down.

"Miss Morris, you'll complete the test like everyone else, on your own, so you can learn. No special treatment allowed."

"Fair enough. What gave you such an impression?" Elissa looked up at her.

Agent Sullivan frowned and pointed to Elissa.

"People like you should be working in telemarketing, not as secret agents."

The students seemed to be quiet in that moment and were staring at horror at the board. Elissa could not believe what she was hearing – because she used a wheelchair to get around she was a different kind of person?

Agent Sullivan placed both her hands on her hips, "If you want to be here, you need to pull your own weight. In a real situation, you can't be carried around by your team."

Katherine looked around Agent Sullivan towards Elissa. Her mouth was gaping open. A heat, an anger slithered in Elissa, waiting to strike, but instead of saying anything, she kept quiet. Agent Sullivan straightened up and walked away.

"Go," Agent Sullivan said. She walked through the rows. Elissa opened the kit and picked two tools. One little lock and one woman was not going to stand in her way.

Once when visiting Grandma's house, knowing her parents were out for a morning run, Elissa went into the kitchen and found Grandma wasn't up yet. Knowing her grandmother needed to eat soon because of her diabetes, Elissa went to her bedroom to check on her. The doorknob was old and had a small hole in it. It was locked, but Elissa could hear her grandmother moaning.

She used a toothpick to jiggle the latch and open the door. When she got into the room, Grandma was on the floor. Elissa's parents had taught her to give Grandma honey or juice to raise her blood sugar levels. By the time her parents had returned, Grandma was downstairs eating the breakfast Elissa made for her. She figured that lock picking experience might eventually come in handy. She just didn't know it would be at school.

The tamper-proof gold doorknob in front of her required her to decide between a tumbler, level or a warded lock tool. Two minutes passed. Elissa heard a squeal in the quietness. A student had successfully picked her lock. Elissa picked up the tubular pins, placed one in the lock, held the other and twisted it. The inner latch was stubborn. Katherine conquered her lock and sat on the floor. Now she felt like a loser and couldn't believe this lock was stumping her.

Agent Sullivan sauntered behind Elissa and stopped. "Trouble, Miss Morris? Time is ticking. Tick. Tick."

Morocco looked up at Agent Sullivan and snorted.

"Thanks for the reminder." Elissa closed her eyes and focused on a mental picture of the latch, determined to open this lock and make this woman change her opinion of her by the time she was through. Then the latch flipped, she turned the knob and opened the door. Relief and justification stayed with Elissa as she looked around the room at the other students still struggling.

After a few minutes, every student was finished, except Jack. All eyes were on him as he frantically fiddled to get his lock open. The clock's second hand ticked frustratingly up to five minutes. With forty seconds left, the tools tumbled out of the lock. Jack picked them up and started again. Fifteen seconds. Elissa willed him on. With ten seconds to go, a smile spread across Jack's face and his lock clicked open.

"Well done. Now you have to get your time under ten seconds. All of you who took longer," Agent Sullivan walked alongside Elissa, "and you know who you are, have some practice to do."

Katherine looked at Elissa and wrinkled up her nose, imitating Agent Sullivan. They both smiled.

"Inside your box is another locked box. You have two minutes. Go."

Her heart sunk at the thought of having to open another lock. All she wanted was to be able to enjoy the achievement of getting into the first door. Inside was a metal box, like a file cabinet drawer with a round silver lock. Elissa opened her lock pick kit and chose two multipurpose picks. This was a more complex lock and an opportunity to polish her skills for the file room. In the keyhole, she wiggled the tools, and a red bulb illuminated above her station, while a siren like at the carnival games rang. This time, Elissa wondered if taking her time would have been the best outcome, as it would've drawn less attention to her. Katherine stopped and looked at her light.

"Everyone stop!" Agent Sullivan charged like a bull to a matador in Elissa's direction.

All the other students leaned and stepped closer to get a look at what Elissa had done. For just a moment, Elissa wished she could disappear as she watched Agent Sullivan get closer and closer. She swallowed and tried to collect her thoughts.

"There is no way that lock would open that easily. Miss Morris, how did you unlock it so fast?" Agent Sullivan glared down at Elissa.

"Multipurpose picks." Elissa held up her picks for examination. Katherine scowled and shook her head as she watched Agent Sullivan tower over Elissa. Morocco snorted again, louder this time. Elissa petted Morocco, more for some support than for Morocco.

"Everyone, maybe Miss Morris would like to come up to the front of the class and show us how she opened it so fast?"

The words echoed in Elissa's head and dread climbed into her heart.

"But I understood we were supposed to learn on our own, without any special treatment?"

Whispers filled the classroom as the students leaned in towards each other, barely hiding their gestures in Elissa's direction. Agent Sullivan's face flushed red and she leaned back on her heels.

"Well, let's make an exception this time," Agent Sullivan smiled and led Elissa, with Morocco in tow, to a locked door at the front of the classroom. Right then, she wasn't sure which was worse, having the entire class know who she was, or being given another opportunity to look so keen and like an idiot in front of the entire class. This time she had really gone and done it. *Way to go girl*, she chided herself.

"Class, let's watch Elissa and then you can try it."

Agent Sullivan stood to the side. Elissa picked up her multipurpose picks and examined her assignment. This wooden door was a double threat with an interlocking deadbolt and a doorknob lock. On the board were no instructions to open the lock so Elissa was going to have to keep in mind all the times she watched Christopher going into music instrument storage room with all his many locks. All the times he forgot his keys and needed to pick into the locks, despite her lack of patience, she did learn a skill that would now come in handy.

"Agent Sullivan, we haven't covered interlocked deadbolts." Elissa innocently looked at her.

"Well, try it anyway." Agent Sullivan waved the students to gather on the floor around Elissa. She felt the hairs stand up on the back of her neck and her palms began to sweat.

Elissa selected the multi-purpose pick and a tension wrench. First, she picked the deadbolt, opened it and left a pick in the latch. Then she moved on to the door knob. All the students were sitting on the floor and were being very quiet, which made Elissa more nervous. A distraction of someone sneezing or whispering would have at least relieved some of the tension. The wall clock ticked. Morocco licked her mouth. As she twisted the knob to open it, the deadbolt mechanism snapped on the pick and stayed open. With light pressure she opened each tumbler in the mechanism. She couldn't believe that the lock was opening, since she just took a lucky guess, but she wouldn't share that fact with Agent Sullivan.

"There you go." Elissa opened the door, picked up the keys on the inside of the door and handed them to Agent Sullivan, who reluctantly took them. Katherine beamed at her and winked. The students clapped and gave a few "woo hoos." At least she didn't embarrass herself in front of the class. Instead she had taken Agent Sullivan's challenge and passed.

"Thank you," Agent Sullivan said stiffly. "Class, return to your desks. You have two minutes to open the lock."

The students sped back to their desks and began on the second door. Elissa packed everything up and went back over to her desk. This little exercise had provided her confidence she could get into the file room, no matter what security they had waiting. One by one, the students glided through opening their locks

"Great job today, students. See you at our next class in our regular classroom."

Elissa and Katherine stared at each other. They were the first two out the door and into the safety of the hallway.

Ten

Expectations

Clanging plates and buzzing conversation emanated from the main dining room before Elissa and Katherine even reached the door.

Jack waved from across the room and yelled, "Thought you weren't coming."

"Yeah, like I'd trust you to save us any food."

"Why break my ravaging tradition? We just arrived too." Jack rushed to sit in the chair before Katherine, who saw him and rushed as well, and they almost both fell on the floor as the chair tipped, but Jack stayed seated.

"Ain't that the truth," Benjamin said

"Oh...sorry...You remember my roommate Benjamin? Benjamin, this is Katherine, Elissa, and..." Jack pointed to the dog as he sat the chair back up and Katherine chose another chair.

Elissa was too busy envying how much time Jack would get to spend with Benjamin to reply.

"Morocco," Katherine jumped in.

Morocco barked as she lifted up a paw to shake Benjamin's hand, but he lunged away.

"Morocco's friendly," Katherine assured him.

"All I see is teeth. Big, sharp, teeth. Sorry, girl." Benjamin looked at Morocco apologetically. Morocco let her tail fall and sat down next to Elissa.

She petted Morocco and whispered, "Give him time."

The food came and the server set a bowl down in front of Morocco. She responded with a tail wag.

"Thank you."

Elissa began gulping the pancakes and bacon to give her more time in the breakfast period to get to her task.

"Excuse me." Agent Larsson stood at the podium. The room fell silent.

"As you know today is the first full day of classes on the Ocean-Alias. Beside every place setting is an envelope with a password and web address. This password gives you access to our network. If you have any questions, please contact administration. Or if you prefer, contact your student representative."

Once Elissa had her class information off the website, all she wanted to do was find the file room and get into it.

"Before Memory and Speech, I'd better take Morocco back to our room."

"I'll join ya. Ta-ta for now," Katherine said to Jack and Benjamin.

Elissa would have usually been glad to have the company, but time alone was essential to completing her mission. She guessed it'd have to wait until later. The ship and its hallways, which were color coded depending on the floor, were becoming more familiar. Not that this place felt at all like home.

"Did you notice the boy at the end of our table? Oh my goodness, he had such nice eyes. Oh, and such a sweet smile. I could just get lost in his eyes. Couldn't you?" Katherine looked to Elissa for agreement.

"Uh-huh." Elissa tried to focus on the conversation but how to get the information and her next plan kept popping into her head. She needed some time to be alone and while she knew Katherine was being nice, she just wished she'd leave her alone.

"At the Sydney Arch table, did you see the tall goth boy sitting on the end? He looked at me and smiled. I think he's crushin' on me."

"Uh-huh."

Elissa continued thinking. As they entered the cabin, Morocco rushed past Elissa.

Katherine dashed into the adjoining room, plopped onto the couch and put the television on.

Elissa ensured her textbook was in her messenger bag, found the location of their next class, and opened up her email. Stephanie's email explained how she was working with a group of scientists on the Tsunami Early Warning System. Her off time, of which there did appear to be some, was filled with trips to the beach and the typical touristy landmarks that travelers visited in Los Angeles.

Elissa couldn't wait to complete her mission of bringing Christopher home. If all went according to her plans, they would all have time to relax in Los Angeles.

She picked up her computer and tried to get access to the Agent Links files, but there was a firewall and router stopping her progress. Christopher's program could get her in, but it was unauthorized so she had to be careful that no one saw it on her computer. Katherine strolled into the room. Elissa left the program running but minimized the window.

"Let's get to class."

By now the silver hallway around their room was familiar and she had understood the difference between the stern and the stem. But to her it was as simple as right or left. When the elevator doors opened at the learning deck, they saw students rushing around, looking at room numbers, and bumping into each other. It was general chaos.

Elissa and Katherine entered their classroom. Instead of desk chairs, the low desks had seats from race cars. Double highway lines were painted on the floor. A pair of eyes and smile from a racing poster on the wall caught Elissa's attention. The man in the poster vaguely resembled

Benjamin. Checkered flags adorned one wall. Traffic signals covered the others. The teacher's desk had a car front, including the hood and front tires. Over in the corner sat a driving simulator. With all the props, she figured this instructor might be fun.

A large window along one wall showed a view of the cumulus clouds. Elissa closed her eyes and took a deep breath. Despite all the secrets trapped below the surface, the ocean seemed calm. With all of Madisyn Academy's available knowledge, the truth about Christopher and his mission was still buried too deep in files she could not get into unless she could get some time alone.

Katherine moved one of the seats so Elissa could pull up to the desk. A man strolled into the room and set a worn brown leather bag on the front desk. He had meticulously arranged short shaggy hair, a blue polo shirt, black pants, and black shoes. As he looked up, his DKNY black eye glasses highlighted his green eyes. Malina entered the room, making a grand entrance, stopped temporarily to model her dress and sauntered to the back of the room to join a group of her friends.

He walked over to Elissa's chair and knelt down to be at eye level with her.

"I'm Agent Maguire. Miss Morris, we are going to be evacuating the classroom. Will you be able to safely follow us up the stairwell?"

"Absolutely," Elissa said as she wondered why they would need to leave the room as they just arrived.

He stood up and addressed Morocco.

"You can't help Miss Morris find her way back."

Morocco tilted her head from side to side at Agent Maguire's comments, lay flat on the floor and covered her face with her paws. He smiled.

"I must witness this stair thing," Katherine said.

"Mr. Smyth, I'm a huge fan of your dad," he said to Benjamin.

Benjamin smiled.

Agent Maguire returned to the front of the classroom. As he talked, Elissa's mind wandered, studying the posters about memorization.

"Welcome to Memory and Speech Level One. Today we'll cover the course outlines and specifics for your assignment. I'll release your outlines." He hit a button on his computer.

Everyone pulled out their mini-computers and looked in their folders with only one assignment, a research paper due Saturday, which made Elissa happy to think there was a smaller work load for one class. But her happiness was temporary when she noticed there was one quiz –Thursday– that had an asterisk by it and an exam, on chapters one to six, also to be completed on Saturday.

"The research paper will be an opportunity to study one of the many memorization techniques in the Mnemonics area. The fairest method of selection is to have each student choose a topic out of a hat." Agent Maguire walked around the room and one by one the students picked.

"Thanks." Elissa pulled out her topic.

"You're most welcome," Agent Maguire said. *Linking Room Method* was printed on it.

"Please email me your name and topic. Switching topics is not permitted," Agent Maguire stood straight. "All the grading information is in the class shared folder. This assignment is due at our last class this week. Are there any questions?"

No one raised their hands. They were all too busy staring horrified at their topics and the essay's required 1,500-word count. Agent Maguire strolled around the front of the table and leaned back. Malina shifted in her chair and then leaned forward, raised her hand and waved as if she was practicing for a parade.

"Why is memorization important?" Malina asked.

An alarm rang.

"That's our evacuation alarm. We need to proceed to the observation deck via the stern stairwell. Leave your bags here and follow me." Agent Maguire grabbed the room keys and strolled out the door.

Outside the room, students rushed to follow their teachers to the bow stairwells. Despite it being just a drill, there was a certain amount of panic in the hallway. Then again, how could there not being some panic when an alarm rang, disturbing the class in progress?

"The stern stairs will be less congested, but during lifeboat evacuation you must use the bow stairs and ensure your lifejacket is properly inflated. Follow the arrows up to the observation deck and wait for me at the spot marked with a star. Elissa, what can I do?"

"I'm good. I'll meet you."

"I'm not comfortable leaving you," he said.

"We'll keep our eyes on her," Jack promised.

"If you're not up in a few minutes, I'll come find you," Agent Maguire said. He slowly walked up the stairs but kept an eye on her, which she found comforting but considered unnecessary.

Elissa drove the wheelchair backwards to the stars, hit a button and grabbed the railing with one hand. Her tires rotated and the wheelchair climbed up one step at a time. Each transfer from one step to the next caused a dull ache in her legs. The boys leaned and gawked at how the wheelchair was achieving the climb.

"Wicked," Katherine said.

They followed the arrows and Elissa counted each step as she climbed. At the main entry they followed the arrows through a maze of hallways and doors. All the other students gathered at the opposite end of the ship with their teachers.

Agent Maguire put on his Prada sunglasses and looked at his puzzled students.

"Well, this was just an evacuation drill for the rest of the student body, but for all of you it was the answer to Malina's question. Why is memorization important? As agents, you'll need to rely on your memory for facial recognition after being shown a photo of your target for thirty seconds or less, learning new languages, recalling license plates, locations, layouts, technology and remembering your assumed identities for each assignment. There is no time for note taking on a mission. In the wrong hands, those notes could compromise a mission or cost someone's life."

"Now you'll be required to find your way back to the classroom. All of the arrows and signs have been removed. You'll be navigating blind, so I hope you remember exactly how many doors you came through and what floor you were on when we started. Even the classrooms on your floor will have the room numbers removed. Once the students have all returned, we will resume the class. You might want to take this time to decide your route and divide into teams."

All of the students collected in small groups of four or five. Jack, Katherine, Benjamin and Elissa huddled together.

"I wasn't paying attention to our location," Jack said.

"Surprising. Boys and toys." Katherine shook her head and nudged him.

"I remember two doors," Benjamin said.

"I came up fourteen stairs," Elissa said.

"All clear to go. The first three teams can go now and two minutes later the next three teams may leave. By the way, the entire team must arrive together. No splitting up.

I'll meet you in the classroom. You each have fifteen minutes to get to the classroom or you will compromise your mission. Good luck." Maguire walked back to the last group of students entering the ship.

When it was their turn, the three teams entered the main door into a short hallway with lighter paint on the walls where the pictures were removed. Any clues that might have given them a hint to their location were now gone. There were two plain doors for them to choose between, which made the choice harder. She wished she had paid better attention to their path.

"Well, ladies, left or right?" Benjamin asked.

The other team entered through the door on the right.

"The flagpole was visible when the students ahead opened the door." Benjamin said. "The left one."

They went through the left doorway and ended up in a small entry area. Again the furniture had been moved as the black Burberry had indents where perhaps a couch once sat. Besides that, Elissa's wheelchair tracks had been brushed off the carpet, she knew they came this way as the carpet attempted to steer her chair in different directions. Waiting for them was Malina's team and three doors. Of all the people on this ship, Elissa seemed to find Malina more often than not.

"Oh man, this sucks," Benjamin whispered so only their team could hear. He checked his watch and glanced at Malina.

Malina turned around. Her face brightened when she saw Benjamin. "Benji, hi. Imagine bumping into you here." When she glanced at Elissa, her smile faded. Somewhere inside Elissa, her smile weakened every time she saw Malina. Maybe it was because she didn't get Malina or the fact Malina just didn't like her, but that girl didn't radiate joy. That was for sure.

"You lost or waiting for us?" Benjamin asked.

Malina's face turned red. "Of course we're not lost. I thought you'd need some help."

Benjamin looked at her incredulously. "Your help is something we don't need." Malina stuck her nose in the air and joined her team through the first door. Elissa fought back the smile at her reaction.

"I tripped on the carpet miter joint when I exited the door," Jack said. They all walked across the carpet looking for a bump. When they found it, they went through the door and found themselves at the very end of a long hallway. As they made progress Elissa's thoughts turned to the program and so wanted a moment to check the progress, but knew she couldn't risk being caught.

"We were next to a table with a tacky flower display on it," Katherine said.

As they searched the hallway, there was no flower arrangement or table. Elissa forced herself to focus as she drove down the hallway looking for indents in the carpet. She pointed at four small compressions. "Here's the door. That's where the table was."

The team entered through the door and into a stairwell. They counted down the steps as they went. Once at the bottom of the stairs and through the door, a hallway with numberless doors waited.

"Any ideas?" Elissa asked.

"Third classroom out of the elevator," Katherine said.

"You can count that high? I'm proud." Jack patted Katherine on the shoulder as he glimpsed the elevator at the end of the hallway. She slapped his hand off.

They entered the classroom to find four of the six teams had returned. Just as they were getting back to their desks, the last team came into the room. If only the last team could have taken a bit longer, it would have provided Elissa a quick check of the progress of her program.

"Good job teams. First let's cover chapter one about the way your brain learns things. To learn, sometimes it's better to complete a quick exercise. Then, even though I'm sure you'll be disappointed, I'll let you go early." Maguire pulled a remote from his bag. A screen lowered from the ceiling and he stood next to it.

"In a moment, a photo of several items will flash on the screen. You have thirty seconds to memorize as many items as you can. Then you'll complete a quiz."

The photo flashed. Elissa tried to visualize the items but her heart sank. The strict polices of the school and all the tasks she needed to complete for this mission seemed overwhelming. Her legs ached and she shifted to get comfortable. She stared at the items on the screen: a wrist watch, a grey Persian cat statue, a plastic clear bandage, a Nature's Sound CD, a small mandarin orange, a blue plastic spoon, a black mechanical pencil, a round green key and a stop sign. The photo disappeared.

"There should be a quiz on your computers. Please complete them and send them to my station."

Elissa looked up where the screen was as if the answers would appear and reveal the items she had not memorized.

Agent Maguire sat as his desk and watched the students struggle.

"Time's up." He typed on his computer. Then he stood. "The average score was eleven out of twenty-four. Several of you managed fifteen and two managed all twenty-four. In a few days, you'll be able to recall all twenty-four items without problem."

Whispers filled the classroom.

"You disbelievers – if all of you get twenty-four correct by this Thursday's class, I will cut your research paper in half. For this offer to be valid, all of you must be in agreement. Raise your hands if you accept the deal."

All the students except Elissa raised their hands. The medications made her brain sluggish and the aching gave her a constant distraction, not to mention the mission and her dad. There was no way she needed the responsibility of studying and screwing up for the entire class, no way. Katherine grabbed Elissa's arm and pushed it up in the air.

Agent Maguire said, "It's a deal."

Elissa pulled her arm back down too late. She leaned in towards Katherine and was about to say something and tell Katherine the mistake she had made.

"If a part of the memorization method confuses us, can you show us?" Benjamin asked.

"Great question. We will cover each topic before your paper's due date. Anything else?" Maguire waited for other questions.

Malina raised her hand. "If all of us ace the quiz and one of us bombs," she glared at Elissa, "Will we all suffer? "

"To ensure that does not happen, you might want to work as a team."

"But that's completely unfair."

"It is what it is. Remember, you're only as strong as your weakest link on any mission."

Every student gulped and looked around the room at the other possible weak links. Malina stared for a moment at Elissa, who in return stared back at her and smiled. Attention focusing was going to be Elissa's challenge, but to throw the memory test, to give up and have Malina suffer did enter her mind, but unfortunately not only Malina would suffer. Her friends and she herself would suffer, along with Christopher, who's mission she was going to complete.

"You may leave now. Please read chapters one to three for tomorrow. And remember the details." He packed his bag. Elissa's mouth dropped open at the thought of knowing three chapters by heart by tomorrow. The assignments were getting in the way of the real reason she was on the ship. If she didn't keep her grades up, she would be booted off before she could get the information. Clearly sleep might have to be a luxury she had gotten too used to at home.

"I'm famished," Jack said.

"Total shocker," Katherine said. Jack slapped her on the arm. "Check out Edmonton Ridge Club Room?" They all agreed as the Edmonton Ridge Club Room was where only Ridge students could chill, study or grab a snack.

Katherine and Elissa waited for the elevator and the guys took the stairs.

On the Edmonton Ridge deck and along the walls, arrows and signs directed them to the end of the hallway. At the end of the hall, on either side of the Edmonton Ridge Club Room metal door, were many small glass bricks providing the room privacy but giving a silhouette of the room's occupants. A large silver metal door with an electronic button blocked the view.

The room had several impersonal, dark wooden coffee tables that wouldn't look out of place in any of the countless hotels Elissa had visited. This room was split into two sections: a games area with pool tables and gaming systems and a study area with shelves built into the wall filled with real books – books that she enjoyed the feel, look and sound of when she opened them. In the game area was a food station, complete with vending machines and an order counter.

At the back, around the order counter, were metal tables and chairs. In the far corner was a home theatre system. *This is almost like home.*

In the far back, next to another door, were chairs, couches and tables. The silver-framed tables reminded Elissa of mother-daughter dates at their favorite restaurant back home. She and her mom had ordered treats they'd been deprived of all month to allow Elissa to keep her dancing figure and Mom her running figure. Then they'd sat in the game room and played until they ran out of change. In the back of her mind, she wondered if Stephanie was safe and having some fun.

Elissa followed Katherine, Jack and Benjamin over to the order window.

"Sugar, what'll it be?" an elderly woman wearing a hairnet and stained white apron asked.

Katherine and Jack ordered pizza. Elissa ordered a fruit salad and Benjamin ordered a hamburger.

"Thumb authorization." The woman reached out a small PDA and handed it to Elissa. Each of them entered their thumb print to bill their orders to their accounts.

"Those'll be up in a moment."

"Let's find a place to crash?" Katherine giggled. "Well, you'll park."

They wove in between the furniture and around the various throw rugs that covered the hardwood deck. Elissa parked her wheelchair out of the main walking path but close to her classmates.

Katherine returned with trays and set them down. Elissa set Morocco's tray, with a bowl of dog food and water down. "Go ahead, girl." She patted her. Morocco shook her tail and dove in. Jack and Benjamin sat next to the table and took out their food.

"That memorization paper is brutal," Katherine said.

"Less than a half if we can all...," Jack said.

Katherine interrupted, "Oh please. Like that's a possibility." Elissa was with Katherine on her thinking, especially when it came to her brain.

"It's possible." Benjamin looked up from putting ketchup on his hamburger bun. Morocco gradually snuck a step closer to Benjamin and his burger. Then she looked at him with pleading eyes. Benjamin slid his tray and himself away, trying to stay a safe distance from the dog.

"The girl next to me got all twenty four." Jack shook his head.

"Seriously?" Elissa asked. Jack nodded.

"Morocco, come," Elissa said. Morocco looked longingly back at Benjamin's burger and returned to her own food.

Eleven

Sharing

Elissa's acoustic guitar stood in the corner of the cabin recreation room. She drove directly to it and picked it up. Seeking some freedom from classwork and worry about Christopher, she threw all of her emotions into her playing. Morocco observed and watched her play for a bit then began howling to Elissa's tune. Katherine leaned against the doorframe, watching the duo in action.

"I wouldn't want to follow your act," Katherine said, clapping. "You really wail. Been playing long?"

"Four years, but seriously since the accident." Elissa didn't look up.

"If you don't mind talking about it, what really happened?" Katherine asked. Elissa set down the guitar and stared at the floor for a moment then looked up at her.

"My dad's recording studio blew up and we were all inside. Dad is missing. Mom has fully recovered. The rubble caused damage and resulting arthritis."

"I'm so sorry. Any leads on your dad?"

"A few."

Katherine walked over and picked up the guitar to examine it. "Did you take lessons?"

"Nah, learned on my own. You play an instrument?"

"Drums." Katherine set the guitar down, sat in a chair and banged away at an imaginary drum kit.

"We'll have to jam," Elissa said with a smile.

Katherine's face drained of all its color. "Maybe one day. In total private. An audience freaks me out." She took a deep breath.

"Got ya. The stage is my normal. My home. Dad gave me that."

"That's wicked to start as a child before public humiliation dawns on you. You're Christopher Morris's daughter, aren't you?"

Elissa looked up at her, "How long have you known?"

Katherine pulled a chair up to Elissa and sat down.

"Since last night; Jack texted me. He went with his mom to see your dad on his last tour. She thinks Christopher is...was hot. It's not my kinda music. He did a search on the net and found photos."

Elissa set the guitar in the stand, then went and looked out the window.

"What's your kinda music?"

"Metal. And although I'll utterly deny it, I'm totally a closet classical music aficionado. Would ruin my image, you know."

She smiled and joined Elissa by the window.

"Mom turned me on to classical – took me to see the symphony. My mom gave that to me before she..." Katherine looked down, her eyes filled with tears and she turned away from Elissa and pretended she was wiping something off her shoes. "We should help each other," she continued.

"Deal." Elissa said. "If you ever need a shoulder…" She patted her own arm.

Morocco charged into the other room.

"I must catch up on soaps for twenty before class," Katherine said as she picked a box up off her bed and went into the other room.

Elissa drove to her bedside table, her fatigued body craving a sugar fix, and was headed for the locked drawer that held her hidden candy stash. But resting on top of her bed was a small white envelope with her name. Wondering what it could be, she picked up the envelope and studied the ink. The familiar handwriting caused excitement as she ripped the envelope trying to get it open. She knew it was Christopher's handwriting, but the time it was written stuck in her mind. There was hope maybe he had broken free from NERD-One and the mission wouldn't be necessary. Hope that faded as she knew this could've been written anytime in the past. A handwritten letter and silver bracelet fell onto her lap. After inspection of the bracelet she read the letter:

> *Dearest Lissy,*
> *Congratulations on all your accomplishments. We're both proud parents.*

Elissa frantically searched the letter for a date: nine months ago, mailed and sent to Helmer Larsson. Her hope dissipated as she realized it was not new and Christopher was not free.

> *If you are reading this it means I'm unable to give it to you in person. I love you.*

She took a deep breath and kept reading the letter.

> *By now you know I'm a secret agent. While my music career is a passion of mine, it is a travel cover for me.*
> *Helmer and I were in Edmonton Ridge together. He saved my life*

Ice Rose

> many times and can be trusted with anything. Should you have any problems or questions, go to him.

Tears streamed down her face. She wiped them away and continued to read.

> Remember our discussion about boys and remember that it's okay to say no.

"Dad," she whispered. A smile spread across her face. Then she turned over the letter and glanced at the other side.

> I know you are wondering why I'm writing this letter. My current assignment is dangerous. Your Mom and I had many discussions about the risks and the future. Due to my subject knowledge, I am the most qualified agent to handle the case. Always know, Lissy, you and your mom are the things in my life that I treasure and am most proud of.
>
> Even though I'm not there to wipe your tears away, hug you when your heart gets broken, or when you're disappointed, I'm always with you.
>
> Here is a bracelet for good luck. The musical note is for the love of music we share, the key is for my heart, the footprint is for all the steps you've taken and all the steps you have yet to take, the heart is for how

much I love you and the stars are for your dreams. I'll always be there.
   Love Always,
   Dad

Elissa wiped the tears off her face as she fumbled with the bracelet and placed it on her wrist. After folding the letter and carefully putting it back in the envelope, she placed it in her locked drawer.

"Everything okay?" Katherine asked as she came into the room.

"I'm such a sap."

"There was one on my bed, so I glanced at your bed. Mine was from my Mom before she..."

As she walked closer, Elissa noted Katherine had been crying and was holding a letter and picture in her hand.

"We're a mess."

They both laughed.

"Mine's from Dad. He also sent this bracelet."

Katherine reached out to touch it. "Oh, it's so beautiful."

"My Dad always did things like this."

"My Mom does...did things like that. She sent this for me." Katherine had a gold ring on her index finger.

"It's beautiful."

Katherine walked to her bed and returned with a photograph for Elissa to look at.

"The ring's for luck. My mom won the Academy Games when she attended Madisyn Academy."

Elissa noticed that there were three teams in the photograph. Under each team was their placing. Katherine's mom was in the first place team. Elissa grinned when she saw her dad was in the second place team.

"So you'll follow in their footsteps. Right?" She gave the photograph back.

"I'm not 100% confident. In six years, Edmonton Ridge has not even managed to place. Sydney Arch has kicked butt the past few years."

Elissa drove over to where Katherine stood.

"That's ancient history. Now you're here." Elissa swept her arms like she was displaying some prize on a game show.

"And so are you. Maybe this'll be the year." Katherine proudly pranced across the room.

"Let's not forget Jack and Benjamin." Elissa stopped driving around.

"Who can forget those two?" Katherine stopped prancing.

Elissa turned her focus to a digital picture frame. Katherine picked it up and brought it over to Elissa. She pressed a button; there was female and male laughter and their voices said: "Love you." Katherine handed it to Elissa.

"That's my mom, dad, and brother, Patrick. We were vacationing in Los Angeles, on our way to scope the beach when we stopped at a red light. A green van, a black van and a car boxed in our van. Mom and Dad yelled for me to grab Patrick and run down the back alley. The van started to fill with a sweet white smoke. Mom opened the back door in the cover of the smoke, and Patrick and I sprinted down the alley."

Katherine walked over to the window and stood there looking out. Finally, she took a deep breath and returned to the bed but didn't sit down.

"I didn't know my way around. I ran from one street to another. Patrick was only three so it was mega hard to keep him still and quiet." Tears filled her eyes and she leaned on the bed. "All of a sudden, a NERD-One operative was chasing me. I kept running and the man followed. At the end of the alley, I was cut off by a white van and when I turned around, the man was no longer chasing me. The van door opened, and Jack's dad grabbed me and Patrick and pulled us to safety."

Standing up, she motioned for Elissa to follow her onto the deck. "He brought us back and we've been living in an apartment above the garage with my older brother Dave for the past two years. Dave works during the summer and is at college on a scholarship. I'm here on a scholarship and Patrick stays with Jack's family."

Katherine shook her head in the breeze.

"Did your ..." Elissa stopped mid-sentence.

"They're deep undercover double agents, but we know they're alive. Knowing the truth is essential. Stupid COOL won't give us any information other than they are presumed alive. What I wouldn't give to read their file. Just to know they're okay."

"I'm so sorry. NERD has my dad. I need the truth. If there's anything…"

Katherine looked at Elissa and a smirk spread across her face. "We could find the truth – find the files."

Elissa stared at the photograph. The combination of the photo and the frame voices reminded her there were two other people, obviously the Bennisons, who left the night of the explosion with Christopher. Inside, her heart sank to think that Katherine and her own family were both missing their family members. And it all had to do with stupid secrets and missions.

"Oh-oh, lost track of time. We better get to class or we won't be able to find anything, being at the other campus," Katherine said. She rushed into the desk area and packed her book bag. Elissa grabbed her large flight handbook and placed it in her bag. This should at least be one class she would enjoy. Morocco rose from her dog bed and joined them by the door.

They entered the elevator, which stopped on the instructors' offices deck where a student on crutches hobbled into the elevator with them. Elissa and Katherine both noticed the "**Do Not Enter. Authorized Personnel Only**" room. Elissa checked out the security and cameras in the hall.

Getting into a room in the middle of a hallway that would be locked after class hours was going to prove challenging, she thought. The girls exchanged a nod and a knowing look.

"Swap horror stories next class?" Katherine asked.

"Wouldn't miss it." The doors closed and Elissa petted Morocco. "Now we just need to bring Dad home."

By following the signs down the learning deck's mazes of hallways, Elissa and Morocco made their way to classroom 425. Sounds escaped from the room where special desks that enabled the students to use their computers sat in front of recliner chairs. In the back of the classroom, Malina and her group were studying and quizzing each other. They appeared to be using candies as a treat for each correct answer.

She looked around the room at the recliners, the painting showing a sky and stars on the ceiling and the counter with a microwave and a mini-fridge. The sweet aroma from two plates of homemade cookies wafted through the classroom. A sign above the cookies read "**Help Yourself**." The walls were covered with posters of the latest gizmos, technology, motorcycles, and fantasy games. Elissa pulled beside a recliner where there was a space for her chair.

She placed Morocco's chew bone next to her on the floor where the dog quietly gnawed on it while Elissa turned her attention to the vacant teacher's desk and the writing on the board. The room was lit by long, unfriendly fluorescent lights.

"Saved me a spot?"

She nodded as she looked up and saw Benjamin holding a handful of cookies in a napkin.

"Want some?" Benjamin asked, settling into a chair.

"No, thanks.

The white board was covered by a projection screen, much like the kind Christopher used to play their ancient family movies, blocking the view of the contents. Then a man appeared on the screen. He was wearing a black T-shirt with the fake tuxedo look, but had matched it with a green blazer and brown pants. A look Elissa wasn't sure he was pulling off all that well.

"Good afternoon. Today we will discuss U.S. databases and national security, The Sentinel program, the Gate Key virus, source key codes and back-up alarms to anti-viruses. Then you will be given a challenge to use your new-found knowledge. First I have released your outlines and assignments, so take a moment to review them."

Elissa noted two multiple-choice quizzes, one before each class on the previous chapters in their tech book and a test on Saturday on the cumulative chapters and lectures to date. That might be a challenge, as each chapter was technical, hard to read, and at least 60 pages long.

Another screen lowered over the white board and it showed a bulleted list about the Sentinel program that is used to protect U.S. databases and national security.

Elissa had heard of Sentinel because Christopher had explained how if someone was to hack into it, he would get access to air traffic control, banking systems, even potentially reactors and water facilities. He had a copy of a similar Canadian program on his websites and home office.

The Gate Key virus was something that Elissa had been hearing about all over the news. It had attacked many personal computers and was the current buzz virus, with threats that it was going to be made bigger and stronger. So far, the smartest minds in computers had not been able to kill it, only quarantine it. The virus had an alarm that thwarted anti-virus software and she knew the only way to get it quarantined it was to use source key codes, which the presentation confirmed. She wanted to get a crack at it because she thought she could break it. Not that she was smarter than expert techs, but she had managed to eliminate several tough viruses and wanted to give it a shot.

"**Good luck, students. Dr. Bunch out**."
The screen rose up to reveal writing on the white board.
Today's class:
- *Turn on your computer and log on to the network.*
- *Go into the Albus file.*
- *Follow the instructions to find me. Remember 2 doors + 1 choice = freedom or a lesson.*
- *When, or if, you find me, I'll give you further instructions.*

Dr. Bunch

A momentary panic caused her palms to sweat and her hands to shake due to the cryptic message and all the expectations she had placed upon herself. If she couldn't track the video call, would she be able to excel in this technology course? Her grades had to stay high, at least long enough to get into the file room and allow her access to the information she required. Not to mention the fact she needed time to play the game and figure out Christopher's password, as it was a rolling one and seemed to be random. All she needed was a few more assignments to occupy her limited time.

"Well, that's a panic attack waiting to happen," Benjamin said as he sat back and looked at the board.

She logged onto the network, opened the file and before she could react, a warning appeared: a virus, The Gate Key, has infected your hard drive. You have a half hour to find it and quarantine it before your hard drive is erased. 29 minutes and 55 seconds.

"Throw us in and expect us to swim," Benjamin said as he looked from his monitor to hers. The room was filled with panicked voices.

Quickly Elissa searched the computer for the virus. It took her few minutes to find the exact location. Benjamin leaned in and looked at her monitor, which she didn't even mind. Elissa knew the Gate Key had an alarm that the anti-virus would no doubtedly set off, which might speed it up, so she didn't try the obvious. She also knew that they were provided two folders, but she was unsure which one would be the right choice.

"Of course," Benjamin mouthed silently.

There was a choice of two files: red or blue. One file will undoubtedly increase the virus's rate and cause absolute disaster, but the other should have the source codes. Which one?

"Girls first," Benjamin mouthed.

"Thanks." She shook her head and took a breath to prepare her to type fast, in case this was the wrong choice, before clicking the blue folder. Up came a box with further instructions. They exchanged smiles. She typed in some codes, which made her able to quarantine the virus but that wasn't enough for her – she wanted to eliminate the virus. It was her chance to have a crack at the virus. She was in a safe environment so she was going to take the opportunity.

Congratulations. You have quarantined the virus. You may move on to the next task.

"Elissa, we can move on to the next task." Benjamin was leaning over and trying to figure out what she was doing.

"I want a crack at eliminating it. You go ahead and move on," she said without turning to face him as she fanatically typed in some codes she had used at home to break into some programs Christopher had written for her. Without Christopher's knowledge, she had found some nasty viruses and intentionally loaded them on their ancient computer and practiced eliminating them. The Gate Key program was one that had come out soon after the accident and she hadn't had the opportunity to search it out.

"As if I want to see this."

Several students walked out of the room, with computers in hands, and seemed to be going to an unknown destination. Usually such things would peak Elissa's creativity, but today she was too busy. Benjamin was following her and typing in codes and going to the same locations she was. After ten minutes of typing codes and more than half of the students leaving the room, she entered the last code and gave Benjamin a glance before she clicked on the enter key. He smiled. The screen went black and then the virus disappeared in the folder. Benjamin hit enter and then, mouth open and chin down, lifted his arm to give her a high five. Elissa usually would have been annoyed at another student riding her coattails but instead she enjoyed the happiness as moments in such a positive emotion hadn't happened all that much since Christopher went missing.

On screen appeared:

Congratulations. You have successfully removed the virus from your hard drive. Your next task: open the lemon folder and do as the instructions show.

Reluctantly she clicked on the lemon folder, wondering what other surprises could be waiting for her. So far, she felt confident she could manage what might await her. A small box opened with further instructions.

Track me in a room, on a deck, on a ship. Explore the consequences of your choices.

Right choice = course outline and freedom :)

Wrong choice = essay and temporary confinement :(

After she clicked on the tracking software binocular icon, Elissa brought up the ship's schematics and floor plans. She scanned the ship for the blinking blue dot. It all seemed too easy, at least for this place, these instructors were keeping them on their toes. She knew something had to be missing. Before settling on the blinking blue dot location, she checked the menu for multiple searches, looking for the heat tracker she had read about when she was skimming the books back at home.

Elissa monitored the blue and red blinking dots at either side at the end of the hallway. Two choices, and only one of them was correct.

"Come on, let's go," she said. She put her computer on her lap, picked up Morocco's chew bone and waited for Benjamin. Only a few students were left in the room, and of course, one was Malina. As they left the room, Malina and her crew followed behind them and attempted to listen to what they were saying.

Elissa slowed up, pulled up to the side of the hallway and stopped to let Malina go first.

"Some of us are leaders. Guess you're a follower," Malina said.

Elissa thought of several things she could say but took a deep breath. "You'd know all about that following people. My choices aren't made by others."

Benjamin leaned back on his heels, looked down at his feet and tried not to smile.

Malina ignored Elissa, and with her group in tow, rushed into the right hand classroom. Elissa waited until they closed the door and then she proceeded into the classroom on the left. Instead of finding a teacher, the room was empty. She couldn't understand how the room could be empty when the blinking-red, heat-seeking dot was clearly in this location. She was so sure and now, Malina would be able to gloat.

"Where's he hiding?" Benjamin asked. They looked around the room for clues to his location. There was a large whiteboard, plain instructor's desk, and rows of desks. Alongside the classroom was a supply closet. The wall was vacant of any doors but was painted with a mural of a beach with palm trees and a desk chair holding a PDA.

Benjamin leaned in and saw her breaking into the ship's restricted network. "You gotta teach me to do that."

"In a room behind the wall mural. Sneaky." They went over to the wall mural and Benjamin pushed the wall and grunted. "Television reruns, don't fail me now."

Elissa joined Benjamin in examining the mural of a beach with palm trees and sand.

Off in the far left corner of the mural was a deck chair and a table holding a PDA and a tech book.

Benjamin knelt on the floor and ran his hand over the book. A door on the top pulled down to reveal a small opening with a switch. Elissa felt relieved when he found the switch. He flicked the switch and stepped away. The palm tree slid to the side to reveal a metal door. They entered the room and the door closed behind them.

"It's about time. Congratulations," a deep voice echoed from inside the spacious room.

When they turned, there was a man sitting in the corner watching several black and white television screens.

"Dr. Bunch at your service." He reached out his hand to shake Benjamin's and then quickly pulled his hand away. "Gotcha."

The television screens along the wall showed views from ceiling-mounted cameras in the classrooms and hallway. In the blue dot room, ten students were sitting at desks, typing and reading off their computer screens. Malina's face reflected her repulsion of the essay assignment on the whiteboard in the front of the room.

"You rock. First students to kill the Gate Key, version 2.0. Great agents are always thinking and preparing for the unexpected – always looking past the easy answers."

He noticed them watching the monitor.

"Suck it up, students. Entrapment until each student researches and writes a four-page essay about heat-signal trackers."

He reached for two CDs and handed each of them one, "Paperless society, you know. Study chapter one for next class's quiz. Now get outta here." He pointed to a door on the far end of the room and gave them the peace sign. "Rock on."

Before leaving, Benjamin checked the screen to ensure no students were traveling down the hallway. Elissa was relieved to have free time for the remainder of the class as they went out the door and headed for the elevator.

"Wanna work on a deck tan?" Benjamin waited by the elevator button for her reply.

"Sounds nice," Elissa said as she tried to keep her excitement contained. She was more excited about being able to spend some time with Benjamin than she was about anything else. For just that moment the world, and the mission she was working on, seemed to melt away.

The lido deck was full of students wandering around, enjoying the weather. Near the side pool, an escape class was being held. Benjamin and Elissa stopped and took their place among the crowd to get a good view of the class. All Elissa could think about was the conversation she had with Stephanie and if this was where she had struggled. A student put on his helmet and harness before he climbed into the driver's seat of a sedan. Slowly the car was hoisted up off the deck and lowered into the water as a large digital clock ticked down. For a minute, Benjamin and Elissa waited for the student to get out.

"Forget about it. The vest buys him time," Benjamin said. He reached into his vest pocket and pulled out a small tube. "Dollars to donuts he has the portable oxygen tank."

The pool water was calm and the emergency divers waited next to the driver's seat.

Elissa crossed her fingers for two reasons: that the student would escape without help and that she wouldn't have to attempt this class, at least not for several years.

In the meantime, the student swam up to the surface. All the students waiting around the pool applauded, so Elissa and Benjamin joined in.

Benjamin pointed to the hot dog stand on the other side of the pool. "Not a New York Deli, but wanna try? How about a nacho dog and cherry coke? My treat." Benjamin looked to Elissa for confirmation.

She handed him her card, and he tilted his head and looked at her.

"Keep dreaming that I'm going to let you pay." His mouth fell open as she looked at him. "This time anyway."

She smiled as a feeling of relaxation engulfed her. They sat at a table overlooking the swimming pool and ocean while they chowed down. The sun was shining despite the odd cloud trying to block its light. Elissa's hair defiantly blew in every direction.

"What'd you do before Madisyn Academy?" Benjamin turned his attention to Elissa.

"Dancer. You?"

"Basketball. Total collision last season injured a tendon in my knee. Still trying to get back to norm. Computers are my temporary focus."

She studied his profile in the sunlight. His tanned nose, eyes and chin all seemed so proportional, just like a model, and his muscles made his shirt fit tight. *He's so completely hot.*

"Look!" Benjamin pointed at the ocean.

She followed his finger's direction and saw dolphins jump out of the water, glide gracefully, and play like carefree children. For a moment they were captivated then he sighed.

"What's up?" Elissa asked as she wished his smile would come back again.

"First Malina followed me here. Then I've got too much reading and memorization. Not great at balancing my time or…" He ran his hands through his hair and pushed his bangs out of his face.

"Time never seems to be our own," Elissa interrupted. "What's with Malina anyway?"

He looked at her for a moment. "Family stuff. She was never the same after her father left. Without his income to supplement her mom's, she had to stay home and she couldn't join me at the school where I played basketball."

They finished their drinks then headed to their next class.

Twelve

Potential

Elissa's feelings when she was around Benjamin reminded her of the times she was taking flying lessons because they were so similar – it felt like she was walking on air. They traveled to the training deck, down the hallway and past a few students just wandering around. The classroom door was open so they entered and found a spot where they could sit next to Katherine and Jack.

Katherine winked at Elissa, referring to her being in the company of Benjamin.

Yeah, even Elissa had to admit to herself that he had serious potential. She heard whispering from behind and wondered if her hair was sticking up, as she lined up with Morocco by her side.

"Benji, we saved you a spot," Malina announced in a voice that demanded his attention.

"Much appreciated, but I need to talk to Jack." Benjamin smiled at Malina and continued to his seat. As he walked past, Elissa found herself smiling at the thought she'd get to see him during this class.

Casually, Elissa turned her head and glanced back at the whispering voices. Three Guess girls, including Malina, and two surfer boys, complete with colorful Billabong shirts, were scrutinizing her. They took turns pointing, leaning in and whispering. Maybe she wasn't wearing designer clothes, maybe it was just her mode of transportation, but the reason Malina was fixated with Elissa was something she would have to figure out or, at the least, ignore.

Morocco faced them and growled.

"It's okay, girl. Sit."

Morocco wagged her tail before sitting down next to her.

Fixated, Katherine stared at the training cockpit in the corner of the classroom. Her fingers were white with anticipation. She pointed at the flight simulator and turned to Elissa.

"Crashing won't be so traumatic. Hitting the floor from that height, and not having the pressure of destroying a real airplane should take away the pressure." Katherine said as she looked at Elissa and rubbed her hands to try and regain circulation. "Tried to opt out of this mandatory class but we all have to take it until asked to leave. For me, with my fear of flying, they should've saved me the public humiliation," Katherine whispered.

Elissa, forcing herself to focus on anything other than Benjamin and the flying program, had trouble deciding whether she preferred the world map wall or the blue sky and cumulus cloud wall. The other two walls had a sunset behind a mountain and a poster about conserving water, recycling, and saving the earth. Across the floor was an aerial view of North America. A box along the window drew solar power for the lights.

"Greetings, potential pilots." The greeting came from a woman wearing the Academy uniform personalized with a T-shirt that said "Tree hugger." As she walked toward her desk, she fumbled half of the large stack of handbooks she was carrying and they tumbled to the newly waxed floor. Benjamin picked them up and set them on her desk. She carefully placed the remaining books that didn't crash to the floor beside them.

"My name is Agent Wright. In one week, some of you will make the Madisyn Academy regulatory requirements to begin your pilot training. Look around the classroom carefully at the people around you. Half will be eliminated from the flying element of the program."

The students scanned the room as reality set in. Everyone was competition. Agent Wright paced the floor in front of her desk.

"These are your handy handbooks," she said, taking the pile of black binder manuals, and placed some at the end of each row. Katherine passed Elissa one and she smiled as she held her Pilot Operating Handbook. She had borrowed Christopher's, but was excited to have one of her very own.

"These are the skills, as set out by the student pilot certification, and private pilot license board, that you will be required to complete. As you can see, you're responsible for always attending class. Should you be unable to attend, it's your responsibility to acquire a copy of the notes from another student. Two classes will begin with a quick quiz on the previous class's content and chapters. Saturday you'll be having a test on the week's lessons, including the simulator flights you took part in. Questions so far?" She looked around the room.

Malina lifted her hand.

"Are the quizzes multiple choice?"

"Each of the fabulous two quizzes, on chapter one to four in your handbook, has forty multiple choice questions. Twenty percent of your grade will be for continuous class participation. Queries? Questions?"

Katherine cautiously lifted up her hand.

"Are we training at our ports of call?"

"We have arrangements to ensure all students have an opportunity to complete sufficient hours of ground school or flight training. As we explore the various ports, we have scheduled time out for your technical training. Be sure personal port exploration time is planned."

Excitement filled Elissa at the serious cool potential this class was going to have. She couldn't believe that she was attending a school where she was allowed to fly and get credit for it.

Agent Wright walked back to her desk and looked at a recycled cardboard-bound book.

"Being able to fly has gotten me out of several sticky situations. I'm looking forward to teaching all of you to be proficient pilots, but you need to jump right in today. Practice performing a flight, using the details on the board, with the program now unlocked in your humble hard drives. We need to evaluate where your skill level peaks." She carefully sat in her desk chair and opened a romance novel to a dog-eared page.

Everyone raced to download the program and after skimming the instructions, they began their flights. A roar of airplane engines filled the room. Some engines sputtered and the warning systems alerted of dives or stalls. Students started to turn down their speaker volume. The format and experience of flying reminded Elissa of her dad's flight simulator. She knew she had an advantage.

Responding to a beep on her computer Agent Wright put her book away. "Ah, good news – student success all around. Congratulations top flyers …''

Elissa's attention wavered as she clicked the minimized window to find the program still running but not into the Agent Links network yet, and there still was no progress indication bar.

"Benjamin, Jack and Elissa. Great going, students. Everyone please open your books to chapter one and follow along with me into chapter two."

She followed along in the book on the chapter about familiarization and preparation for flight. Elissa knew the information well as she had committed it to memory from Christopher's handbook.

"Enough explaining for today. For Wednesday read, review and study chapters three and four as we will be having both the quiz on chapters one and two and referring to chapters three and four. Students, scram."

Elissa, Katherine, Jack and Benjamin decided to try the Edmonton Ridge Club Room for lunch and as the program wasn't finished yet, Elissa decided to join them.

"This hallway's always a traffic jam," Jack said as he made himself skinnier to get in-between the crowd.

As they tried to make their way from side to side, the crush of people became thicker. Elissa flicked a switch to raise her wheelchair and tried to navigate through students engulfing her.

"What's up?" Katherine asked Rachel as she approached. Elissa lowered her chair.

"It's the Aacdemy Games! Remember, they're totally a rite of passage. They posted the first round of qualifiers, in five-member teams. Everyone's running to see if they got on a team with their friends."

"Elissa, wanna check out the list?" Katherine asked.

"Maybe later." It was hard to be excited about the Academy Games as all first-year students were placed in teams based on every activity the students completed to date. Before any of the students were accepted to the academy, they had to complete two missions as part of the Academy Games qualifiers, first round. Those mission results also gave the board at Madisyn Academy their answers as to who would be invited to train at the Ocean-Alias or at Camp Summit.

During the year, there would be additional challenges where the top fifteen teams from both campuses, all-year students, would compete during spring reading week, so there was too much on the line to blow off the challenges. Being on a team and having to compete sounded like so much fun, but yet another activity that would take time away from bringing her dad home. Still, she knew that the challenges would give her stronger skills which could be used on her mission, so she needed to pay attention and learn as much as she could.

"Meet you at the ridge." Elissa navigated around the human fence. By now the students had parted and she snuck through a small path. Elissa smiled and drove into the room. The fresh, air-conditioned breeze brushed against her face providing her the illusion of freedom.

Two small groups of students were eating and watching TV. Elissa parked in the area with tables and soft comfy chairs. Once Morocco was settled with her toys, Elissa checked her email where she found nothing but spam. Suddenly, Katherine burst in the door.

"Elissa you're not going to believe it. Come with me," Katherine squealed. She grabbed the wheelchair handles and tried to pull her.

"We'll stay here," Benjamin said.

"Come on, Morocco." Katherine urged Elissa to come with her.

They went out of the room, into the deserted hallway and up to five students giving each other high fives.

"Check out the last group of five." Katherine pointed it out, squealed and gyrated a hip hop version of the robot.

Elissa scanned the page. She focused her eyes to read the tiny print.

Team 50 Members:
Jack Dancer
Katherine Bennison
Benjamin Smyth
Elissa Morris
Kalan Johnson
Peer—Rachel Abbott

"Awesome. We lucked out," Katherine said.

A smile and nod from Elissa confirmed her excitement. They joined Benjamin and Jack in the Ridge, who were sitting on the floor sharing an extra large order of nachos.

Katherine put some nachos on two plates and handed one to Elissa. Then she lifted Morocco's food and water bowl and set it down next to her.

Anyone met Kalan?" Katherine searched the boys for answers.

"He's our roommate. He's from Nunavut, in Canada – has the best stories about hunting and fishing. If anyone of us gets stuck in the middle of nowhere, we'd struggle but he'd flourish. He's running a bit late this morning," Jack said.

"So which class starts your day tomorrow?" Jack asked. Everyone pulled out their computers.

"Keeping up with family traditions, Jack and I have Field Ops 100," Katherine said.

"I have Tech 100." With a look at Morocco, Elissa smiled nervously and settled in her wheelchair, comforted to have the lab more than ever, as Katherine wouldn't be there. She clicked on her hidden window and the access she had been waiting for was finally gained. She now needed to be alone to review the files.

"With me and you, Tech won't know what hit 'em," Benjamin said.

"Anyone stuck with second class Gadgets?" Katherine asked. They all answered "yes."

When Elissa was sure Morocco was done eating, she wiped out Morocco's water dish and placed it back in her wheelchair bag.

"I'm gonna take Morocco to her room to stretch her legs. Where can I meet you guys later?" Elissa asked, not giving Katherine an opportunity to join her.

"I'm going for a dip. Anyone wanna join me?" Katherine said.

"Guess we're checking out the pool," Jack said.

"Goin' to join us?" Benjamin winked at her.

Elissa smiled. "I'll meet you guys there in a bit."

Thirteen

Solo

Elissa enjoyed being on her own for a few minutes. It gave her time to throw some ideas around in her head. The journey to Morocco's room was uneventful, which Elissa enjoyed. If she never ran into Mr. Russel again, it would make her happy, but she knew he was the instrument to get Christopher home. No sooner were they in the room when Morocco eyed the dog treat dispenser.

"Just one," Elissa laughed.

Morocco pressed down the bone and a few treats fell to the ground. Once she'd eaten them she joined Elissa by one of the trees.

Elissa took off Morocco's vest. "There you go. Have fun."

She drove over to a miniature refrigerator to read the note stuck on the front: "People Food – Enjoy." Unable to fight off her curiosity, she opened up the fridge to find bottled water, cheese, crackers, fruit and juice boxes. Grabbing a bottle of water, she parked next to a picnic table.

Morocco raced around the room and returned to Elissa with a large bone in her mouth. She set it on Elissa's lap and wagged her tail excitedly. Elissa tossed the bone until her arm and Morocco were both tired. She had to keep going and not give in to the urge to return to the cabin and go to bed. While Morocco rested curled up next to her, Elissa pulled out her computer and looked at her custom program's results. A green folder labeled ICE was waiting for her.

"We did it, girl."

Morocco stood up and pressed her nose against the computer to close the front cover. She shook her head from side to side, then looked at Elissa.

"I need to find Dad. I can't move on without him. Please understand." Morocco licked Elissa's hand, poked the computer with her nose and settled down on the floor.

Rather than a complete file, the green folder contained just a summary. The page showed her Christopher's name, simply stating "Missing In Action. ICE ROSE Report in Archives. Confidential."

Elissa knew she would not be able to talk to Agent Larsson because he wouldn't grant her access and then he would make it harder. So, she started searching the archives for the file's location.

Instructor's deck: Authorized Personnel Room.

Well, at least it's on the ship. With a quick check of the hours the various ship areas were open, she confirmed the Instructor's area was open between 7:00 a.m. and 5:00 p.m. It was too late now. The doors and access to the adjacent hallway would also be locked, so she found the information about the power supply for the locks.

She could get onto the floor and cut the power to stop the cameras, which were not on a backup power system, like the door locks. She also made a residence alarm and linked it to her computer so if she needed a distraction, she would have one. Frustrated there was nothing she could do until office hours tomorrow, she decided to go visit the team at the pool.

Due to a long day, she was just too exhausted to get changed and climb into the pool, so she headed straight there to watch from the sidelines. The ship was busy with students coming and going, which helped her to feel less alone.

Elissa followed the student guidebook to find her way to the lido deck and the crowded pool area. Fresh air hit her face as she drove onto the deck and looked at the low sun setting behind the odd cloud. She knew it soon would be dark and this long day would be over.

She saw Benjamin, Jack and Katherine in the pool playing an improvised version of volleyball. Benjamin and Jack were waving to a tall girl posing like a model in a pink bikini. She smiled and winked at them. Malina, in a tight metallic swimsuit, stood on the pool deck scowling. Elissa could not figure out why she wasn't in a bikini and in the pool next to Benjamin.

"Hey Elissa. Not going to join us?" Jack said.

Katherine made eye contact. "Not into swimming?"

"Butterfly stroke's a bit rusty. What are you playing?"

"She'll sink. Probably can't even swim," Malina said, tilting her head to the side.

Elissa looked at Malina blankly and thought how she was not even worth the effort.

"Elissa, this is Marie, Ann, and Dave," Jack said.

"Volleyball. Would you mind keeping score for us?" Marie, an exotic girl with a large brown pony tail asked.

"I'd be glad to." She drove over to the scoreboard.

"Sure, but can you count high enough?" Malina asked.

"Don't you have somewhere else to be?" Benjamin swam to Malina's side of the pool.

"At least I earned my place here and didn't have Daddy buy it for me." Malina looked at Elissa. Somewhere the comment hit Elissa like a punch in the stomach. Christopher was gone and he couldn't have arranged this. Sure, Agent Larsson was family, but that would only get her so far…or would it?

Paying attention to Benjamin, Malina got up off the deck chair she was tanning on and walked closer to the edge of the pool where Elissa was getting her tires lined up in the small space between the pool edge and the scoreboard.

Suddenly Elissa drove her wheelchair backward away from Malina to ensure she didn't bump into her well-toned and tanned legs. Okay, so she was trying everything to make Elissa react, but Elissa wouldn't let her have the satisfaction or come down to her level.

Malina turned around quickly and lost her balance.

Although she was not sure why, Elissa reached to grab Malina before she hit the water but it was late. Malina fell into the pool with a splash.

"She shoots. She scores," Jack said.

Malina swam to the surface with her hair hanging limply. A piercing scowl shot Elissa's way.

"Morris, you pushed me!"

"You should work on that balance," Jack said.

Malina swam to the opposite side of the pool. Her friends, safe and dry on the deck, helped her climb out. One of them wrapped her in a towel and they walked off.

Elissa kept score. Every time a ball flew out of the water, Morocco raced to retrieve it and push it back into play.

As the timer ticked down, the score was tied. Katherine raced to strike the ball. Marie tried to reach it, but missed. Dave unsuccessfully lunged. Ann raced through the water but the ball drifted away from her hand. When the final bell rang, Jack, Benjamin and Katherine had won by three points.

"Rematch another time?" Marie asked, as she exited the pool. "I need to study," she added, wrapping herself in a towel.

"Looking forward to it. I'd better go study, too," Katherine said as she got out of the water.

Elissa waited on the deck for Katherine to grab her clothes. She looked at the sun beginning to set as it disappeared into the ocean and thought about all the chapters she needed to study before going to bed. *I really need to get a better look at the file room tomorrow, too.*

According to the schedule, Elissa knew breakfast would be delivered early to everyone's rooms so they could get to their classes as soon as possible.

So much to do and so little time to do it in, she mused.

Fourteen

Opportunities

Day Three

After a restless night, Elissa watched the clock. At five a.m., she finally surrendered and began getting up out of bed.

Morocco was immediately next to her side. Together, they went into the other room.

Elissa began lifting weights to try and get her arms strong and wake her up. Morocco quietly chased her disk across the room and Elissa played with her in-between arm reps. When she was done and Morocco had settled on the floor with her chew toy, Elissa checked her email and found one from an unknown sender titled: "Unmistakable Proof."

Reading the instructions, she was directed to go to www.chrisishere.com to talk with Christopher via a live video stream, so she knew Mr. Russel must have set it up. There was still a half hour before the call, so she snuck into the washroom to have a shower, knowing that room would provide the most privacy.

When her hair was almost towel-dried, she set her computer on the counter, set a tracer on it that Jon, her dad's assistant, taught her how to use when they were on tour. There was a camera signal box open, but it was not receiving a picture and remained black. With her end set up for the call and trace, she inserted a USB drive and prepared to record.

"Everything cool in there?" Katherine banged on the door.

"Just fixing my face. Need the room?"

"Nope. Going to work out, if you need me." Katherine's footsteps receded and metal music drifted to the washroom door.

All of a sudden a male voice resonated from the computer. "Signal's up. We're a go."

And then his image appeared. Christopher was sitting on a straight-back chair, looking into a camera.

Elissa blinked. Her heart raced as quickly as the thoughts in her head. She hit record and flicked on her computer's camera so maybe her dad could receive the signal.

He looked up and tears gathered in his eyes. His disguise, contacts, and wig was missing. Christopher's face was slim, pale and appeared much smaller than before. His face had a few bruises and wrinkles that accentuated his ordeal.

Too afraid to let her emotions consume her, Elissa took a deep breath and looked at the screen.

"Lissy, girl, is that you?"

Tears gathered behind her eyes and her heart sped up. Happiness, fear and anger waged a war inside her.

"Is there any other?"

He interrupted, "This was never supposed to happen. Two roads – wrong choice."

When Elissa was learning to read, her dad started her reading poetry. She had a favorite poem, "The Road Not Taken," that she made him read over and over. The words and the rhythm inspired her to take up writing poetry and later lyrics. That poem was something they shared, and it became a code to gain entry for backstage and various other places.

With his code phrase about the road and looking into his eyes she knew that was indeed Christopher, but now was not the time to let her anger make her say something that could jeopardize bringing him home. She needed to be businesslike to seal the deal.

"Are you ready to talk?" Mr. Russel asked. Christopher shifted in his chair, hands bound together in his lap by a plastic cable tie. His fingers and eyelids moved in a rhythmic pattern.

"Lissy, no! I don't want you involved."

"Too late," she replied.

The video signal was terminated, leaving only audio. Seizing the opportunity, Elissa turned off her camera.

"I want to see my dad face to face before I help."

She shook her arms and breathed deeply to calm her nerves.

"I'll give you the password and complete the game in your presence. Deal?"

Her legs were shaking so much she was glad that she was sitting down, and the camera was turned off to eliminate any witnesses.

"Miss Morris, I'll contact you with further details."

The connection was lost. Quietly, Elissa surrendered to her frustration and anger. She let the tears flow and tried to absorb everything that had just happened. For months, all she wanted was to have her dad back, but he was still so far away.

With a click she checked to see if the tracker found an exact location for the signal, but it displayed Rome, Brazil, and Italy before the trail ended with multiple signals. Elissa pulled out the USB drive and kept it with her computer.

Disappointment welled up inside her. For all she could do with the computer, sometimes she was still subject to someone with more knowledge. She grabbed some tissues and wiped her face to reduce any evidence of her emotional outbreak. Being unable to confide any details of the video call to anyone was going to be extremely difficult, but was something she needed to do for now.

A knock at the door sounded.

"Can I use the shower?" Katherine tried the door handle.

"I'll be right there." Elissa turned off the computer and washed off her face with cold water. With one last mirror check, she exited the washroom.

"Your breakfast is in our rec room. I ate mine. We have to leave soon." Katherine rushed to have her shower. By the time she came back out, Elissa had eaten her breakfast, and her face no longer showed any indication she had cried.

In silence, they walked to the elevator. Once inside, Katherine stood next to the elevator buttons, but didn't press one. Instead she stared off into space. Morocco looked at Elissa and waited for her cue as to which button to hit. The elevator doors automatically closed. After a minute, Morocco barked to attract their attention. Elissa looked down at Morocco, pointed to the button and then glanced at Katherine.

"Kat, you okay?"

"Sorry, mind's checked out."

"Me too. What's up?"

She took a deep breath and rubbed her face. "I'm just freaking.

What if I bomb as a field op? Let everyone down."

"As if. My dad always said doing your best won't let anyone down."

Katherine smiled. As the doors opened, Elissa drove over to Katherine, reached her arms up and they hugged. Sometimes family expectations and traditions followed the next generations around like shadows.

Tech class was so far Elissa's second favourite class for two reasons: she understood the topics and didn't have to waste too much time and energy and second, of course, she got to spend time with Benjamin. Inside the room, there was the familiar aroma of sugar and sweets. On the counter was what appeared to be homemade chocolates. Of course, that was the first stop for every student, except Elissa, who went straight to where she and Benjamin sat the day before.

Benjamin went to get some chocolates, and Malina ran up to him to talk. He appeared to be humouring her.

Elissa didn't mind, as it gave her a minute to process the video call. It was so good to see Christopher, but as close as she had come, he was still missing – still in the hands of Mr. Russel and NERD-One. The only difference now was she had seen how slim and vulnerable he was, and it added to her sense of immediacy about getting him home.

She opened up her text one more time to check the chapter she had studied. A yawn spread and gave her some energy, but she wished she had more, more of the energy, excitement and anticipation she had before the call.

"Better be careful. Those are contagious." Benjamin set a napkin with three chocolates in front of her and smiled at her yawn. "Thought a sugar rush was necessary." He sat down, popped one of the chocolates in his mouth and opened his text to the chapter quiz. Elissa took a chocolate and ate it, figuring the caffeine and sugar would give her a boost to get through another long day. It was indeed the best chocolate she had ever had, but she wasn't sure if it was the chocolate or the company and the server.

He leaned in to her and said, "Getting 80% might be a challenge today. Man, I don't think I'd love that helicopter ride to Camp Summit."

She met his gaze. "Under those circumstances, a helicopter ride wouldn't be enjoyable." Elissa realised she was staring at him and turned her head down towards her computer screen. The last thing she needed was the distraction of having feelings for some boy she had just met.

Well, maybe I will allow myself the brilliant distraction just for this class, but then I have to get serious, she decided.

Dr. Bunch strolled into the room carrying a video camera and a large bag of headphones and set it all down on his desk. Once he had his computer set up, he sat back in his chair and addressed the students.

"First, we will complete the chapter one quiz. You have ten minutes, and the quiz results will be posted on the network immediately."

Elissa thought that maybe she should have been stressed over the quiz, but she wasn't. There were two areas she felt secure about, and they were computers and aviation. Despite knowing that being overconfident about anything was never an attitude that leant to improvement, she was going with it for now.

As she clicked on the multiple choice questions on very basic computer stuff, she glanced out of the corner of her eye to see that Benjamin was completing the quiz almost as fast as she was. Once the quiz was completed, she clicked on the results and found she had achieved 100% on the quiz. She would have been thrilled, but at the same time she didn't want to set too high a standard that she had to uphold for the rest of their year. Out of the corner of her eye she saw Benjamin's screen had a 100% displayed as well.

Mr. Bunch walked around the room handing each student a headset. Then, each of them was given a program for training, via talking to the computer. It then responded to their voices as they read a paragraph.

"Now we are going a step further. That paragraph had all the consonants and vowel sounds we will need to make each of you say what we need to gain access into our subject's residence. Sometimes a voice activation code should never be the only line of defence."

He had a presentation screen come down and projected the computer screen he was working on where he took a voice profile and edited it. The voice profile then said exactly the phrase to set up the security system and deactivated it.

"You have five minutes to take the voice profile I sent to your computers and to make it say 'alarm off.'"

While Elissa was comfortable with computers, working with voice dictation was entirely a new ballgame. She was amazed at how the instructors had a nasty habit of throwing the students into assignments and expecting them to know everything. Learning through doing was a great way to learn, but she would've felt more comfortable having more than just instructions before she tried all the new tasks.

With the dictation software opened, she followed the instructions and cut, copied, and pasted the recording, then brought it into the screen where the software prompted her to type the phrase she required. Surely it couldn't be this easy.

Benjamin leaned in to see what she was attempting onscreen.

"Too easy, right?"

Dr. Bunch glanced up at Benjamin and up on Benjamin's screen appeared the message "It is that easy." Benjamin blushed and slouched down in his chair. Dr. Bunch and Benjamin exchanged smiles. Once the time was up, Dr. Bunch stood and walked to the front of the class.

"Now we will work on video looping to gain access to monitored areas. Here are the steps. This is a bit more challenging, so we'll walk through it together." He clicked on his computer and the screen showed each student the right way to complete looping.

While Elissa was trying to follow his instructions, her mind was wandering off. If she could get into the ship's security cameras, which she knew she could, then she could get the loop from the hallway and use it too get her access. The pros were that she could ensure she was able to slip in and out of the hallway unseen. The cons were she needed to hack in and record a live feed for at least a half hour as she wasn't sure how long it would take, and that project would consume lots of time. She needed the files and perhaps this lesson would be needed for the Academy Games so she needed to focus. Too much was at stake to screw up and not get into the file room, but this was a skill that could come in handy for the Academy Games. That had to be why they were teaching them the skills.

Focus, Elissa! Focus! she told herself.

The class and instructor were ahead and she had to race to catch up to where they were.

"Great job today. You can keep the headsets. Read chapter two for next class and the quiz," Dr. Bunch said as he clicked off his presentation and opened the classroom door.

"Can I walk with you?" Benjamin asked.

Elissa's heart fluttered in her chest, and while she wanted to let out an enthusiastic *absolutely*, she held back and in a reserved tone said, "Sure."

He walked alongside Elissa, but always went to the opposite side that Morocco was walking on.

Elissa was sure that Morocco was sulking and trying to get close to Benjamin and get him over whatever was making him appear afraid.

In the elevator he stood on the opposite side of Elissa to keep the wheelchair between him and Morocco.

"Benjamin, were you attacked by a dog before? Is that why the teeth freak you out?" Elissa asked out loud before she could stop herself from being overcurious. By then the question was out there, hanging in the elevator. He suddenly was interested in his shoes or maybe some fleck of color in the carpet, Elissa couldn't really tell.

"When I was six, our neighbor's Papillion, Brando, who was my best friend in the whole world," he smiled as he remembered, "got out of his yard. He was the great Houdini of the dog world. There wasn't a kennel, fence, or leash he couldn't think his way out of. Another neighbourhood dog, Kent, a really big German Shepherd, used to bark and chase the smaller dogs. He had his eye on Brando, and this time he attacked him. I ran to stop him from killing Brando, and he turned his attention on me. Brando's owner came out and with the help of Mom, they got Kent off me."

The elevator beeped and they walked out into the hallway of rushing students, but Elissa was so focused on Benjamin, the noise and hustle didn't even enter her mind.

"Oh Benjamin, I'm so sorry," Elissa said as she understood why Morocco would cause him to be apprehensive.

"Brando was treated at the vet's and managed to pull through. Kent was put down. Ever since that, large dogs just give me anxiety."

They walked to the classroom door and he turned to face Morocco.

"So while I'm sure, Morocco, you are a great dog, I just need to work through this on my own."

Morocco sat down, whimpered and lifted up her paw.

He smiled and walked into the room with Elissa and Morocco in tow. Elissa couldn't believe how brave Benjamin had been to save Brando, but then again he seemed like the kind of guy who would help someone or something in need.

Katherine and Jack were sitting at a table at the front.

"Saved you a spot," Katherine said.

"Can't believe we have a detective for an instructor," Jack said.

An investigator is just what I need to get to the bottom of Christopher's mission and bring him home. Too bad I'll have to attempt this mission on my own, Elissa thought.

This classroom was full of police recruitment and police movie posters. Along one wall was a locked cabinet with first edition prints of mystery and spy novels. Stools lined a high counter. The plain white walls, ceiling, and black and white tiled floors gave the room an air of authority. The middle of the floor was empty but some blue mats were piled up in the corner. A woman stood stiffly at the front of the room.

"I'm Mrs. Ackles. Welcome to *Intro Analysis and Investigations*. Watch with me a reenactment of a case, and then we will discuss the outcomes and what, if any, details you would change."

She appeared to be in her late thirties, wearing a grey Mirabelli suit with shoes that contrasted well with her outfit. Her long black hair swayed free about her shoulders. She distributed the course outline and once each student received one, commanded their attention.

"I'm not going to bore you with the outline. You can read it. Essential information is that there will be a quiz today on the class case and on Friday on the highlighted case in your outline. An eight-page essay, including a synopsis, research report, outline, and final draft, is due on Friday. More details are provided in the outline and textbook. You may email or come to my office during my posted hours if you need more help.

"Your assignment is to study a mission and tell me why the team was successful or how pathetic a job they did. Polish your analytical skills. Please use the provided secret agent glossary software to help clear up any confusion on the official reports for your papers. I have provided a list of five interesting missions for you to refer to. Today and in the next class we will have a quiz on the lecture material."

Tensions in the room were suffocating at having more assignments piled on each student. Elissa observed the instructor's rosy cheeks against her blemish free skin while she was talking. She had an air of confidence about her to die for. Elissa envied it.

Essays were an activity Elissa could muddle her way through but writing, other than song lyrics, was just not her thing.

"Next class, bring your essay. Any questions?"

Elissa raised her hand.

"Can the mission be cold and waiting to be completed?"

"Requests to work on cold case missions require permission and file access from Agent Larsson. Be warned, that's easier said than done." She surveyed the students momentarily then leaned on the front of the desk.

"Everyone, you're here because of your special skills. You'll all do great with the assignment. Now let's get down to the video."

She clicked, and while the screen in front of the board started showing a movie, she exited the room. Shortly, she re-entered carrying a tray filled with popcorn tubs and handed one to each student.

Being able to watch anything similar to a movie and eat popcorn was a nice change from all the quick assignments they had been given so far. Elissa enjoyed the opportunity to relax, catch her breath. She quietly reflected on the idea of possibly getting access to Christopher's file, even a censored version, without the need to pass security and observing eyes.

The forty-minute video was followed by fifteen minutes of discussion and a fifteen question quiz covering the video explanation of what had gone right or wrong, and what could have been changed. Elissa knew she might not get the best grades on the quiz, but most of the questions were taken almost exactly from the movie. She felt confident she would not lose any academic ground on this course.

Elissa saw this as a golden opportunity. If Agent Larsson would give her access to the file, that would save her time and energy. Going to the instructor's deck, was at the least, an opportunity to get a better look at the security of the file room. This was her chance and she just needed to go on her own. Benjamin, Katherine and Jack all stood up and were getting ready to leave the room.

"I'm going to go see Agent Larsson about getting permission for a cold case. Meet you guys later?"

"We'll text you when we know where we're going for lunch," Katherine said.

Fifteen

Permission

Elissa went to the Instructors offices' deck, which was all closed as classes were over. The elevator opened up to a medium-sized lobby with stainless steel tables and leather couches. Large hallway windows, recessed in-between the office areas, gave the hallway a spacious feel. The file room was under a bright light at the end of the hallway, close to Agent Larsson's office. She glanced around and spotted one camera by the stairwells, one by the elevators, and one in front of the file room itself.

Getting past the cameras was going to be a challenge, but the doorknob had a combination lock. Those took time to break. While she was confident she could do it, she would need some distractions to buy her time. Not wanting to look obvious, she looked at framed pictures of graduating classes, some in black and white and others in color. She found a familiar face, Christopher's. It caught her eye as he was smiling the same wide fake smile he gave at awards and red carpet events. Younger and slimmer, but with his true appearance; no contacts, no wig, just him.

"I see you found your dad," a voice said. When she looked up, it was Agent Larsson with his hands behind his back, rocking on his heels. For a minute they looked at the picture. "What brings you here?"

"I was going to make an appointment to speak with you," Elissa explained.

"I'm free now. Want to join me in my office?"

She followed him down the hallway to a reception area with inviting black couches. Various tech magazines lined the lobby. The coffee table had a vase with fresh orange Gerberas, just like the pink ones her mom received every anniversary.

"Come on in." He opened the door.

There was a large antique wooden desk that was identical to her dad's desk at home. Matching shelves were built into the walls. Morocco stood next to the coffee table and looked at a small fish tank. A red Beta hid behind the plant and studied Morocco.

"How can I help you?" Agent Larsson motioned for Elissa to join him at the couch while he slid back against the cushions to get comfortable. She wanted to blurt out how she had talked to Mr. Russel, and that Christopher was alive, and she needed access to the file but instead she looked at her wrist and saw her bracelet.

"Thank you for making sure I got this." Elissa flashed her bracelet towards him.

"You're welcome. Christopher wanted you to have that today."

"Why today? My plans didn't include Madisyn Academy."

"But you were planning on attending a dance academy if you didn't join your dad's tour. He bought the bracelet and wrote the letter when he took the mission. If you went on the tour, he would have given the bracelet to you in person. Every student at Madisyn is given a gift during the first week. If his clandestine operation did not resolve with insertion of the agent at the dead drop, he presumed you would be here with me."

"What?" Elissa looked at him.

"If Christopher's undercover operation didn't get our agent into NERD at the secret location and your dad didn't return, he presumed you would be here at Madisyn, under our protection, seeing as you added your fingerprint and password to gain access to the Ice Rose program."

Okay, sure, Christopher did seem to know what she was thinking, sometimes even before she did, this still seemed too planned for her taste. She flashed through some of the secret agent terminology she had seen in movies and tried to use it.

"Is that the entire truth? You know, if his life wasn't kept from me, then maybe I wouldn't have breached the security of his mission. You risked him getting burned or worse."

Agent Larsson sat forward and looked at her. His face seemed to covey no emotions.

"Chatter has not revealed that Christopher's alias has been compromised in the main communication lines, and so far NERD-One has not gotten wind either, but as long as Mr. Russel knows, his identity will never be safe." He slid back in the chair and crossed his legs. "You always were too curious for your own good." He smiled at her.

In that moment, she didn't know whether to take his comment as a compliment or an insult. How could they leave the mission files and information where she could access it and why did she have to get into the middle of this mission? She needed the information, but knowing she was indeed being watched, if not before but even more now, this was going to be more of a challenge than perhaps she had imagined. She just didn't have the time for his game of words and lack of sharing the entire truth with her.

"Can I write my paper on Dad's case? All I need is permission and access to the Ice File."

"Ah – the paper."

For the first time since she arrived, Elissa noticed how tired Agent Larsson looked. He rubbed his face with his hands.

"I knew this day would come." He stood abruptly and strode past the desk and over to his window overlooking the ocean.

"No, I don't think you're ready. Besides, Christopher would not want you involved in this world."

"Why'd you let me come to Madisyn then?"

"An agent gave good reasons for you to attend. Besides, you're safe here."

"It's true, then. I'm here so you can keep an eye on me!"

Elissa turned her wheelchair around, opened the door and sped through the reception area and down the hallway. Anger burned inside while her heart sunk into her chest. Morocco looked up at her and walked fast to keep up. The last thing she needed was another babysitter. Heavy fast footsteps pursued her. Quickly she pointed and Morocco pushed the elevator button.

Agent Larsson yelled, "Miss Morris, stop right there!" He approached her.

She refused to turn to face him, so Agent Larsson came up alongside her.

"I have valid reasons for keeping that file closed. It's what your Dad would want for you."

After keeping everything in, Elissa was tired and the frustration got the best of her. "Stop trying to be him. You're not my dad. You don't know what he wants."

The elevator door opened. She drove in, turned around, pressed the button and looked up at Agent Larsson as the doors closed. His face was filled with disappointment as he turned around and slowly returned to his office. Usually she would have felt sad that she had made him feel that way. Sad she had disappointed him, but right then, all she could feel was the frustration from all the lies and mistrust shared between everyone she once trusted and felt close to. She checked her phone and found that her team was at the Ridge. At a time like this, she couldn't eat and needed some time to be alone.

Once in the elevator, she showed Morocco the button to press to get them to the observation deck, where Morocco's room was located. The hallway was busy with students going to the observation lounge and the mini-mall. The lounge had large windows that stretched for miles, giving a great view of the ocean, which she could see as she entered a side hallway and headed into Morocco's room. At another time she would have jumped at the opportunity to gaze, but all she wanted was to be alone to think. She texted Katherine to say she was working on an assignment and would meet them at class.

In the room she closed the door and took Morocco's vest off.

"Morocco, you have fun."

Morocco ran and jumped.

Elissa's emotions switched from frustration to joy. She pulled out her computer and hacked into the instructors' office hours one last time, then had software compare them and analyze when the floor was open to the students but had limited traffic.

She knew that for this mission she might need some help, but other than Morocco, she didn't feel like she could trust anyone. Well, she could trust Jon, of that she was sure, but if she couldn't get into the Agent Links network, then he couldn't either. The ship's next stop was in Los Angeles, which was a few days away and by then it might be too late.

Wondering if there was a file on Jon, she hacked into the network and gained access to his file. He was on active duty and appeared to be working on a case, but his actual location was hidden and she didn't even have the time to try to find it. The other results came up on her screen. She found that at lunch, and after classes, the instructors were available, but only by appointment. With forty minutes left of lunch, she simply wasn't sure she would have enough time to be able to gain access to the file room, use the residence alarm and use the power outage to short out the cameras, but she was going to seize the moment. With a residence alarm set, and a power outage at the flip of a button, she put Morocco's vest on again, and they headed back into the hallway to meet the team.

Sixteen

Access

While in the elevator, Elissa prepared by getting out her flashlight; when the doors opened on the instructors' floor, she drove out, hitting her button to cut power. Darkness covered the area until the ships' generator kicked in to give the floor limited lighting. It was like being on an airplane, with aisle floor lighting. Fortunately for her, the door locks were also lit up. She drove up to the door and pulled out her code breaker since there was a code required to gain room entry. She attached the suction cords to the keypad.

Morocco looked up at her, turned her head towards the staircase, and quietly barked.

Please hurry. Beads of sweat ran down Elissa's neck. *Gross.*

One number at a time, the combination popped up on the display and revealed the five digit code. Elissa quickly typed the code on the keypad, the door beeped and she turned the handle. Morocco pushed the door open and Elissa drove inside to see the three walls lined with black file cabinets, two additional rows of cabinets against the back wall and no windows. Several large servers were along the remaining wall. Using the light from her flashlight, she turned her wheelchair and navigated behind some cabinets that hid her from the door. Morocco used her front paws to close the door and rushed to Elissa's side.

Hidden behind the cabinets, Elissa opened her computer. Sitting in the glow of her computer screen, Elissa and Morocco listened to the stairwell doors open and footsteps thunder down the hallway towards the door.

"Please don't let me get caught yet," she whispered to Morocco.

The door beeped and Agent Larsson pushed it open. He was holding a folder in his hand. Elissa swallowed, hit the alarm key she linked to the tab key and closed her computer. Agent Sullivan rushed up behind Agent Larsson, jabbering as she tried to push herself into the file room behind him. The limited light from the hallway snuck into the room and Elissa could see high, wall mounted book shelves filled with thick orange and red binders. Despite her squinting, she couldn't make out the labels describing each binder's contents.

"You getting a file? In a power outage?" Agent Sullivan strained to look into the room around Larsson's shoulders.

She doesn't have access, Elissa realized. Morocco looked up at her questioningly, when suddenly, the alarms in the hallway let out a scream like an ambulance siren, only high pitched like an opera singer's high note. Elissa covered her ears as it seemed to reverberate in the hallway and the small room. Morocco, who was sitting on the floor, lifted her paws over her ears.

"Checking security. I was updating a file, in fact," Agent Larsson replied loudly over the alarm and looked at the flashing light in the hallway. "But I guess it'll have to wait until later. Looks like a security breach on the residence level." As he gently guided Agent Sullivan back out the door, he ensured it was locked securely. Above the door was a digital clock that showed the time, she now had less than a half hour to be at class.

Whew.

Elissa drove over to the numbered, alphabetized file cabinets. From her lock picking kit, she chose the multi-purpose tool and slid it into the lock. It was exactly like the first lock she got into in Agent Sullivan's room, so she knew with a bit of patience and visualization, she could get in. Visualizing the lock helped her to turn it and she worked until the drawer glided open. Elissa pulled open the drawer and quickly thumbed through the files, singing the alphabet to herself, K, L, M, Morris. She searched for her dad's file. She knew she was safe as long as she had the security of the blaring alarm.

Finally she pulled the file and rested it on the other files in the drawer. There were about twenty pages in the folder. With her mini computer attached to an equally mini portable scanner, she slid each page under the scanner light. Suddenly the alarm went silent, although a persistent echo rang in her ears. The light wouldn't be far behind, but the cameras would have to be set again before they taped. She quickly grabbed the Bennison's file and started scanning. With two pages remaining, she heard two voices and footsteps approaching but she wasn't leaving without the information for Katherine. She wasn't going to sit idly by and watch another family suffer like hers. Morocco nudged Elissa with her nose.

As the last sheet was scanning, in the light of her flashlight, she threw the sheets back in the folder, hoping they were in the correct order, and placed the file back in the drawer. Her eyes closed and she winced as the lights came on illuminating the room. Her heart was racing as she closed the file cabinet door and went back to her hiding spot. She raced to the back of the room, next to the letter Z file cabinet and tried to hide, wishing herself invisible. The door opened to reveal Agent Larsson.

He opened the cabinet, replaced the Morris file with another and exited the room with her dad's folder in hand. When the door closed, Elissa took a deep breath and placed the computer and scanner in her bag. Then she listened for movement in the hallway. After Morocco opened the door, they snuck out and raced to the elevator.

Back in Morocco's running room, Elissa removed Morocco's vest, got a bottle of water for herself and parked by one of the tables. The dog helped herself to a treat and settled down next to Elissa.

Elissa clicked the Morris file and came upon photos of the recording studio after the explosion with pieces of rubble everywhere. The forensic examination revealed explosive residue and components including trigger boxes and timing devices, which led to other explosions that NERD-One had clamed responsibility for. The second photograph was an aerial view of the studio and smoke.

Three photographs were from red-light traffic cameras at intersections, taken shortly after the explosion. In one of the photos, there was a black SUV with tinted windows which made it impossible to identify the driver. A report detailed that the SUV was rented to a Mr. Russel, who had paid for it in cash. The vehicle was later found in the lake with no paper trail. It contained a prepaid "burn phone," also paid for with cash to eliminate the possibility of being traced. Pictures of Mr. Russel showed him in sunglasses with his eyes always hidden. Underneath his photos, a note on the file stated that Mr. Russel's true identity had yet to be determined.

The official mission report was in an Arial font, but had the COOL logo, as background. With all the official jargon, she ran it through the glossary scan to clear up the details and liked how the terms appeared in italics next to the meanings. This gave her a new insight into the world in which she was working.

Agent Morris had been without agency support, *naked,* on a secret mission to ensure communication on a, *clandestine exfiltration* operation to act as a bridge agent to the Northern Elimination Retaliation Detail (NERD). He was to contact Agents Jason and Hamari Bennison, who had been unwillingly extracted by NERD-ONE, three months prior.

The Bennisons kept their identities, posing as agents working for both COOL and NERD-One, *(double agents)*, to use for COOL's benefit. Morris was taking the program to a secret location, a *(dead drop)*, to meet the Bennison's NERD-One handlers, when an explosion at Agent Morris's music studio compromised the mission. Agent Williams was to provide NERD-One with inaccurate information while retrieving correct information for COOL, *(playback)*, as a tech and become an agent providing information, *(mole)*, but he was not successful.

If Jon, or Agent Williams, was working on this case as the file indicated, then Jon would be someone Elissa could trust with her mission. Morocco put her paws on Elissa's lap and licked her hand next to her watch. Elissa tore her eyes away from the case documents and noticed that it was 12:45 p.m. She had to hurry if she was going to make it to the training deck and her flying class in 15 minutes.

"Thanks, girl." Quickly packing up her stuff, she helped Morocco into her vest before rushing out of the room. In the elevator she focused on the information. The knowledge that she could contact Jon, and maybe get his help with her mission, was a huge relief. The weight of this mission and all the secrets and ideas finally was taken off her shoulders.

Now she knew that Jon was the agent that Agent Larsson spoke of, who helped get her access to the ship. He was how Mr. Russel had gained access to the Ocean-Alias and to her. Elissa knew that while Mr. Russel had been on the ship, Jon would have been tracking his movements. Other than when he was in the elevator with her, which she was sure the camera moving was a sign, the meetings had all been with other people around, ensuring her security. She was so relived to have flight class next because her attention wouldn't be on the lesson anyway, and really, flying came as second nature, so she could make it through this class with only a review. Her heart raced as she approached the classroom.

Her team was already seated and Agent Wright was arranging her presentation. Quietly Elissa pulled into place and took out her computer.

"You have fifteen minutes to complete the quiz on chapters one and two. If you score below 65%, I'll expect a six-page paper on pertinent flight documents and the aircraft. Essentially everything studied in those chapters. Good luck." With the click of a button, Agent Wright released the quizzes to their individual computers.

One at a time, Elissa went through the chapter questions. The questions were not as straightforward as she presumed they'd be. *Please, let me pass.* She double checked her answers and hit submit.

While the students worked, Agent Wright had set up her lecture slides on the board and was now watching the class. Elissa considered emailing Jon, but she knew right now she wouldn't have time to encrypt the email for the security she would require to ensure Mr. Russel would be unable to track it.

"Students, five more minutes." She sat down at the desk. Katherine's hand was shaking as she clicked submit.

Agent Wright watched as the second hand of the clock sealed her students' fates.

"Time. In a few minutes your marks will be sent to you privately. For the remainder of class, we are going to embark on a serious study of ancillary controls and taxiing. No class tomorrow, but on Friday we'll have a quiz on chapters three and four and take a simulator out for a spin. First, take a five minute break to recharge those brains."

Elissa tried to pay attention but her mind kept thinking about Christopher and Jon and the program and when she should show Katherine the Bennison's file. She hadn't opened up or looked at their file because it was not her parents and she just felt like she would be snooping into Katherine's business.

Benjamin had his memory book on the desk with him and for a moment Elissa's throat became dry thinking how the class would hate her when she failed that memory test and they would pay for her mistakes and Malina would never let her hear the end of it. Staying on this ship was the only way she could get to Christopher, and Mr. Russel had warned her to stay on the ship. She forced herself to take notes and pay attention.

Everyone checked their marks and left the room – everyone except Elissa and Katherine.

"Kat, I need to show you something," Elissa whispered. "But it's seriously hush-hush, deal?"

"Deal," Katherine agreed, leaning over.

Pushing her computer to Katherine, Elissa scrolled to open the Bennison's file. A shocked expression spread on her face and she looked up at Elissa.

"How did you get it?" Katherine looked up at her, awestruck. Then she put out her hand before Elissa could say a word. "Deniability! Don't tell me."

Katherine continued to read the file and her face frowned, smiled and once in awhile looked up at Elissa. Students begin to trickle back into the room. Jack and Benjamin returned to their spots. Katherine turned the computer back towards Elissa and smiled.

The email icon on Elissa's computer flashed. As Agent Wright set down her blue sky coffee mug, Elissa opened her mail.

Jack told Katherine about the aroma of cinnamon buns wafting down the hallway.

With a deep breath, Elissa opened her quiz grade — 88%. She let out a sigh of relief. She had another email from Agent Larsson telling her to go directly to his office after her classes.

Elissa gulped and shifted in her chair as she wondered how they found out so fast. She could jeopardize her entire mission.

Katherine peeked at her screen and mumbled, "Busted."

Although there was nothing in the Madisyn Academy student guidebook about breaking into files and sharing them, she was sure she had broken at least several security violations. Violations that she was sure could be used for expulsion to Camp Summit at the least. Her heart sunk into her chest as Agent Wright pointed to the slides and spoke. She didn't hear much of the hour-long lecture, as what the instructor was saying was more like the sounds the teachers made on the Charlie Brown cartoon.

Seventeen

Disclosure

She made her way to the next class as she was in no hurry to get to the meeting with Agent Larsson. With instructors and students everywhere all the time, she had to be careful when and what she did. Benjamin sat with Malina for the memory class. A small piece of Elissa was thinking how nice it would be to have him sitting next to her.

Then there was the meeting with Agent Larsson. How could he possibly expect her to study and think about the class when she had the meeting hanging over her?

"Before next class, can you please read chapters four to six? Now, I hope you found chapter one interesting about how the brain stores and retains information. Let's discuss chapter two about the rhyming scheme and three about the Linking Room method. Before I begin – any questions?" Agent Maguire glanced around the room for any student who might have any confusion so far, but no one raised a hand. He seemed almost disappointed as he clicked on his computer to have a PowerPoint presentation come up on the screen.

Elissa yawned. She had read the chapters, okay, maybe not as thoroughly as she should have but chapter three she did because her paper topic was on that one. Now all she had to do was force herself to focus on the screen.

"First let me cover pegs. A peg is any item, either a number, say in a list, or an item in a room where you will be placing any information for better retrieval. Like using your brain as a giant file cabinet and knowing exactly where to find that information." The instructor was smiling and clearly delighted by the content, but Elissa was not so sure.

He walked to the front of the desk, leaned and began to read off the presentation screen. Elissa found herself staring at a small poster on the wall that had some information about the Madisyn Academy Games and underneath was a picture of a class, which when she studied it closer, had Agent Maguire sitting in the front holding the trophy. By the looks of the big flowered disco shirts, she thought it was sometime in the seventies when he attended. She smiled with excitement and wished that it was Thursday so she could be working on a Games challenge. She only hoped that she wouldn't be sent packing for her security breach.

"In this chapter, you learned about how to take everyday items that are in a home, school, anywhere and link information to them," he said as he referred to his presentation.

She opened her computer screen and was working on creating some malicious software to use against NERD-One when she finally got them into the Ice Rose program. She was aware she would be in trouble for creating a sniffer and worm and not paying attention, but she was trying to improve her time to program them. Then, the instructor started to move around the room and glance at the students notes so she clicked back to her other screen and typed some notes.

"Chapter Three. Linking is more than just linking random information on each spot. You need to use pictures or animation to make it stick in that head of yours," he said as he tapped his head and walked back over to his desk.

Elissa noticed that Katherine, Jack, Benjamin and even Malina were intently typing notes and following along in the book. Then Benjamin caught her eye and smiled. She smiled back and was content to keep her head down and take notes for the remainder of the class.

After class, before the rest of the team were ready to go, Elissa slipped out of the classroom, into the hallway and straight to the elevator. She preferred not to explain what she had done to the team or why the guilt she should have been feeling wasn't anywhere to be found. Alone, in the instructors' offices hallway, Elissa pulled herself together by looking at the awards of previous classes and residences displayed on the desk and walls, realizing finally that on this ship with these people, she just felt right. Since the accident, she hadn't felt much like she belonged anywhere, but here she did. It would be sad if she had to leave all her friends. Anger welled up in her stomach with the realization that she had screwed up her mission to bring Christopher home.

With a deep breath she sat straight and remembered Christopher telling her to take responsibility for her actions, so getting suspended might actually have made him proud. At least, that's what Elissa told herself as she drove down the hall.

Agent Larsson's door was closed when Elissa reached it and his older receptionist, with a tight perm, bright nail polish and lipstick, was typing. She looked up and smiled as Elissa drove into the reception area.

"Agent Larsson mentioned needing to talk with you." The receptionist stood, straightened her arms to her sides in a modified stretch, and strolled into his office.

Elissa took a deep breath.

"You can go in now." The receptionist flashed Elissa the "oh-you-poor-thing" look.

"Miss Morris, come in." Agent Larsson motioned for her to join him in his office. On the lowest speed, she drove into the room. The moment the office door was closed, he turned to face her. She had seen his face straight and his laugh lines gone when he was disciplining his children but never had she seen that look directed at her. She didn't like it.

"I'm glad you're here. Tell me what aspect of 'no' you do not understand?" His eyes were steely cold. The room that seemed so friendly a few hours ago now had a decided chill.

As he stared at Elissa's face, she could feel all the rosy color drain out of her cheeks.

"I was ready for the truth."

"Rules need to be followed. Wishes need to be respected."

Elissa fidgeted with a zipper on her vest, looking around the room at the images of renowned places depicted in black and white travel photographs. She still couldn't meet her godfather's gaze.

"I'm sorry if I disappointed...I just don't know what to do...who to trust. I'll pack and leave when you tell me to."

"Young lady, you're not giving up that easily."

Tears gathered in her eyes making his silhouette blurry. Right then, she wanted to feel protected and to know that everything was going to be fine – to just for a moment feel safe, like she did before the accident. He walked over to his desk and returned with a sheet of paper, which he handed to her.

"When the qualifying Academy Games are over next week, and campus selection is complete, I expect a seven-page report on various security level clearances and the potential hazards of reading classified materials."

He watched as she wiped the tears off her face and tried to hide her vulnerable heart from him.

Elissa glanced around the room then blurted out. "Is this room secure?"

"The room is regularly swept for all bugs and recording devices. You're safe here." He sat on a chair at her height.

"I spoke to Dad yesterday – and Mr. Russel. It seems NERD-ONE requires my services."

"What are you talking about? Are you okay?"

Elissa handed Larsson the USB of the call she recorded in her bathroom.

"The night at the recording studio – they took him."

"What are you talking about?" Agent Larsson looked at the Madisyn USB.

She grabbed it back and loaded it into his computer.

"That is highly unlikely. It's been eight months and our efforts to locate him have been unsuccessful."

"I need answers, truth."

Agent Larsson joined her by the computer. "Is it possible to stop you from searching?" He looked at her.

"Maybe, but they've already contacted me. I'm going to bring him home with or without your help. Why don't you want him back?"

He stood up, walked around the room and stopped in front of the windows.

"Christopher, your dad, was my best friend. I would have given anything to take his place." He returned to the couch. "You know he might not be..."

"He is. Here's proof." Elissa pointed to the computer and watched as her conversation replayed. Behind Christopher, her lethargic father, was a wall with brown and orange flowered wallpaper. Unexpectedly, the wallpaper sparked a memory, reminding her of Mr. Jenkins' wallpaper in his basement. She began to wonder if the location where Christopher was being held could be the Jenkins' house. A glimmer in the back of her mind, made her question whether Mr. Russel and Mr. Jenkins were somehow related. That was something she'd have to figure out later.

Christopher's fingers moved in an odd pattern, but Elissa was unsure what he was trying to communicate. His blinking eyes, on the other hand, spelled out a message in their shared code, usually used for saying hello across a room crowded with press. This wasn't a message of apology for taking so long or laughter at the throning fans. It was simple. And terrifying.

F-I-N-D M-E.

As the message played, a cautious smile appeared on Larsson's face and he cleared his throat. Then he typed on his computer to start a retina and finger signal scan.

The search came up with a profile of Agent Christopher Morris, including his identification number and his profile photograph. Elissa smiled. With a couple of strikes on the keyboard, he brought up Elissa's schedule.

"Will your friends get suspicious if you stay here for the remainder of the afternoon and evening?" Agent Larsson asked.

"I know the memory method for my paper, so yes. Kat thinks I'm here because of my security breach."

He halted mid-step, turning to face her. "I hope the file gave Miss Bennison answers."

Elissa looked down. "She read the original. Not the one you planted."

She braced her shoulders as she waited to be scolded.

Instead, Agent Larsson sat down at his desk.

"But you are only a security clearance one. That knowledge is dangerous. Miss Morris, this is not a game. There is too much to lose."

Elissa looked at her legs, straightened her body, and met Agent Larsson's gaze.

"The mission needs to be completed. Mr. Russel and NERD-ONE needs to be accountable for their actions." She adjusted herself in her chair.

"Please text Miss Bennison and request she does not share any information. Tell her you have to stay here until nightly curfew."

While she was texting Kat, Agent Larsson called his receptionist and arranged for Agent Jon Williams, the onboard tech expert, to join them.

Elissa turned to face the agent when he entered the room.

"Twinkle Toes!" she squealed.

"Well, Miss Morris." Agent Williams, Jon to Elissa, stopped and looked at her. He was in his late teens, tall and was wearing worn blue jeans and a Glass Tiger vintage T-shirt. His blue eyes sparkled as he raced over to her, messed up her hair and gave her a hug. The strong scent of his cologne made her remember sound checks, when they would tango across Christopher's stage. More often than not, he stepped on her feet. Once, she tripped and they fell in a pile on the stage, their laughter echoing in the large stadium and messing up the sound adjustments. The Namibia trips to his parents' safaris and racing down the sand dunes were some of her favorite memories. Memories from when the world seemed safe and simpler.

Jon set a silver case on Agent Larsson's round table along the wall. He also had various disks, USB drives and other wires and equipment Elissa was unfamiliar with.

"Thought you might require an old friend about now," Agent Larsson admitted, joining them.

Elissa shook her head and looked at Jon.

"Loser." She held an L in front of her forehead. "Great cover – Dad's assistant. Thanks." She hit his shoulder.

"You can't talk, Miss Secret Agent – passing as a dancer." He pointed at her and tweaked her nose.

"Agent Larsson, Jon – you could've trusted me."

"Miss Morris has been contacted by NERD-One and has spoken with Christopher," Agent Larsson explained. He handed Jon the USB. Elissa drove over to the sliding patio door to look out and get over the fact these two people, who had been such a huge part of her life, were keeping secrets from her. In that moment, she wondered if she was getting the entire truth or still just what they thought she could handle. Anger bubbled up inside her. Behind her chair, footsteps approached. She turned to face Agent Larsson.

"You knew he was...?"

Agent Larsson reached out his hand to touch her shoulder and she drove away and back over to Jon.

"Jon, Agent Larsson," she made sure they were both looking at her. "Trust isn't a one-way street."

The two men looked at Elissa and smiled.

"Stubborn, isn't she?" Agent Larsson said.

"Just like her dad," Jon said.

A large smile spread across her face.

"Your file room needs better security – simple door system, cameras, one lock and a cabinet? Please."

Agent Larsson turned to Jon.

"She hacked into the network, found the file's location, broke into the room, opened the cabinet and read her dad's file."

"No fair. I taught you everything I know." He held his palms up. A smile spread across her face and they both laughed.

"Let's get him home," Elissa said.

"You're not field ready," Jon said.

"Then get me field ready. I'll get them through your game and provide them the password. They'll give me Dad."

"Elissa, it's not that simple. Your dad would never approve." Jon placed his arms on his legs, hunched down and rubbed his face.

"I'll put out an alert to bring them in." Agent Larsson walked towards the door.

"Stop! I'll never get Dad back. Besides, that'll compromise the mission. Compromise all the work and everything that has happened since...the price we've paid will be for nothing. You owe it to my family to see this through." Elissa raced after Agent Larsson. He walked out onto the veranda. She drove over to Jon.

They turned their eyes to the computer screen and saw the location for the signal of the call was blocked. It gave a radius where the call came from.

"Jon...I mean," she took a breath. "So much for the case being cold. Agent Williams, you're working on my playback and your NERD-One infiltration, aren't you?"

Elissa winked at him and he squirmed in his chair like a child caught with his hands in the cookie jar.

"Thanks for ensuring my success attending Madisyn."

"I shouldn't have let you borrow my computer knowing your curiosity. Now you're involved." He rubbed his face.

"I added the fingerprint and password thinking you needed more of a challenge," Elissa said. She leaned in towards him, "The wallpaper behind my dad. It's in Mr. Jenkins' house...well, it was before he leased it – our neighbor. Can you check there?" He nodded to her.

Agent Larsson entered the room.

"Stupid tracking software. Doesn't work when it's supposed to," Elissa complained, scowling at the screen.

Two years earlier, Elissa had been excited to receive a BlackBerry for her birthday to keep track of all her appointments. A couple of months later, she had secretly met with a friend to buy a present for her dad's birthday. When she got home, her parents had grilled her about where she'd been, but she didn't crack. A few days later, she went to retrieve homework files off her dad's computer and did a little snooping. She found a file that tracked her location over the past three weeks. Apparently her birthday gift had a tracking device inside. Instead of confronting her father, she'd carefully packed her BlackBerry in a box and sent it with a friend to their cabin in Canada. After two movies and some much needed shopping, she went home to find her parents livid that their daughter was in a car on its way to Canada. They were caught so off-guard by her reappearance that they couldn't even yell at her for dodging the tracker.

"We've kept you long enough. You better get back before curfew," Agent Larsson announced. "We'll contact you tomorrow. And remember, Elissa – keep our discussions classified. They're for our ears only."

Elissa smiled. "I'll write my paper on a different mission."

"Thanks. If anyone contacts you again, let us know immediately."

"With you both looking out for me, I'll be fine."

"Catch ya later," Jon called, turning his attention back to his computer.

Elissa drove out of the room and into the main hallway. Most of the rooms were dark as she passed. She wondered what Jon would find in Mr. Jenkins' house. She always knew he was more than just a bad neighbor.

Back in the hallway while they waited for the elevator, Elissa pulled out her computer and checked her email. She opened a bulletin from Agent Larsson.

"I would like to officially open the Acdemy Games. Individual challenges will begin tomorrow. At 7:00 am, you will disembark and be taken to your challenge area. Team challenges to follow later. I believe the challenges will be both testing and *fornøyelse*."

She knew that word meant "fun," reminding herself that Lisa had told them about his constant testing of their vocabulary. Her second email from Agent Larsson explained that Sam would pick her up in a van and take her separately to her challenge. While she was excited about the Academy Games and the opportunities to polish her skills, skills she could use to bring Christopher home, she wondered when she would find all the time to study and brush up on the Ice Rose program. She couldn't actually load it as she didn't have either Jon or Christopher's fingerprints or passwords, and she couldn't have Christopher's entry virus take down her own and Madisyn Academy's. The next few days were going to be very busy indeed.

Eighteen

Vulnerability

Day Four

Elissa had all of about two hours sleep the night before. Instead of sleeping, she spent the night studying and trying to understand what she needed done for classes. Katherine was asleep in front of the television when she came in, so Elissa had climbed into bed to avoid having to discuss what had gone on with Agent Larsson and Jon. She was a terrible liar and trying to think of a cover for their meeting was just another item she didn't want to tackle. She had waited until Katherine moved from the couch to her bed and was snoring before she got up, with Morocco in tow, and studied in the cabin's rec room.

In the morning, both of them had to race to get ready. Each student was given a breakfast sandwich and a juice to have en route to their individual Game challenges. After getting off the ship somewhere along the Pacific Ocean, somewhere on the United States coastline, she was taken in a black van, while the entire student body, including Katherine and her team, left for the individual challenges on buses. They were all given blindfolds before boarding their bus.

Elissa rode in the van listening to heavy metal music on headphones. The music helped to drown out any traffic noise and sounds that might give the students clues to where they were heading. She wondered if all of the students were having music pumped into the bus while driven to their individual challenges. She wore a black leather blindfold so she couldn't see where they were traveling. Instead of listening to the music and daydreaming or catching some much needed sleep, she paid attention to every turn the van had made. There were two stops, each for about one minute, as she counted with one hippopotamus, two hippopotamus between the seconds. She used that method when she used to play tag with Jon at the venues. Each time the van turned, she swayed in her chair and figured each turn was a corner and estimated traffic lights by the amount of time they stopped. So far seven songs had played on her player, and with each song running no more than five minutes, she figured they must have been driving for about thirty minutes.

When they finally stopped, Sam, who had driven her and Katherine from the airport to the Madisyn Academy Camp Summit location, gently picked her up and carried her out of the van. Warmth from the sun shone on her face and the aroma of spruce gave her an indication she was in a wooded area. Each step he took was not a smooth one – it was more like he was walking on a gravel surface. A gentle breeze tossed her hair and he held her tight as he jerked her a bit and gravity pulled her downwards, which must mean they were on a hill.

Next, he gently placed her on a soft seat that felt like a car seat, and the sun that was shining on her face no longer provided heat. Sam fastened her seatbelt and patted her arm. There she waited for the signal to start the challenge.

"Miss Morris, you can begin now. Your scenario is that you and your fellow agent were on a dead drop mission when you were pursued and ran off the road. You still need to make the dead drop with the package. Check the glove box and trunk. Good luck," Agent Larsson said into her headphones.

She was hung up on, by Agent Larsson saying she was with another agent. Maybe Katherine, but secretly she did hope it could be Benjamin so she could spend some more time with him, one on one. She'd be happy as long as it was anyone but Malina, though. Her understanding was that all of the students had individual challenges, so she didn't understand why there was another person in her scenario.

Immediately she ripped off the blindfold to orientate herself with her location and find out where Morocco was. As her eyes adjusted to the limited lighting, she took off the headphones to give her some peace and quiet. Morocco stood next to her wheelchair outside of the van at the top of the hill. Morocco was allowed to come with her and help with doors but not navigation.

Elissa was in the driver's seat of a vintage sports car at the bottom of a small embankment. The windshield was cracked. To her right, Malina sat in the passenger seat, with a bump on her head and very realistic blood dripping down her face and a gaping gash on her leg. Her heart sunk when she saw the one person she hoped wouldn't be there.

Although she knew it was not real, she couldn't help but admire the make-up. Medical stuff was something she always enjoyed learning about. In that moment, Elissa hoped Malina would be unconscious because then she wouldn't have another distraction. Not only would that test Malina's acting skills, but it would make her task easier. Despite the fact she knew that Madisyn would never make any task easier, she just for a moment hoped as she gently tapped Malina, silently wishing to the universe that she wouldn't talk.

"Malina, you okay?"

"Of course not. My leg. My head." Malina held her leg and rocked.

"I'll get the first aid kit," Elissa said. She attempted to unclip her seatbelt but it wouldn't budge. Of course not, that would be too easy. From her bag, which Sam had set in the back seat, she pulled out her neon orange multipurpose car tool. The tool had a sharp cutter tip to break the window glass, and a flashlight. Elissa freed herself with three snips and rolled out of the car and onto the cold dirt. Using her arms, she pulled herself toward the trunk. As Elissa pulled herself up on the back bumper, Malina pulled a package out of the glove box and maliciously beat it against the dashboard. She knew Malina didn't like her, but why she had yet to figure out.

From the trunk, Elissa grabbed the rope, first aid kit and blanket. When she slammed the trunk, Malina put the dented package back in the glove compartment. Before approaching Malina's door, Elissa looked at Morocco for some support. The lab barked and wagged her tail. Elissa struggled to move around as she opened the passenger side door and carefully placed a splint on Malina's leg. She had learned basic first aid last summer when Christopher and everyone on the tour took a class. Clearly she was no nurse, but she could do the basics, that would hopefully be enough until help arrived.

"Ouch, you're hurting me. Oh my head," Malina said.

"Maybe if you're still, your head won't hurt so much." Elissa gently rested on the passenger car floor next to Malina's leg while she put a dressing on Malina's head wound and scanned the hillside, searching for a path to get them up.

Malina was reading her scenario sheet with instructions on how she should act. She curled up her nose, mumbled and looked at Elissa. "Just leave me. I can't walk or help you. Sorry." She said as she seemed to be enjoying the fact she couldn't help Elissa to get her out of this challenge.

Elissa had to admit that leaving Malina was an appealing idea, but two things stuck in her mind right then. The first was her Grandpa, who served in the Canadian Army, and would tell her stories about how his friend had saved him after he was wounded in battle and that they never left another soldier. The second was Agent Sullivan explaining to Elissa how she would drag the rest of her team down and be dead weight. Malina, in this scenario, was indeed dead weight. Elissa had to get her out and prove to not only everyone else, but to herself, that she could complete this challenge.

"The people who ran us off the road may come back. Besides, you're hurt and team members are supposed to stick together." Elissa dragged Malina, via one pull at a time using the hooks on her vest, out of the car and over to safety. Then Elissa returned to the car to retrieve the package from the glove box and placed it in her vest before she rejoined her partner. The letter taped to the package instructed her to deliver the package within three hours to a warehouse off of the interstate. Elissa knew that she needed to pick up the pace to get them to the destination in time. It would take too long, and use up all of her energy to try and get Malina up the embankment, but if she could get to her wheelchair and use the winch to get Malina up, it would solve both problems.

"You need to keep talking. Head injury. Tell me how you know Benjamin." Elissa threaded the rope through Malina's vest.

"Like I would tell you," Malina huffed.

"Just trying to make conversation," Elissa said.

"Benjamin lived next door to us. We grew up together. We went to school together and we were rarely apart. Until last year."

"What happened last year?" Elissa pulled herself up the embankment using old roots and rocks. Elissa could distinguish trees thanks to Stephanie pointing out the various trees when they would go hiking in the various parks. The combined effect of the shades of green of the tall Douglas firs, Hemlock and Spruce trees, that seemed to reach all the way up to the sky, provided the hill a green umbrella, keeping the possibility of nasty weather away. They also served to keep the sun from shining down on them and gave some much-needed warmth. Her hands were covered in mud from the ground, perhaps because a coastal town, this city which she guessed to be in Oregon, had a limitless supply of moisture in the air. She was shivering, more from the effort of trying to pull herself up and using muscles she hadn't used in awhile than from the cool breeze settling in. The familiar chirping of a robin and sparrow reminded Elissa of home and how she could be in the safety and warmth of her bed right now, but that wouldn't bring Christopher home.

"He left to play basketball at a sports school. Said he'd keep in touch but he didn't. Not enough anyway," Malina looked at Elissa.

"You know boys." Elissa slid herself over to the wheelchair and Morocco got down and helped her transfer.

Malina looked up at Elissa. "He was different though," she mumbled. "Then he got hurt and came home. It wasn't the same."

"Hold on. I'll pull you up." Elissa threaded the rope into the winch and got it started pulling her partner. Looking down at her smarting hands, she found them cut up from the rope.

Just then, Malina stood up and began walking up the embankment as the rope pulled her.

"Please, like I'm gonna get mud on my pants."

At the top, next to her wheelchair, Elissa stopped the rope and pulled out the extra seat.

"You can't expect me to ride on that." Malina looked up her nose at the seat. "Of course you have an advantage." She looked at Morocco.

"If you'd rather walk." Elissa put the rope in her bag and started to drive off.

"Wait!" Malina limped over and sat down.

"What made him different?" Elissa handed Malina the emergency blanket and she wrapped herself up.

"Life just changed. My parents officially separated. Dad moved away and we only got supervised visits. His work was mysterious and he always seemed jumpy. Preoccupied. Benji and I just didn't share everything anymore. He didn't like me after that. Stupid boys," Malina said.

Elissa remained on the forest bike path, away from the road. Morocco followed behind them but didn't interfere.

"Here, I'm safe. I mean…we're both safe from Dad's secrets. Where are we going?"

"You're going to the hotel up ahead," Elissa said. "I'm going to the warehouse." With Malina's extra weight, she would never make it to the warehouse in time. Morocco growled and nudged Elissa's arm. A black sports car drove slowly along the highway and a bright beam of light attempted to chase them down. Elissa veered her wheelchair behind some trees and brush as her heart raced and fear threatened to cloud her judgment.

Malina stared towards the car and scowled.

"Dad?" Malina whispered. "Until I know what he's up to…I just can't see him right now, Elissa." She ducked down as much as she could. The car kept driving and didn't spot them.

"Shh," Elissa said as she studied Malina's body nearly stiff while she tried to hide. This was the confirmation she needed about Mr. Russel's identity. Mr. Jenkins identified as being Mr. Russel explained his weird behavior. Also, it gave her information she could use to blackmail him. Despite the fact that Malina knew he was up to something that wasn't right, she didn't know the real truth. Elissa was sure Mr. Jenkins wouldn't want his daughter to know that. They sat, quietly watching the car drive away. Elissa wondered exactly who he was looking for, but she knew that he couldn't find either of them. She also entertained the thought that maybe he was there to have her get him into the Ice Rose program.

Elissa put her wheelchair on high speed and charged towards the small hotel.

"What did you and Benjamin do before the Academy?" Elissa idly chattered while she tried to figure out the next step, as the security of this test had now been compromised.

"We were ballroom dancers. Don't you even remember me? I competed against you last year in the individual competitions."

For a moment Elissa tried to place Malina's face. She thought about her last few dancing competitions. There was that snobby girl who always seemed to come in second…

"I'm so sorry Malina, I…" Elissa pulled off the path and behind some tall Spruce trees.

"You wouldn't remember. Second isn't important." Malina followed Elissa's eyes. The black car was parked in the hotel lot. And the driver was clearly visible: Mr. Russel.

Elissa studied her map again.

"Why're you avoiding him?" Malina scowled at Elissa.

"I thought we weren't supposed to be found," Elissa replied. "Want me to drop you off here and you can visit with your father?" Elissa stared at Malina.

Malina smirked. "I thought we weren't supposed to be found."

"Guess you'll have to come with me to the meeting." Elissa changed direction, crossed the road and drove onto a bike path on the other side of the secondary road.

"Regarding dancing, second place is great," Elissa chattered, trying to get back to figuring Malina out and said quietly. "Besides, I'm no competition now."

"You got that right," Malina scoffed. Then her face hardened. "Benji likes you. I don't get what he sees." Malina studied Elissa up and down.

Elissa felt anger bubbling up but focused on traveling past a steep ditch. Birds were singing, and the breeze blew the trees. The road bumped beneath her wheelchair. For a moment she wondered if Malina had given the location to her dad, but by her reaction, that couldn't be possible. That said, why would Agent Larsson team them up? It wasn't like Malina would help her without some compensation.

"What're you getting out of being my teammate?" Elissa asked.

"Twenty minutes off my individual time." Malina sat up straight. "You weren't expecting me do this out of the goodness of my heart, were you?"

"You…no. What does your dad do?"

As the warehouse came into view, Elissa noticed her power reading dropped from full green to warning red.

"You know, a reputable job, undercover with the government. Saving people. That's right, you wouldn't know," Malina said.

Elissa thought about how the truth would shatter Malina's entire view of her dad. Just like the truth had shattered Elissa's world. She exited the path, looked around to ensure no lurking Mr. Russel, and then pulled onto the back road. She negotiated over a narrow path spanning a deep ditch towards the warehouse parking lot.

"Benji will leave you once you don't need saving. Then he'll come back to me," Malina said. Elissa took a deep breath, but sitting and staring at Malina didn't help calm her down.

"Well, right now I'm not the one who needs saving," Elissa said. She pulled into the parking lot.

Morocco barked and growled. She turned her head to see Malina reaching towards the joystick and pushing Elissa's hand off.

The wheelchair, under Malina's control, veered towards the ditch.

Malina's elbow struck Elissa, in the face, as she fought to regain control of the wheelchair before they both went into the ditch. Her cheek and lip throbbed after the impact. Elissa grabbed Malina's wrist and twisted her arm behind her back. With her other hand, Elissa switched the power off. Morocco stood by Malina growling and baring her teeth.

"Elissa, stop it. Let go!" Malina struggled and stood up. She pulled away but Elissa didn't let go immediately. A flock of birds in a nearby tree flew away from them.

"Morocco down," Elissa said calmly. Morocco stepped away but kept her focus on Malina.

"Maybe Benjamin was the same and you changed. Maybe he just needs you to be his friend." Elissa flicked her power back on and let go.

Malina stood and rubbed her wrist. She looked at Elissa. "I'm outta here."

"We're not going to finish together?" Elissa asked, hoping that Malina would storm off and leave her alone. Although she wanted to prove to everyone she could finish with her, she just didn't have the energy and time to get Malina back.

"We were never working together. Never will." Malina stomped away from the ditch and to the side of the warehouse.

Morocco looked at Malina, snorted and looked up at Elissa.

"It's okay, girl. Let her go." Elissa tried to move but the wheelchair's batteries were now dead. She flicked it to manual and began pushing herself away from the ditch and towards the warehouse but paused for a minute, as she knew an explanation would be required for her cut lip. Any acts of violence directed towards another student were an automatic reason for expulsion. Despite the fact Malina was not one of her favorite people, as she had said, she was safer at Madisyn from Mr. Jenkins.

The front entrance had a few steps and with no power, the steps were not an option. She just wanted to get inside the warehouse where she could wipe her face and have a moment to process everything. Now with confirmation of Mr. Russel's identity, she could set up a computer file and have it in a secure location. A secure location where it would be sent to Jon should something happen to her.

"Guess we'll try the back," Elissa said to Morocco, who pulled Elissa and her wheelchair towards the back of the old blue-and-gray cement warehouse. The dirt parking lot had tire tracks leading towards the back of the warehouse, but the overgrown grass and weeds along the building told her it had been abandoned for some time. Douglas fir trees towered and kept the sunshine from finding this place.

Above a small rusted ramp was another door. Elissa tried the knob but was disappointed to find it locked. She wiped her lip, got blood on her hand and wiped it on her black pants. Morocco licked her face.

Elissa took out her lock picks but her hand was shaking – shaking from having someone hit her and from her muscles fighting the exercise. Even worse was her mind recalling over and over again how vulnerable she was outside the ship. After three attempts, she got the door open and placed the pick back in her pocket. Then she shook her shoe to ensure the file she hid there earlier was still inside. It shifted slightly and she felt a bit more secure.

Morocco ran ahead and flipped on the lights to reveal a large warehouse. In the middle sat an old fashioned chrome table with matching chairs. Empty pallets were stacked in the corner. The air was filled with a mix of old dust and rusty metal. On the floor were puddles of dirty water. Every window allowed light to enter diffused through a milky film.

She pulled up to the table, set her bag down, opened her computer and pulled out the dented package from the glove box. Morocco settled on the floor next to her. The package contained a small, locked silver box. She rushed to open it to see if the contents were damaged in Malina's little stunt but then changed her mind and went to getting Malina and Mr. Russel's relationship typed in a file. If she could set up the computer file and have it time stamped and sent to Jon's address, she would feel more secure.

She got the information posted, including the file she had taken from the Ocean-Alias. She set the file up so that if she didn't check in every twelve hours, the file would be sent to Malina, Agent Larsson and to Stephanie.

Morocco lifted up her head, growled and barked at the door behind them, where they entered. Elissa hid the box in her vest and turned to greet the visitor, knowing who she was going to find before she turned.

"Hello, Miss Morris," Mr. Russel said, strolling into the warehouse. The fuzzy light reflected on his gun.

Morocco stood up and lunged towards him.

"Down, girl." Elissa said, though she would have loved to tell her to attack.

Morocco looked up at Elissa and growled. At that moment she knew exactly how Morocco felt. She thought that she and Mr. Russel had an agreement to help each other, but he seemed to need her to feel intimidated. Then again, maybe the gun was to protect him from Agent Larsson and Jon, who she thought should be at the warehouse soon.

"Morocco, down!" Elissa said firmly. Morocco finally sat, but kept her eyes on Mr. Russel as he sat down next to Elissa. His blue jeans were caked in a layer of dust and fresh blood. His green hoodie appeared dirty enough to stand up by itself.

Elissa's heart was racing and she tried hard to lick her lips and move her tongue around to get some moisture into her dry mouth. She wasn't going to give Mr. Russel the satisfaction of knowing he was getting to her.

"Get me into the program," he demanded, setting a laptop on the table and opening the screen.

"My team is coming soon," Elissa told him. She wondered if between Morocco and her, they could overpower him and tie him up until help arrived.

"Too bad they're having car trouble," he said. Mr. Russel pulled a remote trigger box out of his pocket and set it on the table next to him. "I'll decide if they make it here. I can get us more time if needed." His wide eyes sparkled.

Elissa shifted in her wheelchair as she thought about Jon and Agent Larsson. He and NERD-One had taken so much away from so many people and now they were threatening two of her family. For a moment she thought she could throw him across the room, but she knew reality wouldn't allow her the satisfaction.

"There isn't time for both the password and fingerprint clearance," Elissa said.

"True you missing for too long will raise suspicions. Just Christopher's password, we'll get your pertinent information later." He opened up the program for her but didn't let go of his gun. In the far right corner of the screen was a video, taken from a light post camera, of Jon and Agent Larsson working on their van. It seemed as if they were working hard.

"What if I can't get in?" Elissa asked.

He pulled his chair over to her. Morocco stood up and tried to block him. He aimed his gun at Morocco's head. Having the gun pointed at Morocco made her wonder if she could grab the gun, aim it at him and pull the trigger. All this time she had wanted to get alone with Mr. Russel and make him pay for all he had taken from her family. Yet to try and grab that handgun was a step she wasn't ready to take.

"Say goodbye to Morocco and Christopher." His warm cigarette breath choked her.

"Morocco, down," Elissa said, forcing back tears. Anger welled up inside her. Her heart raced and adrenaline boosted her confidence. She stayed close to him and looked in to his cold brown eyes.

"Hurt either of them and you'll never get the program." Elissa slid in closer to him. He leaned back and wiped the blood away from her mouth and onto his pants. His touch sickened her.

"It's your choice as to how much longer, Jon, Larsson and Morocco keep on breathing," he said, reaching out to pet the dog.

She lunged to bite his hand.

"Let me give you some added incentive." He abruptly stood and left the warehouse.

She took a deep breath and looked at Morocco.

"You okay, girl?" Elissa petted her. Morocco licked her face. Then a rumbling noise drew her attention to the large door behind them. Mr. Russel's black sports car drove in.

A shadowy figure sat in the passenger seat. Elissa drove towards the car as Mr. Russel hopped out and opened the passenger side door. She watched him pull a mask off of the quiet passenger, whose hands and legs were cuffed and hooked into a ring in the dashboard.

Oh my gosh. DAD?!

His face was slim and covered in dirt and some bruises. He looked up at her and a cautious smile appeared on his face, despite hiding behind the duct tape. Then, as if noticing Elissa was in a wheelchair for the first time, as if the consequences of that night had finally absorbed into his subconsciousness, his eyebrows and face tightened in anger. All she wanted to do at that second was rush over to him and give him a hug. Morocco barked and tried to run towards Christopher but Mr. Russel stopped them from approaching.

"Dad?" Elissa tried to believe and comprehend what she was seeing. Then the barrel of a gun pointed at his head. It was being held by a black glove protruding from a black clad arm. The gunman was entirely shrouded. The presence of that gunman made any attempt to overpower and keep the kidnappers in the warehouse, until help arrived, an impossible choice. The odds were against Elissa, Morocco and her dad. Keeping them alive, at least Christopher, was no longer necessary for NERD-One.

Christopher's eyes teared up as he looked at her. Mr. Russel ripped off the tape around his mouth.

"Are you okay?" Elissa's voice cracked as she absorbed the essence of his spirit with him sitting so close to her. Powerlessness blanketed her as she realized she could never get Christopher away from two men with guns using only Morocco's help. The odds of all of them getting out alive were drastically reduced now.

"Don't help him. If he gets what he needs we're both dead and…" Christopher was trying to say when Mr. Russel interrupted his warning by pushing between him and Elissa to stick more tape around his mouth. Then Mr. Russel stepped out of the way so they could see each other once more.

Christopher's eyes pleaded with her.

She knew he would die before he gave NERD-One that password because while he was to get the software to NERD-One as part of his Ice mission, Jon was supposed to infiltrate NERD-One. He wouldn't blow the mission.

She wished that she could explain to him, reassure him, that she knew about the mission and that she was going to bring him home to them. Her heart ached at the thought of him spending one more day or night with that man and his goons.

Elissa considered the possibility that he might kill her and her dad right where they were. Then she quickly reconsidered and decided that Mr. Russel still needed the passwords and fingerprints. *Perhaps I'm still of some value to him,* she thought. *It's Christopher I need to be concerned about.*

"If you get me the password, I'll let Morocco, Agent Larsson, and his young sidekick live to breathe another day. When we have more time, you can run and disengage the entry intruder virus and get the Ice Rose Program fully operational so I can gain access for our plan. You have my promise," he said.

Making a deal with him, for some NERD-One plan of which, she was sure was no good, was the very last thing that she wanted to do, but she needed to have everyone safe. Mr. Russel's word was something she couldn't trust and yet she had to. There was no way she could complete Christopher's mission and get Jon into NERD-One with the program if he wasn't alive.

"I want the trigger box when you leave. I want Christopher," Elissa drove back to the computer and took a deep breath trying to focus her attention on finding the password. At home it had taken her quite some time to get into Christopher's computer due to his rolling password, which he had set up to change everyday but she had all the time in the world as no viruses were set to attack the operating system pending the codes and fingerprints being entered.

"That my dear, you'll get when you get me to the end of the program." He again reached to wipe the blood from her cheek, only this time she lifted her arm and slapped his away.

She leaned away from him. "Don't touch me."

His face highlighted his surprise to her reaction.

"You should get that looked at."

He sat down in the chair next to her, leaning into and almost touching her shoulder as he watched her figure out the password. Usually Christopher used her mom's or Elissa's name but she was sure that NERD-One had some of the best hackers and would have tried the obvious like family names, birthdays and favorite things. Still she tried them to buy some time until she figured out what the password could be. Casually she looked at the time on the bottom of the screen. She had a half hour before Jon and Agent Larsson would arrive, maybe more if the car trouble was something permanent. She saw the live video of the van showed the lights on and Jon and Agent Larsson bringing supplies from the back and fixing something.

"Miss Morris, are you having trouble focusing? Let me help," Mr. Russel waved to the car.

The man in black got Christopher out of the seat and dragged him towards them.

Christopher's one leg seemed reluctant to follow his body. He was dragging it.

The man roughly tossed Christopher into a chair next to them. His arms and legs were handcuffed, just like the kind of restraints they used to transfer prisoners, which she knew from television crime shows. His mouth was gagged, but he was sitting next to her and she loved that.

Elissa's mind was racing as she frantically typed in old pet names, places they had visited around the world. But every time the same stupid screen cane up: "Access Denied."

Mr. Russel pulled a large knife, out from a strap hidden on his leg. She gulped as she looked at the blade.

"Every five minutes that you don't get the password, I will use this on Christopher." He jumped up from his chair and lunged towards Christopher.

"Stop!" Elissa yelled as she watched in horror as he grabbed Christopher's left arm and sliced the top until blood was dripping out onto the ground. Christopher showed no sign of pain or discomfort on his face but she knew otherwise. Blood was never something that made Elissa sick, but her stomach churned to think this man was so heartless. She knew she needed the password but she needed time. Mr. Russel wiped the knife on his pants and set it on the table. The man behind Christopher set a tarp that was resting on the floor under him to catch the blood.

"How's that for motivation?" Mr. Russel asked as he sat back in his chair and crossed his legs.

Then she had an idea. She typed TROUBLEMAKER— the name of their family plane – into the program. No change in the screen came up. Her heart sank at every attempt that gained the same results. She could see that the clock was coming up to the five minute time again. Mr. Russel casually picked up the knife and began to stand. In that moment she was so very glad that she had a Dad who was a good man. That was it.

"Mr. Russel, I get the point. I assure you I will get you in, but you might want to consider something before you use that knife again. I want my dad alive and in no worse condition then he is now."

Mr. Russel walked over to Christopher and grabbed his other arm.

"You are not in position to make demands." Mr. Russel held the knife to his arm.

"Actually, I believe I am," she said, trying to sound innocently confident, but struggling to keep her voice from shaking. "Keep in mind that I'm on the same ship with your daughter. It'd be a pity if she knew what her father really does – knew that Mr. Jenkins and Mr. Russel are the same man. Her dad doesn't work for the government, but for NERD-One."

Russel's face flushed red and he charged over to her with the knife in his hand. Morocco ran to stand between them.

"Don't you threaten me, you little…" He held the cold knife to her throat.

Her heart raced and she wondered if she had taken it too far. Christopher tried to get up from the chair and come to her rescue, but the armed man threw him back. The knife's blade was cool against her neck and she reluctantly swallowed slowly to keep her skin from putting any pressure on the blade.

"If I do not check into my timed file, it will be sent to Malina and COOL So I suggest you take that knife away before you do something you'll regret."

He leaned down so he could see her face.

"I believe your success depends on me staying alive." She met his cold eyes, held his stare and smiled at him. "So maybe you should put that thing down." Elissa tried to control her breathing and sat still. Christopher's hands were clenched into fists and his chest rose as he breathed fast.

"How do I know you've done that?"

"You saw me typing when you came into the warehouse. Try me."

He was so close and his arm smelled like he hadn't had a shower in a long time. Between that, her heart racing and her stomach still swimming from watching Christopher being sliced, she tried to keep down the breakfast she wished she had not eaten at all.

"You're wasting time. Do you want the password or not?"

Christopher blinked at her and tilted his head down towards his hands. He did it subtly so no one would notice, but she knew it was a message for her. She thought back to one summer when Christopher was learning sign language so he could go and speak to a special school where the students were all deaf. The word ability was that sign. That must be a possibility for the password.

Mr. Russel pulled the knife away from her and sat back down on the chair.

She was not sure whether to be relieved or disappointed to have given Russel what he wanted. Stalling him any longer would be too dangerous as he might really use that bomb. She knew he wasn't a person to make idle threats.

"Ability." She said as she typed in A-B-I-L-I-T-Y, and took a deep breath. A welcome interface appeared.

"That wasn't too hard, was it, Miss Morris?" Russel smiled creepily. "Get Chris back in the car." The man abruptly grabbed Christopher and dragged him back to the car.

"I'll keep Christopher with me until you complete our other tasks. You'll be hearing from me. Till then, don't contact the authorities or you'll lose everyone you've ever loved," he said.

"If you so much as touch anyone who matters to me, I'll make sure Malina gets a front row seat to her father's downfall," Elissa hissed. "Aren't you forgetting something?" She held out her hand for the trigger box. He handed it to her.

"Go say bye to Daddy." He motioned to the car and kept his hand on her bag.

As she drove towards the car, the person in the back raised the gun to Christopher's head again.

Christopher, in response lifted up his head and watched her approach.

Elissa slid out her lock pick, covering it with her hand. Maybe she could give Christopher an advantage. As she drove up to the passenger seat of the car, Christopher reached his hand out as far as the chains would let him so he could touch his daughter's hand. She grabbed his hand and pressed the pick against it. She saw him smile despite the gag. He reached his other hand up and brushed it against her face, showing concern at her bloody lip.

"Everything's going to be okay. You'll be back home soon," she said, making sure he had a good hold on the pick. A presence behind her caused her to quiver.

"We must go," Mr. Russel announced. He pulled the wheelchair away leaving Elissa to stare at the deep bleeding cut on Christopher's arm.

"You better take care of his arm," Elissa said. She winked at Christopher and followed Mr. Russel back to the table where he was collecting his computer.

"NERD-One has agents on the Ocean-Alias. Keep that in mind." Mr. Russel rushed over to the car and climbed in.

Christopher fought to lift up his hands and give her the heart signal before they pulled out into the sunlight and sped off. She followed the car out of the warehouse and watched them speed down a small embankment and onto a gravel road below. When they were no longer in sight, she took a deep breath and let the tears stream down her face.

Morocco put her paws up on Elissa's lap and brought a smile to her face.

"Thanks, girl. We'd better check the package. Time will be up soon." Elissa drove back into the warehouse and over to the table. She grabbed a tissue out of her bag and wiped her face. She wasn't ready to have Agent Larsson and Jon arrive yet; she needed more time to collect herself and work on the story of what happened with Malina and her lip. Still Elissa felt a rush of relief when the van full of familiar faces pulled into the warehouse parking lot.

Nineteen

Competence

The drive back to the ship seemed much longer than the ride out to the challenge. To Elissa's surprise, Malina had confirmed her story as to how she got the bloody lip, and Agent Larsson let them off with a lecture, a twenty-minute time penalty for Elissa, and thirty minutes for Malina as she attempted to destroy the package and was warned if she tried sabotage again, she would be expelled.

Elissa was relieved to pull into the main dining room full of students. She quickly wound her way through the crowd until she saw Katherine, Jack and Benjamin at a side table. She wheeled their way when they waved her over.

"Glad you made it. Oh, how'd you get that?" Katherine said pointing to Elissa's bruised face.

"Wiped out."

Elissa looked at the menu and her mind wandered.

Katherine elbowed her, leaned in, pointed at the tall athletic waiter and whispered, "I'll have an order of that."

They looked at each other and smiled.

"Tough choices," Benjamin said.

"Um hmm." Katherine's eyes were still fixated on the waiter.

Elissa thought about Christopher and wondered where he was and if they had wrapped up his arm.

"Is there something particularly exciting on the menu?" Katherine asked Elissa as she examined the front and back.

"Just daydreaming about L.A."

Jack reached into his bag, pulled out his sunglasses and slouched back in his chair.

They each took turns typing in their order and scanning their thumbprints into the small computer while they talked about the day and their assignments.

Malina walked past Elissa, but ignored her when they made eye contact. Neither girl spoke.

While Elissa wasn't sure if Malina was grateful or bored with her, she enjoyed the temporary reprieve. It was never Elissa's intention to get in-between the war that Malina seemed to have with Benjamin. Feelings, especially romantic ones, were something that she thought couldn't be faked. Instead of being angry, Elissa found herself feeling more patient with Malina.

"After that challenge, I don't know if I have the energy for field ops," Katherine whined as she slouched in her chair.

"Back at ya. The weight-sensitive floors and climbing gear can be exhausting," Jack said.

"No worries. Elissa and I have tech. How bad can that be?" Benjamin teased the group.

Katherine and Jack managed a meager scowl in Benjamin's direction.

"Shall we go, my lady?" Benjamin asked as he reached out his arm and half curtsied to Elissa.

She smiled and they headed out of the room and to their class.

As they walked into the room, an aroma of blueberry muffins greeted them. Benjamin joined most of the class as they went over to the counter, and helped themselves to the fresh muffins that were individually plated with a plastic knife and small container of butter. Benjamin set one next to Elissa.

Dr. Bunch was eating his muffin while sitting at his desk.

 Malina, sitting with her usual group of friends, was laughing and enjoying her muffin as well. Although she saw Elissa looking their way, instead of making a comment, or pointing at them, she turned her head and ignored her.

"At some point you have to give in to your cravings," Benjamin said.

"Thanks," Elissa said, as both she and Benjamin dove into their muffins. She had to admit that she was still hungry since she didn't eat much at lunch. Besides, pastry was one of her biggest weaknesses.

"Five minutes to complete your quiz. Good luck."

Once the quiz was completed, Dr. Bunch began his lecture.

"Today we will be exploring wireless PIR motion detectors or Passive Infrared sensors. The detectors basically work because they have two sensors that have to be tripped before the alarm sounds. They also have a power-saving feature, for the lithium batteries, that render them inactive for a period of 15 seconds or one minute, every ten minutes, on the hour. The sensor range is approximately 10 to 40 feet. Each has a system that can transmit information by email or instruct a camera to turn on. These use a remote to enable or disable the alarm," Dr. Bunch said as he finished the last bite of his muffin and washed it down with a sip from his mug. Then he stood up from his chair and strolled over to the front of his desk.

He held his hand up over the table, imitating the ladies who highlighted the exciting prizes on the game show called *The Price Is Right*, where there were three different models, but all were the Shepard design, numbers 40-45. Each was white, had a rectangle box with a rounded piece of plastic in the front, and was roughly eight inches long and four inches wide.

"These all have the benefit of being wireless to make selection of the area convenient. Each uses batteries, and has a tamper-proof system, animal-immunity control for both large and small animals, so animals won't set it off, but these two…" he picked up one that was slimmer and one that was fatter, "are for outdoor use. They have an additional feature of not being enabled by natural elements such as sunlight, rain, etc."

Dr. Bunch clicked on his remote and a screen lowered from above the white board which showed an example of a room with a detector in one end and the area highlighted by red lines where the sensor completed its monitoring.

"Information is in all of your files on the various detectors available on the market and their features. This is your in-class assignment."

He referred to the room on the white board. "This is your room. You need to get to the door at the other end. The room has a Shepard PIR detector that's tamper proof and animal immune. The sensor is set at a one-minute power-saving feature. Break into teams of two or more, make a plan of action, and be ready to share your findings in fifteen minutes." He picked up the remote for the one sensor and held it up.

"This allows the owner to engage and disengage it when they want to. Good luck." Dr. Bunch clicked the remote. After a light illuminated on both the remote and on the detector, he returned to his desk.

Benjamin opened up the screen to look at the specs and turned towards Elissa. As she tried to focus on the task at hand, her thoughts slipped to Christopher then Stephanie, who she would have to tell soon, and how her mom's reaction could jeopardize the entire mission. It hovered above her like a dark cloud, but she needed to focus. Benjamin, her teammate in this class, deserved nothing less.

"This is just an impossible task. If you crawl over to it, you still can't dismantle it. Could intercept the transmission of an intruder but an alarm would sound giving you only a small window. What do you think about going during the one-minute power-saver window?" His green eyes pierced her for an answer.

She was thrilled he had chosen her and was enjoying having another opportunity to work with him. She only hoped that she would not say something to look like a total dork. Then again, if he liked her it had to be for her, dorkiness or not.

"Could go in the one minute, but what if a person returned and we needed to leave before the minute was up? What about capturing the rolling code the remote is sending out and retransmitting it? Then the alarm would be disengaged. We would have to follow it up by sending a message to the control box that it is not disengaged. Make the owner think they are still protected," Elissa said matter-of-factly, as if she did this kind of thing everyday.

"Do we have something to intercept that signal?" Benjamin asked as he searched his computer screen.

"If we have time, the code breaker will pick up codes."

Benjamin glanced at her and raised his eyebrows. Elissa smiled as she thought about Stephanie inventing the gadget on the garage door after her little test for the code breaker. She only hoped Stephanie hadn't worked with this company on the rolling codes, or fifteen minutes might not be enough time. Then using the remote would not be an option on such a tight deadline.

She pulled out the code breaker and set it to find the signal for a remote device within the room, then watched the clock. Benjamin leaned in as they saw the screen running though the number possibilities.

"So how do you know about the code breaker? We haven't used it in classes yet," Benjamin whispered as he smirked.

Even his smirk was cute. Elissa leaned over to him. "I tried it on our garage. My Dad has a collection of Harley

Davidson's and had the best security remote control door system – turned out it wasn't so top of the line afterall."

He shook his head and opened his mouth in shock.

"You little prowler. You didn't?"

Elissa nodded.

"It took ten minutes to get the rolling code and gain access. When I told Mom about the security breach, she invented a special rolling code for the remote and by the time I had left, I hadn't yet gained access."

They both looked at the clock for the time they had remaining. Elissa's heart sank thinking how it had been ten minutes and they only had fifteen total.

"I'll get the location for the control transmitter and we can intercept the signal indicating the sensor is inactive. So when we get the code we are ready to go," Benjamin said as he typed on his computer and waited for the search to finish. Then he redirected the messages to come to his computer email instead.

She looked in Malina's direction and the group she always worked with was talking and seemed to have the task completed. Great, that would allow Elissa and Benjamin to both look like idiots when they had no ideas to share. Having another opportunity to look like an idiot was one too many for her tastes. Not to mention having to drag Benjamin down with her – that was just an experience she could live without.

Benjamin noticed her surveying the room and Malina.

"Malina is very good at very many things, doing them almost effortlessly. It was a trait I always admired, but don't get me wrong, I'm not about competition between friends."

Elissa nodded and stared at the code breaker, trying to will it to find the answers. The codes stopped rotating and one code was displayed on the screen. Elissa smiled with relief and held the box up to Benjamin.

"Should we save the disengage until when we present?" Elissa asked.

"Totally. Let's floor them," Benjamin smiled.

Dr. Bunch sat up and surveyed his students.

"Last row first. Share your ideas." He sat back, grabbed a pen and paper and began making notes as each team shared their mission plan. The majority of them favored waiting until the sensor was on the power-saving feature for both entry and exit. Malina stood up and referred to a pink recipe card with her notes.

"First, we intercepted the signal where the sensor was sending messages so we could ensure if we needed to leave at a time the sensor wasn't in the saving mode, an alarm would only sound at the location and a message not go to the owner – thought that should buy us some time."

Malina smiled at the rest of her team. Dr. Bunch made notes on his sheet of paper and continued to listen to Malina.

"Then we used the power-save feature to gain access."

"Very good job. You always need to ensure that you have both a way in and out of any location."

Benjamin smiled in Malina's direction. Her face lit up as she saw him beaming at her, and she smiled and sat down at her desk. Elissa thought she'd feel jealous that Malina and Benjamin were sharing a moment, but she didn't. After all, they were friends, and the world would be a very lonely place without friends. Benjamin leaned into Elissa, as it was their turn.

"We have this. You want to disengage the remote and I'll present, or vice versa?"

She was relieved to have him complete the presentation as she liked to have a reason to study him a bit more.

"You present. That'd be wonderful."

Benjamin stood up and confidently addressed both the class and the instructor.

"First we found the location that the sensor was relaying messages to and changed the report location to our email, then Elissa used the code breaker to find the rolling code." He referred to Elissa and sat back down.

"As the detector can be engaged and disengaged by the remote, we only needed to access it and we can enter the location, complete our mission and then disengage it when we leave."

Dr. Bunch stood up and walked over to their desks. "Can you give us a demonstration?"

Elissa looked at Benjamin who was smiling so confidently that it almost calmed the butterflies in her stomach. Sure, it had worked at home, but sometimes things just didn't work when there was an audience present. Take, for example, her fourth grade science experiment, a potato battery, that no matter how many times she tried at the exhibit, it wouldn't work despite having just worked at home. She pressed the code breaker button and the little light on the remote blinked and the sensor light went off.

Dr. Bunch walked over, picked up the sensor and showed the class.

"Absolutely awesome. Was the message of disengagement sent to your email?"

Benjamin beamed as he held up his computer email with the message from the sensor confirming it had been disengaged. He turned towards Malina, and they shared a smile.

Something in Malina's face made Elissa wonder whether she really was being sincere.

"All the examples given will indeed get you into the location. Exposure is my concern as you were depending on being able to leave when the power saver is on, on its schedule. Missions don't always go as scheduled, so having another exit strategy is important." He smiled at Malina's group and then to Elissa and Benjamin. "Good work today.

It's been a pleasure to teach all of you, and I look forward to having you in my classes on the Ocean-Alias."

"So memory class next. We need some details on the test." Katherine said.

Dread filled Elissa as she entered the classroom. This was going to be the quiz that would decide the length of their research paper. The entire class was going to potentially be angry with her if she botched it up. She had studied so hard and didn't want to be the weak link in this class.

The room that had seemed so fun and filled with joy was now consumed by a lingering silence. Rather than the students chatting about assignments, music, or anything, everyone filed in, sat down and looked at Agent Maguire, who was sitting at his desk, smiling at each one. She wondered if that smile was their cold comfort to urge them to do well.

Once everyone was seated, he stood and clicked on his presentation. "We will cover chapters four to six and then have the quiz. You all are going to do fine," he added with a smile. She wondered if it was meant to convince the class or perhaps himself. Nonetheless, the stakes were laid out and it was time for the students to sink or swim.

Malina raised her hand and was a distraction to the panic everyone was feeling. Agent Maguire walked around to the front of his desk.

"Malina, isn't it? How can I help you?"

Malina glanced at her computer and then returned her attention back to him. "As this is our last class with you before our test on Saturday, can you tell me if it will be strictly on the textbook or will we be using the techniques?"

He nodded, rubbed his chin and gazed out the window. Then he returned his attention to her. "The test will be based on the textbook only, multiple choice, 25 questions. I suggest studying the test examples in the back of your textbooks and the presentation notes in your class folders. Anything else?"

Everyone seemed to send out a resounding no with head shakes and glances around the room. With that, he began to lecture on number shapes, the story method and more advanced linking systems. He pointed to the presentations, walked around the desks, and then leaned on his desk.

Elissa followed his movements with her eyes but without her mind even noticing. She kept thinking about Stephanie and how she was going to react to the news of her daughter's meeting with NERD-One. In all their years together, Stephanie had always been quite open to letting Elissa try new things; still she was cautious.

Convincing Stephanie to allow her to attend Madisyn had taken several long discussions and promises that she would be safe. That warehouse meeting with Mr. Russel was going to ruin everything, all the assurances and secure feelings that Elissa had given Stephanie.

Despite running through every single scenario in her head, it always came back to one thing – the truth. Stephanie and Agent Larsson were going to find out about it. Maybe, if she acted like an adult and told Stephanie first, she would see Elissa's viewpoint and let her continue on at Madisyn.

"Now for the quiz! I'm going to put three paragraphs up on the board and you have ten minutes to read it and then I will put up the quiz, which you'll have five minutes to complete. Good luck." He sat at his desk and was reading something off his computer.

She read the three paragraphs, trying to memorize the 24 items mentioned in the story and placed them in the room list she'd made in her head. When the story flashed off the board the room was filled with a silence as everyone waited for the quizzes to appear on their laptops. Twenty-four questions flashed on the screen about various items. She replayed the story about a woman who was making a quilt and all the fabrics in her head as if watching a video. She quickly entered as many items as she could remember. To her surprise, she listed all 24. Being able to visualize the story and place each item in a specific location in her bedroom and then walk through it in her mind was a great help. She checked the clock and hit send while watching the second hand tick down to pass the three minute mark.

As she looked around the room, she saw that only she and Malina had completed the quiz. Malina noticed Elissa and shook her shoulders. Perhaps the shrug summed it all up. Elissa had done the best she could and now there was nothing more she could do to make the answers right if any of them were wrong.

"Fifteen seconds, everyone." Agent Maguire watched the clock and then clicked a key. Every student's computer monitors returned to their screensavers. He typed on his keyboard and then referred to his presentation screen. There was a list of the top ten students, rated by time, to finish the quiz. Malina, Elissa, Benjamin, Katherine, Jack, were the top five.

"Malina how did you remember the items?" He asked as he leaned on the front of his desk.

She sat up, clearly basking in the attention.

"I used the story method and visualized the items. Then I just retrieved them when the quiz came up."

"How many of you used visualizations?" he asked the students.

Everyone raised their hands.

He smiled as he clicked a button that revealed the test results for each student. Elissa's heart raced to think that in front of the entire class she was going to be humiliated but she scanned her name and 100% was after it. She sat back in her wheelchair and let herself relax as she savored the moment of not letting anyone, including herself, down.

"As you will notice, all of you achieved 100%. Congratulations. Your paper has been cut to 750 words, or 3 pages. Despite no more classes before the test, if you have any questions, just email me or come see me during my office hours. You may go."

Elissa processed how quickly the classes had gone by. She hoped that she would be asked to return to the Ocean-Alias to attend classes with all the amazing instructors and students she had met, but the accident had proven to her that sometimes life doesn't go the way she planned.

Elissa gathered her things while Benjamin checked his phone.

"The team is going to Ridge for some chow. You coming?"

Twenty

Promise

Elissa wanted nothing more than to follow Benjamin to the Ridge and have some time studying and hanging out, but she knew she should call Stephanie and tell her the news. Then she decided that the news of her visit from Mr. Russel could wait until she had some time to process the meeting herself.

"Wait for us," Jack said. "How about we study before the ultimate billiards challenge?"

"Sweet," Katherine said.

Once they found a quiet spot next to some comfy couches, they all cracked open their books and munched on their lunches. Thanks to a speed-reading course Elissa took two years ago, she could read material quickly, but with all the distractions, retaining information was challenging.

Elissa read the two tech chapters and moved on to her flight study. The flying book was interesting so she read an extra chapter for good measure. As everyone was still reading, she started a search on mnemonics and the room method to add creditability to her research paper.

With a rough outline of her mnemonics paper completed, she researched cold missions from the list the instructor had provided. All of them were boring until she found one about a missing government portfolio and an unfavorable outcome. Her computer beeped to signal her of an upcoming video call.

"Video call. I'll be back." Elissa drove over to a booth in the corner. The booth was similar to a street phone booth only there was no break in the bottom to allow airflow; it was self contained, other than the door, to add security. It was a challenge, despite the extra room allowed for the wheelchair, but she got inside and closed the booth door. She drove over to the small table that had a telephone. Then she set up her computer, ensured she had a signal and prepared to talk. Stephanie came up on the screen. She looked happy but black rings under her eyes told another story.

"You save the world yet?" Elissa asked.

"The project's going well. I should be done by tomorrow. We can hang out in L.A. That is, if you can stand hanging with your mom."

"I can't wait."

"How're your classes coming?"

"Good. We had an individual challenge today. I had another student with me – that awful girl from the Mike's line-up who challenged me. Apparently, my wheelchair is somehow insulting to her or something," Elissa moaned. She wanted to be face-to-face with Stephanie to tell her what was going on. She tried to hide the results of the long day from her.

"Honey, she just hasn't gotten to know you." Stephanie smiled. "Anything special tonight?"

"Just studying and playing pool with my friends."

Stephanie smiled. "Now want to tell me what's really bugging you?"

"Something's happened, Mom. Can you sit down and chill out? And don't say anything until I finish." Elissa looked at her mom. Stephanie sat down and looked at the screen.

"Mom, NERD-One contacted me. They have Dad. I need to help them get into a computer program and they'll let him go." Elissa awkwardly sat back and watched the news travel the distance to Stephanie.

Stephanie's face lost all its color and her eyes went cold. Elissa knew that look as she had received it several times before, when she let her stubbornness overwhelm her common sense.

"Elissa, I want you to come home," Stephanie said firmly with an almost eerie calm. "You're not safe there." She clenched her fists.

Elissa fought the tears gathering in her eyes. She needed to make her understand.

"I'm safe here. I met them when I was off the ship. Besides, if they wanted me, they would've done something sooner. I know what I need to do," Elissa explained. She thought if Stephanie could see her confidence and lack of fear then maybe she would let her continue.

Stephanie leaned into the camera. "It's not your responsibility to bring him home. I can't lose you, too." Tears streamed down Stephanie's face.

"I understand. Please let me stay. Sleep on it. We have a team challenge and I don't want to let them down. I finally fit in, Mom."

"If you promise to tell Agent Larsson about your meeting, I'll think on it." Stephanie stared at Elissa with a straight face and wiped her eyes.

"If I tell…if I leave the ship…they said they'd kill him." Elissa began to cry, completely frustrated at the position Stephanie was putting her in.

"How do you know they haven't already?" her mom says.

"I saw him," Elissa whispered. "He talked to me – gave me our 'road' password. I looked into his eyes." Elissa wiped her eyes and sniffed. In that moment she was glad the glass was frosted so no students could witness her crying.

"Was he…" Stephanie gazed into the camera. "Was he…?"

"Skinny, tired, but alive, Mom." Elissa smiled.

Stephanie took a deep breath. "Talk to Agent Larsson tonight after your game and I'll think about it."

They both said their goodbyes and Elissa, once her face wasn't as red, joined her friends again.

"Enough brain torture," Benjamin said, shutting his computer. "Any billiard rookies?"

"I'm a little rusty," Katherine admitted.

"We'll refresh your memory." Jack flashed a crooked smile at Benjamin who nodded. "Check out the professional table." He walked around the table and admired it.

Jack set up the balls and handed out the cues. As Elissa picked up the pool cue she suddenly felt as if she were being watched. Mr. Russel did warn her that NERD-One had spies on the ship but, despite a million reasons, she didn't feel unsafe on the Ocean-Alias. She turned her head and casually surveyed the room. Many other students were gathered but none were looking her way. But the door to the kitchen was slowly closing.

Katherine bent down and petted Morocco. As she did she whispered in Elissa's ear.

"Gotta watch those two." She stood. "How about girls against boys?"

"As if there's any other choice," Jack said.

Elissa remembered past pool games in backstage areas with her dad. Christopher was a great player. She did a quick inventory of the Ridge room and all the breakable vases and remembered backstage at the arena, hitting the ball so hard it bounced off the table and crashed against the cement floor. The 'Granny Stick' reminded her of stretching across the green felt table as a kid and attempting to make an impossible shot.

"Let's start with eight ball," Jack said.

"Stripes are so last season," Katherine said. She glanced at the striped balls and Marie, the exotic girl from the pool, who was wearing a low cut, blue and grey striped jersey knit dress.

Jack and Benjamin looked at each other and Jack rolled his eyes.

"The first ball you pocket is what you're stuck playing," Jack said. Katherine motioned for Elissa to go first. As Elissa lined up, Katherine picked up a cue and twirled it around like a giant baton. The cue made contact with Jack's hand and crashed to the floor like a gun shot. Everyone in the room looked up to track the abrupt sound. Kat turned red as she picked up the cue and moved next to Elissa.

"No, you break." Elissa backed away.

Katherine lined up across from the racked pyramid of balls. A loud crack filled the air. One of the solid balls, the seven, rolled towards the right pocket.

"Come on, go in." Katherine ran to the edge of the table closest to the pocket and watched it. The ball teetered at the edge of the pocket and fell in with a plop.

"Figures. You'll be aiming at all the solid balls," Jack explained. He walked around the table and lined up his shot.

Katherine came over to Elissa. "Aiming…that's easy for them to say."

On Elissa's turn, she drove up to the table and aimed for their ball closest to a pocket. She leaned the pool cue on her hand and then shot. The last time she played pool, she was standing. The view was different from her chair. A cue ball struck the four-ball which hugged the edge of the table as it rolled towards the pocket. Then it struck the three-ball and slowed up a bit, but continued rolling. It passed the edge and then dropped in. Katherine attempted the 'moonwalk' and gave Elissa a high five.

"Morris, you've played before," Benjamin said.

"Maybe a few times." Elissa glanced up at him and smiled.

They played the game and the score, with an advantage, went back and forth, with the boys winning, then the girls, then the boys again.

Katherine strolled over to the table to aim for the eight ball.

She shot but the ball rolled just short of the pocket.

"Call the police. You were robbed!" Jack whistled. He flashed a lame sympathy look her way.

Benjamin lined up to make his shot and sunk the eight ball. The boys gave each other a high five and then moved on to some handshake that involved fists, thumbs, and snapping. With boasting and eye rolling all around, they decided to go back to their cabins to finish their reading. She wanted some time to play Jon's game so that she could get NERD-One in quickly, which would allow her to place a tracker also. While most of her assignments were under control, it was going to come down to the wire to get them done. First, she had to make good on her promise to Stephanie and talk to Agent Larsson.

"See you tomorrow," Jack said.

"Group task coming soon. Watch out for our team," Benjamin said. The girls and Morocco went to the elevator.

Katherine asked, "Did you get your research done?"

"Not quite. I'm going to go talk to Agent Larsson now."

"You're such a keener."

As Elissa came out of the elevator, she saw a small area with two couches, a wooden door surrounded by glass bricks showing the shadows that lived behind them, and a video intercom system. She drove over to the child-height intercom system and pressed Agent Larsson's button. Elissa felt bad contacting him after 8:00 pm, but she had made a promise, so despite procrastinating as long as she could by playing pool, she was making good.

"Miss Morris, how can I help you?" Agent Larsson appeared on the screen.

"I need to talk to you. It's important," she said.

"I'll be right out."

She drove over to the table and picked up a National Geographic magazine and looked at the photographs of far away places. Each picture reminded her of the trips her family would take to see the world. Maybe one day they could travel as a family once again, but they needed to get Christopher back first. A beep signaled the door opening and Agent Larsson walked up to her. Instead of the formal clothes that were required during the day, he was wearing khaki pants and a green golf shirt. This was how she was used to seeing him, casual and relaxed.

"How can I help you?"

"Can we go to your office?" Elissa met his eyes.

"Okay," he responded as he followed her to the elevator. Morocco looked up at him and he bent down. "Hey, girl."

This time, as they walked down the hallway to his office, she wished it would take longer. She knew once he knew she'd come face-to-face with Mr. Russel, everything would change. The truth always had a way of interrupting, and she was not the best at keeping any secrets, a skill she was going to have to polish to be a competent secret agent. Agent Larsson opened the reception door, turned on the lights and she followed him to his office. He sat down on the couch with his arms rested on his legs and his hands were clasped loosely together. Elissa took a deep breath and, in a steady tone, said what she needed to say.

"NERD-One, Mr. Russel, promised they'd keep Dad away from us if authorities got involved. Mom made me come tell you. Thought you could be trusted. At the challenge yesterday, when the cameras were out, a NERD-One operative came to the warehouse. He brought Dad and I talked with him. I helped them get into the Ice program."

She sat back in her chair, waited for the proverbial bomb to drop, and squinted as she waited to be reprimanded. Larsson stared at her as the meaning to her words settled into his consciousness. He rubbed his face with his hands, his eyebrows plunged into an intense scowl and he leaned forward and held her hand.

"Did they hurt you?"

"No, just made threats. They need something from me. I'm too valuable to them." Elissa squeezed his hand and made eye contact to convince him. She felt like her entire future was waiting on some decision Stephanie was going to make and she had absolutely no power to change it. That feeling sat on her shoulders like a weight she could not lift off.

"You told your mom?" He let go of her hand, stood up and walked towards his desk.

"On my video call this evening. The booth scrambled the conversation and she well…she knows me. Knows when something's up." Elissa drove up to him and knew that her success was dependant on him understanding. She needed to be as convincing as she could.

"You were to tell me if they contacted you. Was that ever your intention?" He turned around and the scowl had once again taken over. She backed away to put some space between them – space to give her room to think and breathe.

"When I was ready. This is our best lead. I couldn't risk him being taken away because I trusted someone who never trusted me with the truth. Trust isn't a one-way street."

He raised his eyebrows and crossed his arms. "I'm going to contact Stephanie and see what she wants to do about this situation."

Her heart sank into her chest. She knew exactly what Stephanie wanted Elissa to do – come home where she could keep an eye on her. After all the work Elissa had done to get on the Ocean-Alias and stay here while she found the truth, to come so close to having Christopher home, and to have two adults, who at that time had no clue what was going on, decide for her was going to kill her. Tears of frustration ran down her face.

"Please don't jeopardize my chances…our chances…of getting him back."

"Come back tomorrow morning and I will have a decision."

Elissa returned to her cabin and watched the colors of the setting sun ignite the ocean. She could hear an entertainment show telling the details of a movie premiere, something she used to be interested in, but now that world seemed so far away from the reality she was dealing with. With the wheelchair on low, she drove into the rec room to find Katherine, with her book resting in her lap, reading, but a make-up commercial had enticed her attention away. She turned to Elissa.

"You get what you needed?"

"Think so. Adults sometimes are so clueless."

Katherine rolled he eyes, "Tell me about it."

"I'm going to study at my desk." Elissa turned around and parked at her desk. She took off Morocco's vest. "Go ahead and enjoy yourself. You've earned it." Morocco ran over to her bed and grabbed her favorite squeak toy, a blue stuffed monkey, and played with it.

The sun plunged into the ocean to end the day, a day in which she still did not have Christopher home, safe with Stephanie and her. She opened her computer and got into her email. To her disappointment, there were no new messages. Hours slipped by as she practiced imbedding a sniffer to steal and spread NERD-One's passwords unwillingly to COOL and a worm. The very last step to get her sniffer and worm working was still hanging her up.

In the moonlight, she noticed movement in the water. Squinting, she saw it was only a fish. Of course it was a fish, they were in the middle of the ocean, what else could it be? Really, all this secret agent nonsense was making her paranoid.

Frustrated with the game, Elissa opened her study list and started to place images on her pegs with the pictures in her mind – pigs dancing on top hats and other nonsensical items. After about an hour, she found herself yawning and looking out the window at the moon dancing on the ocean, and wanting nothing more than to get some sleep. She put away her computer and book and went into the other room.

"I need to crash," Elissa said. She covered a big yawn.

"I hear you. One chapter left, then I'll be there," Katherine said.

Twenty One

Consequences

Day Five

As it was the last day of classes, Elissa was tired. Her brain wanted to play and think about anything other than classes. Every day brought another possibility, if not an opportunity, for an encounter with Mr. Russel, but today Elissa knew that would not be the case. They were on the ocean and he couldn't risk being trapped and potentially caught. She was stuck on the ship with fellow classmates, going to classes and working on the assignments that were daunting to them. Soon there was also going to be a group challenge, which would provide clues as to which students would be allowed to permanently stay on the Ocean-Alias. It also provided statistics that revealed which students would be invited to participate in the Academy Games to be held during the year.

Anxiousness grew more each hour as Elissa waited for Mr. Russel to contact her. But his silence made it difficult for her to focus on studying her cold case and completing her assigned papers. Katherine, Jack and Benjamin all were focused on their assignments, but Elissa knew her heart was miles from homework, flight simulations and formatting bibliographies.

Elissa tried to complete her exercises to keep her body strong and take away the powerlessness she felt from the encounter with Mr. Russel the day before. Elissa got some water and food out for Morocco before closing the door to their rec room. She didn't want to wake Katherine who seemed lost in peaceful dreams. Morocco stood on the treadmill, looked at the switches and, pressed her nose on one of the workout settings. Written in permanent marker was Morocco's name. The treadmill started and Morocco strolled on it comfortably.

Elissa poured all her energy and frustration into the weights and lifts. When the treadmill had finished the workout, Morocco ate breakfast. By the end of the workout Elissa's body ached and her frustration was released into the universe, which Elissa was sure would allow her to focus a bit better. After a quick shower, she wrote Katherine a note to remind her of the meeting and opened the cabin door.

"Come on, Morocco," Elissa whispered. Outside the room, she secured the dog's vest and leash. An uncomfortable silence blanketed the hallway. As no one else was up yet, the elevator proceeded straight to her deck. When the doors opened, the hallway was lit but each room was dark. As she passed one, she swore a shadow moved by one of the empty desks. Chills ran down her spine. Morocco looked around, ears at attention, sensing something.

"You spooked too, girl?" Elissa stroked her softly, sped up, and headed to the end of the hallway. As she entered Agent Larson's office, through the reception area, Jon's voice startled her. She was supposed to meet Agent Larsson and there was no mention of Jon. This got her wondering if Jon was there to soften the blow of the news or maybe to escort her off the ship. Instead of being thrilled to see him, his presence only made the weight of the next few hours seem almost unbearable.

"You're here early."

"Couldn't sleep." She turned her head to look back towards the hallway and the door to the stairwell was closing.

"Agent Larsson went to get a coffee. How're you handling this?"

"I'm trying to grow eyes in the back of my head." She smiled as she tried to keep the fear of having to leave, and her frustration, from bubbling up and making her seem less composed than she actually was. If they thought she was not handling all the stress – that might give them another reason to send her packing.

Agent Larsson walked in all decked out in his formal Academy uniform.

"Good morning," he said, as he closed and locked the door.

Jon and Elissa sat near his computer and Agent Larsson pulled a small disk out of a brown envelope and showed it to Elissa.

"Christopher signaled a location. We followed it to a locker on Catalina Island. This disk was in the locker and we wanted you to view the contents. We weren't sure you'd want us to look at it. It could be personal," Agent Larsson said.

"It's fine. We're like family."

Jon loaded and ran the tiny disk in the computer. The screen prompted them to enter a username and password. Agent Larsson looked at Elissa and Jon slid the keyboard over to her.

"What makes you think I know these?"

"The message he sent using Morse code, a version we have not deciphered before, via his eyes, was meant for you, Elissa, not for us. Some code we were unable to decipher," Agent Larsson said.

"You're his insurance the contents didn't get into the wrong hands," Jon said.

Now Christopher wanted her help and all at once she was thrilled and yet, she didn't want to let him down. She typed in username 'rock star' and password 'find me' before pushing the keyboard back to Jon. She hit enter.

Elissa turned back to the screen, pressed enter and a sniffer notification box popped up. She squealed.

"That'll fix em. It's a sniffer to give us access to NERD-One's system. But it'll take time to intercept the streams, hours to pinpoint the exact information we need." Elissa slouched in her chair.

"Want to meet your friends for breakfast? Probably best that they don't get suspicious about you going on early morning excursions," Agent Larsson suggested.

Elissa looked down disappointedly. "Promise to keep me posted?"

"Absolutely. I'll email you reports," Jon said.

"Your help has been invaluable," Agent Larsson said. "Wait, did Agent Williams fill you in on the house raid?"

"No."

"We checked Mr. Jenkins' house. It was leased to a Mr. Russel after he moved out. We found the Bennisons there, along with two NERD-One operatives. The operatives were setting them up to be terminated as their true identities had been discovered and they had provided all the intel that NERD-One required."

"Are they…?"

"A bomb was detonated, but our agents were able to secure them in time. They're being treated for dehydration, but they'll be fine. We're going to contact Katherine soon."

Elissa wanted to tell Jon that Mr. Russel and Jenkins were the same man. After all she agreed not to tell Malina, but Jon and COOL were two different things.

"Jon, you know that Mr. Jenkins and Mr. Russel are the same person, right?"

He looked up at her and shook his head no.

"If you tell anyone, he'll release Christopher's I.D. out into the world. It'll wreck Dad's career. Jon, you need to keep it on the down low. That's our deal to have him not expose Dad's real identity to the press."

Jon looked down at the floor then slowly raised his head to make eye contact with Elissa.

"I'll tell you what. I need his identity to remain unknown to get me into NERD-One. For now, it'll remain between us. When I get into NERD-One, we'll think about releasing his identity later. I'll keep an eye out for chatter about Christopher and intercept any that gets into the main lines of communication."

Elissa took a deep breath and enjoyed being able to share a small part of the secrets she had been keeping locked up inside her. Before leaving the room, Elissa checked to see if Katherine had texted her. Sure enough, her friends were saving her a seat in the dining area.

"I'll walk with you. I'm going to make an announcement at breakfast." Agent Larsson walked alongside Elissa to the elevator. "We'll be giving out the group Game assignments for each group this morning," he said.

"Agent Larsson, was Dad good at the Academy Games?" She glanced up at him.

"We were teammates. He was amazing at adapting to whatever challenge they threw at us. Is there an area you are anticipating learning about?" he smiled.

"Computers and gadgets."

"Just like your parents."

She smiled. As the elevator doors went to open Elissa pushed and held the "close door" button. "Have you contacted Mom?"

"She was notified that we have a lead, but she was not surprised."

"Any decision as to my future here?" Elissa hated to ask, it was as if it had all been forgotten about, but the suspense was killing her.

"That we will discuss and have a verdict on later."

The elevator started to ding so she released the button and they went into the main hallway. As Elissa entered the dining room she could see Katherine and Benjamin waving to her near the door.

"Talk to you later," Agent Larsson said as he walked toward the head table. She got settled and noticed an empty chair at their table. Jack watched both Katherine and Elissa staring at the empty chair. The thought of meeting a new person made Elissa feel a bit uneasy. The team had such a good dynamic and she hoped this new member wouldn't jeopardize that, but she was intrigued by a new person.

"Kalan's going to join us today."

"Check out Kalan's carving skills." Benjamin opened his bag and pulled out a stone bear sculpture. He handed it to Elissa. The bear appeared to be dancing. The lines and curves were very detailed.

"I can't wait to meet him." Elissa gently passed the sculpture to Katherine.

"Here's your chance." Jack directed their attention to a boy approaching them. Though he was short, he walked with an air of confidence. His dark straight hair and oval face emphasized dark twinkling eyes and rosy cheeks.

"Elissa, this is Kalan. He completes our team," Jack said.

"Pleasure to meet you." Elissa stretched out her hand to welcome this new addition. So far he seemed to be artsy, and according to Jack, his skills in hunting and exploring would complement their team.

"I'm excited to be a part of your team," Kalan smiled. A dimple appeared on his left cheek.

Agent Larsson stood by the podium. "Today is team challenge one of two. If you have been paying attention in all your classes, this challenge should be exhilarating. Right now, all of your team missions are being delivered. Your first task is to select a team leader and email us the name. Good luck." He joined all the other instructors at the table and they ate breakfast.

Rachel walked over to the team, set a leather portfolio on the table, and wished them good luck.

"I nominate Benjamin," Kalan said. Everyone agreed.

Elissa opened the file and read aloud. "Three tasks. Enter a room alarmed with heat detectors, pick into a safe door, hold your team's weight and retrieve a card from the lap of luxury."

"How about we divide into sub-teams? One for communication and tech and another for field ops?" Benjamin suggested.

As the trays of food were cleaned off the tables, the teams quietly made plans before heading to the lido deck. Despite the lack of information, Elissa was fairly confident about completing the task. In class, they had been given the information she figured they would need to successfully complete the tasks.

"Brutal. There are more than three tasks on this group team challenge," Katherine said.

"Tasks are irrelevant if our time sucks and we can't get through the detectors and traps," Benjamin said.

On one side of the deck, large and bulky cubicle rooms choked the freedom of the open space and sunshine. A main table, with a sign above, highlighted the team challenge area registration while velvet ropes blocked off the entrance.

"We have to sign in," Katherine said, pointing to the table.

"You are assigned to work on section eleven," said Agent Davidson, who was tall and wearing an empire waist dress with the Academy vest. She flashed her hazel eyes at the team. "Results are measured on successful completion and time. Registering in and out here with a representative will allow us to keep track of your task time." Agent Davidson handed Benjamin a black knapsack.

The team headed to their assigned section, excited to see the task ahead of them, to stand under sign 11 and survey their challenge. The first room resembled a country kitchen, with a black and white tiled floor surrounded by three eight-foot-high walls covered in bright rooster-printed wallpaper. The ceiling, made of clear glass or plastic, had large silver tracking, like for track lights only super heavy duty, to enable climbing equipment and people to hang from it, running along either supporting wall and grounded at each corner by a big support beam. It criss-crossed into an X at the center. At the end of that room was a large orange safe door with a menacing lock, providing a break from the wallpaper. There was a small area in the front of the kitchen that had "Welcome" spelled out where the team stood to survey the room.

Elissa opened her computer and swept the area around the safe for any security traps.

"What surprises are waiting for us?" Jack asked.

Kalan checked Elissa's computer screen and said, "There's a wireless detector, just before the safe door, beside the chrome switch plate cover by the safe entry, but I have to check which kind." He tried to get a better look without settling off any alarms. Most of the kitchen was accessible, as the detectors only monitored a set area, but there was a start line painted on the floor to allow the students an entry zone to get their plan together and allow them the opportunity to not engage the alarms before they got going.

"Yikes," Katherine mumbled.

"Jack and Kalan, you two look up the detector sensitivity? Katherine, check out the lock specifications on the safe. Elissa and I will figure out a path through the room." Benjamin pulled up a chair next to Elissa. While she tried to focus on the task assigned to them, she was a little excited having Benjamin working with her. He was very special and she enjoyed every opportunity to spend time with him. If only the nervousness, like numb tingles that appeared in her limbs as they went asleep, would get out of her stomach and stop clouding her judgment, she'd enjoy spending time with him more.

"Guys, we found the detector. It's the Shepard 45, heat sensitive," Kalan said as he walked over to the team but stayed clear of the detector area.

Elissa was relieved it was a detector they had covered in classes. At least the experience would give them a sneak peek into the world of detectors.

"The sensor is tamper proof, so we can't disengage it or it will provide a warning as an alarm for us and send a message to the owner's email. "

Benjamin reassured the team. "Elissa successfully got past a detector like this in class with the help of a code breaker and a redirection to my email. We will get this done."

Elissa worked with the code breaker to get it searching while Benjamin found the owner's email location and redirected all messages to him. After completing a first survey of the area and coming up empty-handed with what might be behind the safe door, Jack tipped their mission bag out onto the floor to reveal its contents: one harness, duct tape, two helmets, a smaller empty knapsack and rope. The small table, before the start line, had a small bag on top. Benjamin opened it and emptied the contents on the floor: two compact mirrors, a screwdriver, a flashlight, pens, paper, and a measuring tape.

Katherine read her intel on the safe. "The Lock-Up 10 has a double-locking spinner. Its electric charge prevents tampering. Any explosions will cause the second lock to engage."

"Locks are Kalan's specialty. Rocked them in fields ops the other day," Jack said.

Elissa clicked the code breaker the moment the codes stopped rolling.

"Detector's disengaged," Elissa said to her team. She was glad to be able to help as she knew there would be parts of this challenge that would be too physical for her. But then again, all of the team members had their strengths and weaknesses.

Benjamin smiled and picked up his computer. Kalan pulled out his code breaker and plugged it into the lock. The device sped through the number combinations.

"Jack, scan for traps beyond the door," Benjamin called out.

Elissa watched Kalan use the code breaker to get the safe combination.

"Bad news," Jack said. "There's an alarmed, weight-sensitive floor – one person, maybe a hostile, in the middle of the room."

The team gathered around Jack's computer to look at the heat reading inside the safe. They decided to let Kalan open the door anyway. Kalan carefully unplugged the cord and handed it to Elissa. Then he entered the code and pulled the door, disconnecting the seal, and making a suction noise as it heavily swung open. In the middle of the room was a high-backed velvet chair. Rachel was tied to the chair and gagged. She was wearing her climbing harness and helmet, and her head hung down limply. A blue key card was on a red velvet pillow in her lap. A support beam ran across the ceiling from the door to the far wall.

"Use the climbing kit to string an anchor and rope across. One of us will have to climb," Jack said.

Elissa was relieved that she didn't have to try the climbing gear. While she had been a dancer, having to gracefully hang and move through climbing gear with her limitations would be exhausting.

"You mean I can climb, don't ya?" Katherine placed her hands on her hips and winked at him.

"Can you support Rachel's weight?" Jack asked Katherine.

"With a little help from my team," Katherine said as she nodded to the team.

Benjamin, Kalan, Elissa, and Katherine got to work. Jack and Benjamin readied the mechanical climber. Kalan strung up the climber on the poles. The climber was a silver box, about the size of a box of five CDs, had four buttons, and slots to attach it to a rope. Elissa helped Katherine into the climbing harness. Then Jack and Kalan shot the attachment and rope to the other side of the room.

"The mechanical climber's ready for you," Benjamin announced. Jack and Kalan snapped the climber up to the rope.

"You ready? Time's a ticking." Jack said.

"No pressure, thanks." Katherine walked over to the safe door. The boys pulled the table over by the door, and Katherine climbed up on it. She locked her harness into a slot on the side of the mechanical climber and pushed a green button. It smoothly propelled her along the rope until she hit a red button to stop over Rachel. Then she pressed a blue button on the climber, twisted a release on the harness and flipped upside-down. Her long hair hung down onto Rachel's shoulders. Katherine carefully reached down, picked up the key card and zipped it in her vest pocket. Once that was secure, she examined how Rachel was tied up.

Elissa watched how Katherine moved around so gracefully and competently with the climbing gear. *Katherine has such good control over her body*, she thought. It made her miss the days when her body moved gracefully and easily. The boys were also using their skills to ensure Katherine was supported by counter measures with Benjamin as her spotter, keeping slack on the rope. All of them were working so well together and for that second Elissa felt a little bit left out of the physicality of this phase.

"She's unconscious. If we lift her, it'll trip the alarm."

"Hang in there, Kat. We're working on your extraction," Benjamin said. Jack rushed back to the kitchen and started to fill the empty knapsack with as many recipe books as he could shove into it. Katherine secured Rachel's harness clip into her climbing gear and untied Rachel's arms and legs. Jack closed the bag and brought it over to the table. Elissa marveled at how fast the boys were coming up with ideas to help Katherine.

"This should match her weight," Said Jack, as he and Benjamin sent the knapsack along the rope. As the bag hovered over Rachel, Katherine grabbed it, unclipped it and set it behind Rachel's back.

"Okay, take her up." She lightly rested one foot at a time around Rachel on either side of the chair with her legs securing the heavy bag into place on the chair seat where Rachel was seated. With her hands she eased Rachel's limp body up and away from the chair. Elissa held her breath for a moment as she waited for Rachel to clear the area of the chair. She listened for an alarm but it didn't sound. Rachel briefly peeked and smiled when she saw their progress. The buys manually pulled Rachel over to the table and while Jack held her stationary over the table, Benjamin and Kalan gently brought Rachel down and set her on the floor.

Using the climber to get around seemed like a ride and a half that could be fun, but Elissa decided she would keep her feet on the ground and use her electric wheelchair any day.

Kalan examined Rachel for injuries and checked her breathing. Black and blue make up on her face gave the illusion she had been interrogated. Katherine very slowly raised herself back up the main rope. She pressed the green button on the mechanical climber and sped back to the group. Jack unhooked Rachel, and Kalan and Benjamin carried the table back. Elissa helped Katherine get the harness off. With a push of a button, the mechanical climber rolled the rope around the pole.

"Elissa, you and Katherine go ahead. Can I have the code breaker and I'll engage the detector? We'll bring Rachel and meet you by the sign-out table." Benjamin gently placed Rachel over his shoulder. Elissa drove over and handed the breaker to him.

While the boys were closing the safe, the girls proceeded to the main table where Agent Davidson was waiting. The other rooms were quiet and Elissa wondered which room Malina and her team were in. She wondered how they were doing, although she was sure they were doing well.

"What an intense challenge," Katherine said. Elissa nodded in agreement. With the key card in hand, they waited for the boys to approach the table.

"Team 50, signing out," Benjamin reported as he handed Agent Davidson the key card and watched her swipe it through the scanner.

"Congratulations. At lunch we'll be posting the teams moving on to the next task."

Rachel clapped and squealed as Jack set her down carefully. After congratulating each other, the team decided to go to the Edmonton Ridge lounge to celebrate. Katherine walked with Elissa to the elevator.

"How can you bend like that?" Elissa asked.

"Years of gymnastics."

"I learn new things about you everyday." The elevator door opened and they went down the hall to the Ridge, where eight other students lingered. "I'd better check my messages," Elissa said.

"Me too. I hate being out of the loop," Katherine said.

The quiz results she'd been waiting for were in her inbox, but Elissa's heart skipped when she saw a new email from Jon. It read:

Analysis complete. No transmission signal yet. Return to office ASAP.

She looked at the timestamp. The message arrived an hour ago.

"Hello, ladies," Benjamin said.

Another male voice came from behind Benjamin. "Miss Morris." Elissa turned and saw Jon looking at her intensely. Usually that look never was related to anything good. When she had him give her that look on tour, it was usually followed by a punishment of some kind or having to clean the tour bus. "Your presence has been requested in Agent Larsson's office. We need to discuss a missing file."

Katherine raised her eyebrows at Elissa.

"Everyone, this is Agent Williams," she said as she put her computer in her bag.

"Can't this wait until after classes?" Jack asked.

Jon shook his head. "Miss Bennison, Agent Larsson will also be requesting your presence later today." Katherine slouched and flashed her best puppy dog eyes at him. Elissa made sure she had everything, and without another word, she drove out of the Ridge and into the hallway.

"Sorry to take you away from your friends," Jon said when they were alone.

"So what can you tell me?" Elissa asked as they entered the elevator.

When the doors closed, Jon filled her in that the sniffer was one that her dad engaged, but they presume it wasn't loaded as they couldn't get into NERD-One's passwords. Jon avoided eye contact with Elissa. This tipped her onto the fact he was trying to hide something from her. As he was a secret agent, he needed to be able to keep things quiet, but there was something about the slouch in his back and the way he dragged his feet as he walked that told her he knew something was coming and she wasn't going to like it one bit.

"What's up?"

"I'll let Agent Larsson tell you."

Letting someone else tell her was all the confirmation she needed that something bad was coming. She wondered if Mr. Russel had intercepted the call with Stephanie and knew she had let out his alias…or worse. No, she couldn't allow herself to play all the worst case scenarios in her head. She just needed to wait until she heard the news. Of course, she also needed her stomach to understand that and stop throwing around its contents.

Changing the topic, Jon said, "Your team did great this morning."

The elevator doors opened to reveal several teachers in the hallway. Several students were sitting comparing notes. As they entered Agent Larsson's office he glanced up from his computer.

"Miss Morris, I talked to your mom. Neither of us are comfortable with NERD-One continuing to contact you alone. You will either need to go to Los Angeles to an undisclosed location with Stephanie, and be under 24/7 surveillance, or have Agent Williams be your shadow here." He stood up straight, arms crossed and meaning business.

"But…" Elissa started to say as her heart sunk into her chest.

"Those are the only choices. It's up to you." All the kindness she usually saw in his face had been replaced by a stern, cold stare. There was no arguing, no other options for her to suggest and she knew it. Just select one or the other.

She drove over to the sliding glass door and searched the ocean for an answer. No matter which choice, she would still be stuck with someone around her, but having Jon, who was still working on the mission, might not be a bad thing. It might even work to her advantage if she could convince him to let her help him get into NERD-One. Then maybe he could also help her get Christopher safely home with them. She turned to face them and crossed her arms.

"I'm not leaving the Academy."

"I made a promise to your mom to keep you safe, so Agent Williams will be your personal bodyguard until this mess blows over."

"You'll just have to put up with me," Jon said, reaching over to mess up her hair.

Elissa did her best acting impression to appear annoyed then smiled.

"Trust me. It'll be the other way around. So what's our cover for me having a shadow?"

"Agent Williams is with you as punishment for breaching security. For your safety, due to the potential for danger and your hereditary stubbornness, Agent Williams will hook you up with some technology."

"Here's your communication." Jon passed her a small ear bud device. "To turn it on, just touch your ear." Jon placed one in his ear.

"Try it," Agent Larsson said as Jon left the room.

Touching her ear, she asked, "Was it something I said?"

"Isn't it always?" Jon said.

This device was really cool. She used to watch the secret agent shows and movies and had secretly wished she had some devices she could use, okay, play with, and this was one of them.

"I wouldn't go there." She glared towards the closed door. As Jon was older, it seemed that when something went wrong during the tour, like changing Christopher's

backstage rider to include only green jelly beans, she was always blamed before the truth came out.
"Ready for flight simulation class?"
"Flying? Born ready."

Twenty-Two

Rhythm

Elissa joined Jon in the reception area, and they proceeded to the flight classroom, where she pulled over to the desks by her friends. Katherine raised her eyebrows and flashed her best flirting smile at Jon. Elissa nodded to the side towards Jon.

"Everyone, Jon will be joining us," she said.

"Why?" Benjamin asked.

"She broke into a locked room and scanned a highly classified document. We want to keep an eye on her," Jon said. "Katherine, Agent Larsson needs to see you now." He settled in a chair in the far corner.

Kalan, Benjamin and Jack all grinned at Elissa.

"Wanted to write my analysis paper on a cold case file. I found 'no' to be an unacceptable answer," Elissa said, raising her eyebrows.

"Shucks, there won't be time for my flight." Katherine's face beamed as she walks out of the classroom.

"You hear the news? We advanced to the next round of the Academy Games," Benjamin said as he and Jack gave each other a high five. He passed Elissa a printed list of all the qualifiers from each residence. At the top of the Sydney Arch residence was Malina and her team. It seemed as if Malina was going to be a student she would be challenged by, and Elissa was not sure she would have the energy to take on that consistent challenge. Maybe it was because she didn't think winning was that important, but she would never let her team down. She just thought that fighting over anything, let alone a boy, wasn't worth it. Still, Elissa was thrilled they had moved on to the next round of the Games, as it gave her opportunities to polish her skills for real applications.

Agent Wright came in and smiled at Jon, but addressed her class.

"Remember to study all four chapters and the notes from classes for the Saturday test. Today we'll be taking the flight simulator for a spin. How many students have soloed in an aircraft?" Agent Wright asked as she surveyed the classroom.

Without looking around her, Elissa raised her hand. She was the only hand in a sea of students. Feeling self-conscious, she quickly pulled her hand down and hoped that no one saw it. If she could be invisible, right now would sure be a good time.

"Could you tell us about your experience, Miss Morris?" Agent Wright asked.

"Of course," Malina groaned. The three girls sitting with her laughed.

"My dad was teaching me how to fly before he..." Elissa stopped mid-sentence as she figured how to finish her thought without breaching security.

"Before he kicked the bucket," Malina blurted out. Her group snickered.

"Miss Jenkins, that's quite enough. You're deliberately disturbing this class. One more outburst from you and you'll be paying a visit to Agent Larsson's office. Clear?"

"Perfectly." Malina slid down in her chair and stared down at the floor.

"Miss Morris will start us off. We have a simulator in the adjoining room. The class will watch your progress via a camera." Agent Wright motioned for Elissa, Morocco and Jon to follow her into the classroom next door. "Come on over."

Elissa immediately noticed the absence of the rudder foot pedals. Instead there were hand controls. The addition of those hand controls would allow her to be able to fly. To be free and still enjoy a piece of her life that brought her joy.

"Want a hand?" Jon offered.

"I think I have it, thanks," Elissa slid into the simulator. With the seatbelt secured, she oriented herself with the hand controls. "What would you like me to do?"

"A 'touch and go.' You have confirmed clearance to take off. I'll be watching." Agent Wright started to walk away, turned back to face Elissa. "Remember, flying's fun." Both Agent Wright and Jon walked over to a desk and sat in front of a monitor to watch her progress.

Elissa closed her eyes for a moment to focus and remember Christopher's flight checklist. Her mind then wandered to him and Mr. Russel. She wiped away the images of him in the car driving off with Mr. Russel and thought about the two of them flying in an airplane once again. Taxiing down the runway gave her an opportunity to focus. The flight simulator tilted up into the artificial sky.

Her dad had been showing her touch and go's the week before the accident. No sooner was the simulator at the specified altitude when she had to descend. She heard Morocco, a distance away from the simulator, shift positions to get comfortable.

Her palms started sweating as the runway approached. She remembered the last flight with Christopher, with her at the controls, and the landing attempt when the airplane bounced like an out of control basketball across the court. As the runway got closer and closer, she gently grasped the stick and prepared to give this simulator a better landing than the one she tried a few months ago. She could hear Christopher telling her on their last flight, "You control the airplane." Her landing gear touched down and she took control of that airplane and made sure that it went straight and stayed down on the runway. She taxied down the airstrip to the hanger, and parked the airplane. Joy filled her heart as she had managed to make it through a task that had been digging away at her confidence ever since that flight.

"Excellent, Elissa. You can join us in the classroom." Agent Wright said into the simulator intercom.

Morocco raced over to the simulator and was ready if Elissa required her help. Jon followed her and watched Elissa transfer to her wheelchair. "Great landing. Your dad would be proud." Jon added.

Agent Wright, Elissa, Jon and Morocco went back into the main class room where Elissa pulled over to Katherine's empty desk. Jack and Benjamin raised their hands to give Elissa fives. She glanced Malina's way and earned herself a bitter glare. She had to admit to herself that she was a bit disappointed, as she thought they had moved past all the petty behavior.

"Class, your next chapter and all-inclusive assignment are on the board. Please read, review, and be prepared for a quiz. After your flight simulator turn is completed, you may leave."

Each student took a turn. Everyone knew how to take off, but only some students knew how to land. Elissa stuck around, anticipating Malina's go at the simulator. She could not wait to see Malina's great landing and have a challenge to beat the next time she flew.

"This should be entertaining," Benjamin said as Malina walked over and climbed into the simulator.

Malina successfully achieved the correct altitude but stalled and was unable to pull out. As she started to dive, she panicked. Agent Wright calmly instructed her on how to get control of the aircraft but she was descending fast towards a farmer's field and alarms sounded.

Katherine snuck into the room. Her face was beaming and her nose was a bit red. She met Elissa's gaze and gave her a thumbs up. Agent Wright pressed a button and the simulator shut off. Malina climbed out of the simulator, kept her head down and walked back to her seat where her group consoled her.

"Great take off." Benjamin clapped, just as every student had done for every other student before, and Jack, Elissa and even Katherine added support until the class was clapping for her as well. Malina lifted her head, smiled and shared a wink with Benjamin.

As Katherine settled into her desk, she leaned into Elissa. "Thanks for bringing them back. You rock."

"It was Jon." Elissa smiled.

Katherine made eye contact with Jon and mouthed "Thank you."

He smiled.

Jack scanned Katherine's face, Elissa and Jon for what was really going on and what he was missing out on.

"Mom and Dad are safe. I'm going to see them soon," Kat said.

Jack beamed at her.

"You'll have a vacancy above your garage when the Bennison siblings go back home," Katherine teased.

"I have a feeling we'll stay friends." Jack patted her head, making her hair appear disheveled.

Agent Wright said, "Miss Bennison, please take your place in the simulator."

"You'll do great," Elissa assured her, knowing full well how much she hated flying.

Katherine blanched as she slowly walked towards the simulator.

"I hope you're right, or she'll be even more freaked next time," Jack said.

Katherine took off, got up to altitude, and smoothly turned to come in to land. Agent Wright gave her the landing steps as she had for each of the prior students. Elissa's heart was racing, her fingers were crossed, and she was thinking positive thoughts in Katherine's direction. With the landing gear down, she touched the simulator down with a bumpy landing. Jack, Benjamin, Kalan, and Elissa all clapped and whistled when she came to a stop.

Proudly, Katherine hopped out of the simulator. Elissa gave her a congratulatory hug. Everyone in their group got through the flight without disaster. Then they dragged themselves up to their next class where Elissa grew more concerned about handing in her essay.

Elissa had her completed essay in her hard drive when they all filed into the room. At her old school, her mark, which was usually a 90%, was measured by her effort, but she hadn't been marked by Academy standards yet. Keeping that in mind, she tried to put a little extra effort towards research, grammar and rhythm. With all the other assignments, and preparing to get Christopher extricated from Mr. Russel and NERD-One's destructive hands, while getting Jon infiltrated, she had too many distractions taking away from the effort she would've usually put into her schoolwork.

The reason for coming to Madisyn Academy had been to get the truth and find Christopher and along the way she had a found a new world, a world that until the truth came out about her parents being agents, she knew nothing about – one where she now felt comfortable. On the Ocean-Alias, it was accepted to be good at computers and flying and curious about the world in general. Then there were her amazing new friends, and Benjamin with whom she hoped to be able to spend more time. Now the thought of leaving this place and these people was something she didn't want to have to even contemplate. This essay should grant her the opportunity to stay.

Mrs. Ackles was seated at her desk and greeted each student with a reassuring smile. Once everyone was seated, she stood up and strolled in front of her desk.

"Let's get our video case study going and have a Q & A session. Then you can give me your essays."

They watched another video of a mission and ate fresh popcorn. Benjamin, sitting two seats down from Elissa, occasionally caught her glancing in his direction and smiled at her. She returned his smiles rather than tilting her head downward. Their team mission was scheduled for tomorrow, and she was curious to know what skills were going to be asked of them. This past week had been a blur of challenges and new activities that the students were supposed to know or learn quickly. Elissa hoped that she had learned and retained enough to be a successful member of her team.

After the questions and answers on the video they were given the quiz. Elissa had done a better job taking notes since she knew which questions might be asked.

"Please send your essays into my class folder. Then you may go. It has been a pleasure to work with all of you. I look forward to working with you throughout your studies at Madisyn Academy. Have a good evening."

Elissa dragged and dropped her essay into the folder and with that, the expectations for this class were over.

"Main dining area, cafeteria or the Ridge?" Jack asked.

"The Ridge is quieter," Kalan said.

"We did the main room for breakfast. That's plenty," Katherine said.

"Ridge it is," Jack declared.

To celebrate the last day of classes, the team agreed to have a feast. In the Ridge, Elissa stared out the window at the sun setting. The red and orange sky made her feel as if a battle was brewing – a battle, perhaps one between her and Mr. Russel in a fight for Christopher. A battle she was going to win.

"The colors like to fight," Kalan said from behind her. She turned to face him and noticed him gazing at the sky. Her stomach growled, breaking the somber moment, and they laughed before they joined the team at a table. Jon walked over to the corner and sat down.

"Agent Williams, get over here and join us," Jack motioned with his arm.

With a nod from Elissa, he joined them. "You sure? I don't want to intrude." Jon looked at Elissa. She smiled.

"Numbers, man. We can use another guy against these girls," Benjamin said.

"That's for sure," Jack said. Katherine reached over and gently swatted Jack's arm.

"Oh, the pain, the agony." He leaned back in the chair, rubbed his arm and smiled.

With her permission, Jon slid a chair over next to her and sat down. Kalan pulled two bear statues from his bag. "One for each of you." Kalan handed Katherine a bear standing on his hind legs. As he handed Elissa her bear statue with the bear standing on his hands he described it, "Ability is in the journey, not the ways in which you travel. My elders say grace is found in spirit. Both bears have ability and grace, like all of us." Kalan smiled.

Gently they took the carvings and marveled at the detail. "I'll treasure it always." Elissa gently placed it in her bag. Katherine got as close to Jon as possible, to take advantage of having him in the team's company.

"So, Jon, how old are you anyway?" Katherine asked.

"Eighteen. Why?"

"How'd you graduate the program at fifteen?" Katherine batted her eyelashes and leaned into him. Elissa wondered if Katherine's flirting would be a bit much for Jon to take.

She glanced at Jon to see how he was responding to the flirting and, surprisingly, he was enjoying it. Elisa couldn't help but smile, as Jon was attractive, or at least the teenage girls on Christopher's tours found him so. Jack was shaking his head at Katherine's flirting, but they were all enjoying his stories.

"Actually, I was seventeen. My previous school gave me a head start." In the Ridge there were a few students walking around. Elissa drove over to the food order counter and Jon joined her.

"Sorry to be a clinger."

"Now that you mention it…" Elissa had a smile on her face. Jon feigned shock then smiled before he arranged a pathetic Mohawk in her hair. She smoothed it back in place.

They got Elissa's food and joined her friends. She put down some water and food for Morocco, who was sniffing Jon's burger. Then Morocco snorted at the veggie burger and walked over to her bowl of food.

"Did you guys check the postings to see if your team advanced to the next level of the Academy Games?" Jon bit into his veggie burger.

"I totally forgot. I'll go check," Jack said.

"I'll come with you." Katherine raced Jack out of the Ridge.

"I hope we made it." Kalan put a mouthful of nachos in his mouth. Jack and Kat ran back into the room.

"We made it. Top five," Jack gave everyone a high five. Benjamin breathed a sigh of relief. Elissa was thrilled to be in the top five. That placing, getting to the next round, would allow her another chance to earn her place at Madisyn Academy. All of them returned their attention to the food.

"So Jon, how many missions have you been on?" Kalan asked. Katherine sat intently and waited to hear his answer.

"Three so far," Jon said as he bit into a celery stick.

"Stories, man. Give me stories." Benjamin shifted to get more comfortable.

"Well, one case I was working on took us – my handler and me – to use a computer program, as bait, to get us into our enemy agency. The loaded program worked to freeze computers. It made the network vulnerable to outside hacking and attack. Our main concern was the program being used to hack into national security, banks, air traffic control or the Internet."

"Wow." Katherine held a fork full of melon salad in mid air.

"Luckily for us the software had an entry level virus engaged if fingerprints and passwords were not entered in a special time frame. There were only two people, well three, who knew the programming."

"How'd it end?" Katherine asked.

He glanced at Elissa.

The boys were listening almost as intently as Katherine.

"A new agent saved the day."

"How about we study and then hit Rock-it to blow off some steam?" Katherine suggested. Everyone agreed, including Elissa, but she wasn't sure how it would feel to be at a dance club and not be able to get up and dance like everyone else. Any kind of occasion where there might be dancing, such as the monthly or holiday dances on the ship, should she be invited to stay on the Ocean-Alias, made her unsure if she could handle them. She still had her arms, which she could move to the beat, it had been so long since she had tried to dance, she wondered if she had lost her rhythm. Rock-it was the ship's equivalent to a dance club, but with supervision, as everyone was underage.

After studying until she couldn't cram any more items into her head, Elissa started to put her books into her bag.

Benjamin was staring out the window and saw Elissa. "Elissa you ready to get your groove on?" He smiled.

She only hoped that she still had her groove.

"Think so. You?"

Katherine and Jack started shoving their books haphazardly into their book bags and stood up to stretch. The Observation deck, the main hall away from Morocco's running room, had duelling pianos coming from the Observation Lounge. At the nearest corner of the hallway, a muffled drum beat was enticing all to come to Rock-it at the end of the hall next to the Academy Mini-Mall. One day Elissa was going to check out the deals there.

Nearby, the See-U movie theatre had flashing lights highlighting the two movies that were playing, while the arcade had a large screen highlighting the games. Elissa really liked the main hallway, as there were students coming and going and everyone was smiling and happy. As they passed the music room, there were students in private cubicles practicing their instruments. Just for a moment it reminded Elissa of her old school and climbing into the soundproof booth, about the size of a phone booth, to complete her vocal exercises. It had been some time since she sang vowels up and down the scale, and she kinda missed it.

Benjamin opened the glass door to the club and an electronic song jumped into the hallway and passed them. At the end of the room, along three of the four wall-length windows, was blue tile. A DJ was in a booth built into the fourth wall along with a food and beverage counter. Four adults, two men and two women, in black suits with the Madisyn Academy Logo, with ear communication devices, were stationed in the room by the exits and washrooms. By now she was used to running into security all over, as everyone was, but these were highly concentrated in one area. Jon came in with them. They walked over to an empty table made from a large drum created from a drum kit, and pulled over the drum stools alongside. There they could watch the dance floor and take in the view of the star filled sky, or if they had come earlier before sunset, a view of the ocean. The ceiling had small lights that danced in the patterns of the music beats. Elissa thought this room was probably her favorite, so far anyway. If she was accepted to the Ocean-Alias, she would enjoy exploring the entire ship.

"Oh, I love this song. Jacks, dance with me." Katherine pulled Jack onto the dance floor as the beat made Elissa's foot tap.

Benjamin sat next to Elissa and smiled as Jack and Katherine danced. Jon sat in a chair at the next table to give Elissa and Benjamin some space to talk. Elissa would have been glad but she could see him smiling condescendingly, that smile you give to a child when they are doing something cute, but she tried to ignore him.

"They're having fun, aren't they?" Benjamin said referring to Jack and Katherine.

"Yes, they sure are," Elissa smiled and remembered her feet dancing across the floor.

Malina, sitting at a table at the far end of the room, was smiling and laughing. When she caught sight of Benjamin, her eyes filled with sadness and her smile faded.

"I never wanted to break her heart," Benjamin said, leaning in to Elissa. "I still want her as my friend."

When Malina saw Benjamin leaning into Elissa, she turned her face away.

Elissa felt a little guilty.

"Did you tell Malina that?" she asked. "That you still want to be her friend, Benjamin?" Elissa waited to hear his answer. Maybe Malina wasn't her favorite person, but she knew what it was like to lose your friend. Elissa had lost several of her friends from school when she was injured.

Benjamin frowned and turned his head to Elissa.

"I thought she knew. Girls are usually more perceptive. What did she tell you on your individual mission?" He rubbed his legs and sat straight.

"Let's just say she feels like she has lost her friend."

He shook his head and searched the room for Malina, who was walking towards the exit. Benjamin nodded to Elissa, got up and went running to meet Malina by the door. They walked to the dance floor and were grooving to an upbeat song. Benjamin and she were talking.

"That was a nice thing," Jon said as he came up to Elissa's side and squatted down. Elissa bit her lip and smiled at Benjamin and Malina.

"Everyone deserves to have a good friend." She smiled at Jon.

"Back at you. Later tonight, after curfew, I'll drop in and come get you to prepare you." He glanced up, stood up and walked back to the table behind. She wondered what dropping in meant and how he would evade the hallway cameras. Then again, Jon always did enjoy a good entrance, especially if it involved the element of surprise. Katherine came over to the table and grabbed Elissa's wheelchair.

"Girl, get out there with us."

Elissa was excited and somewhat horrified. They got out to the middle of the dance floor and Elissa began to nod her head, and tap her feet, getting what little motion she could out of her damaged legs to move back and forth in the wheelchair. The rhythm was still in her and while she could not brace her own weight, she could still move her wheelchair and arms around.

Katherine grabbed the chair and spun Elissa around. Soon enough Kalan and his girlfriend Karma, who was a slender Asian girl, joined them. Malina and Benjamin joined the group, too, but Malina left after one dance.

Benjamin grabbed Elissa's chair, and they were spinning and doing improvised versions of the Waltz box step and turns. Elissa laughed and enjoyed the great music and being able to just be fifteen. They danced until the announcement came on the speakers that the Rock-it club was closing and there was fifteen minutes to curfew. The word curfew sent a shiver through her, as she wondered exactly what she and Jon were going to do, but now she and Katherine had to get back to the room.

Twenty-Three

Advantage

Later that night, Elissa lay in her bed and listened to Katherine's rhythmic breathing. Of course, Katherine unwound by watching an hour of television before bed, and Elissa felt as if she had been sending silent messages, willing her to go to bed. She presumed Jon wouldn't come until Kat was asleep so there wouldn't be witnesses. She glanced at the ear bud communication device which she was going to start a habit of taking out every night and putting in every morning. In the darkness, she stared at the veranda and saw a black rope slide down. Out of curiosity and wondering why she didn't feel a twinge of fear, Elissa slid out of bed, keeping an eye on the rope, as she transferred into her wheelchair and went to the other room. She knew that security would be watching her and the only person who could sneak around the ship unnoticed would be Jon. Morocco followed her and watched, standing at attention with her ears up.

"Shh. It's just Jon, girl." Elissa petted Morocco.

A dark shadow, all dressed in black, slowly and quietly landed on the veranda. That shirt and frame, even without her seeing his face, provided Elissa proof that it was indeed Jon. For a moment, Morocco lunged towards the patio door, but as soon as Jon removed his mask, she wagged her tail.

"Morocco, close the door." Elissa pointed to the room's door. Morocco ran and quietly bumped it closed with her nose. Jon unhooked his harness from the climbing apparatus. Elissa slid open the door and the cool sea air slapped her face.

"Nice of you to drop in," she joked, staying in the warmth of the room.

Jon knelt down and placed his climbing gear and rope in a bag. Morocco licked his face. He laughed and ruffled her ears. "It's good to see you too, girl."

He quietly stepped into the room and closed the sliding door behind him. He slid off his dark vest and jacket to revel a worn Haywire T-shirt.

"Sure you want to bring Christopher home and get me into NERD-One? No one will think any less of you if you don't," he asked with a smile.

Elissa took a deep breath.

"Absolutely. Teach me what I need to know."

"We need some freedom to talk and move. Morocco's room will suffice. As we're under curfew lock down, we'll need a security card to gain hallway access and elevator entry." He took a small credit card-size keycard out of his bag then glanced up at Elissa.

"Sometimes this job has perks."

He quietly opened the door to the next room where Katherine was sleeping blissfully. Elissa's heart was beating fast and she took a breath to try and calm it down. He grabbed his bag and they slowly proceeded through the darkness. Suddenly the quiet was shattered by Katherine rolling in her bed. Agent Williams threw himself onto the floor. Elissa froze. Morocco got low on the floor, thinking they were playing a game. She slowly took a step towards the door. Katherine turned away from the door and soon her breath returned to its slow rhythm.

Elissa wrote a note saying she'd taken Morocco for a walk, left it on Kat's bed, and met Morocco by the door. She was wagging her tail in anticipation of a late night stroll. Jon opened the door and they stepped out into the semi-dark hallway.

"All my gear is in Morocco's room. You have the key?" Jon asked.

Elissa reached in her bag and pulled out her keycard.

He smiled and patted his key card. "Every time you use that card they know where you are. These can't be detected."

Morocco pulled on her leash as the elevator doors opened. Elissa let her run free. While she headed to the end of the hallway, she kept an eye on Agent Williams and Elissa.

He opened the door and they proceeded into the dog's bright room. Morocco ran over, grabbed her plastic disk, and brought it to Elissa before she'd even made it all the way inside. Elissa tossed it and Jon walked over to the table where his laptop was waiting. There were several blue mats on the floor. Elissa drove around them making her way to the table, but Morocco made it there first. Jon tossed her disk again then he turned and stared at Elissa. His smile was gone and the black circles under his eyes were visible.

"You don't have to do this. I can get in on my own," he said.

"NERD-One took so much away from me – from Dad – from Katherine, too. How is this mission going to work? Give me some details."

Elissa wanted details so she could fill in how everything was going to go. She always asked many questions, especially before each test that the doctors had put her through. Knowing what was coming allowed her to prepare herself. This was going to be no different, but she knew that he was still finalizing the details and wouldn't be able to provide her the specifics she required.

He looked at her for a moment shaking his head.

"Your dad will kill me for letting you help me."

"He won't know until it's too late. Listen, NERD-One needs to be held accountable for what they've done. You know Mr. Jenkins, a.k.a. Mr. Russel, needs to be stopped. Promise me you'll see this through." Elissa searched him for reassurance.

"Pinky swear." He held out his little finger. "We can go through with this mission on one condition. You have to play by my rules. If you do not, the safety of both you and Christopher will be jeopardized. Deal?" He pulled his laptop in her viewing range and reached out his hand.

Elissa shook his hand. "Deal."

Jon opened a bag and pulled out a small black pen. "This is your gear. These are for emergency situations only. It's all Third Year Issue."

Elissa pulled out a roll of duct tape and looked at him. "Dad never left home without this stuff."

"Watch this training video. It'll be faster than me explaining everything." He loaded a disk into his laptop. The Tormentor resembled a mini-flashlight key ring until the agent on the screen pressed the light end into another person, sending him to the ground. The narrator explained an electric charge renders the victim immobile for five minutes.

The next item was called the Agonizer. It appeared to be an ordinary glue stick. When opened, it released a quick stream of pepper spray. An agent held up a ruler, called the Hibernator, and broke it. Gas discharged, rendering the video's standard bad guy unconscious. The narrator warned that agents must hold their breath during use. While the gadgets were all welcome in Elissa's life, it made her stomach squirm at bit. The reality that she might have to hurt someone in order to get Christopher and her out of this mess was a cruel one.

There was also a pencil that shot tranquilizer darts and a calendar containing a taser. When it hit its target, the assailant jerked in pain and was temporarily paralyzed.

"These items won't permanently injure anyone, will they?" Elissa asked trying to convince herself that using any of these items to ensure safety and success was a good thing.

"Everything is meant to buy us time, not to kill. These items will complement your lock picking kits and the gadgets you already have." He glanced at his watch. "You must be ready to use everything. You and your father's lives depend on it."

"I'm not going to let anyone down." She sat up straight determined that she could not only convince him, but the little voice inside her head that kept telling her that she was not ready, too.

"Now you get to kick my butt." He led her to the middle of the floor by the mats. She followed him but tensed as a momentary panic entered her body.

"Remember the self defense class Christopher made you guys take?"

Elissa remembered the day Christopher informed Stephanie and Elissa that they were going to take karate so they could defend themselves against attackers. Her dad arranged private classes with their own sensei. They were taught about using voice, ensuring boundaries, escaping, anticipating and diffusing an attack before it began, and avoiding looking like victims. Once they were comfortable being forceful and aggressive, the lessons got more fun.

At home, she and her mom practiced arm and striking positions. Some of the arm movements were fluid and reminded her of dancing. Others were sharp, short punches used to protect.

The very last class was a test for both of them. As Stephanie was taking her test, Elissa sat at the front of the studio and waited for her turn. A lump sat in her throat as she listened to her mom yelling and then she heard scuffling. Then Stephanie came out of the room with sweat on her forehead and a smile on her face.

"Good luck." She walked over to Elissa and gave her a hug.

Into the room she walked and her sensei was nowhere to be found. She stopped in the middle of the room. Suddenly someone was behind her, grabbing and trying to pull her down. For a moment she was shocked and afraid, then she completed all the blocks, kicks and strikes she could. Her heart was racing and her palms were sweating as she worked through the moves he had shown her. Using a combination of her arms and legs she was able to get him onto the ground and get away to the other side of the room.

The sensei stood up and came walking over to her. He bowed and smiled at her. She bowed back. At the time those skills made Elissa feel prepared but now, sitting in a wheelchair, below everybody, she just felt powerless.

"Yes but…" Elissa scowled down at her legs and at the wheelchair.

Jon leaned down in front of her. "Use it as a weapon. Stop me." He stood up, moved behind her and shoved the wheelchair.

Morocco barked at him then got between Jon and the chair, and wouldn't let him push her.

For a moment Elissa felt safe having Morocco there and yet, her new-found friend and protector was getting in the way of her being able to handle whatever was thrown at her.

"Morocco, I'm trying to help."

He let go of her wheelchair.

"Morocco. Come here now!" Elissa shouted as she tried her hardest to be stubborn and command Morocco to do what she asked. Morocco came up alongside the wheelchair with her tail down and Elissa petted her.

"Girl, I'll never hurt Elissa. She's like family to me." Jon sat down next to Morocco and petted her. "Trust me."

She barked and then licked his face.

He got up and Morocco went back to playing with her toys, but she kept her eyes focused on them at all times. He pushed the chair hard. Elissa rolled a bit before she slammed on the brakes. The chair tipped and Jon got an armrest to his stomach, doubling him over.

"Good job," he said, still hunched over as he walked off the jab.

"You okay?" Elissa asked guiltily.

Morocco looked up at them and tilted her head.

"Next, keep your hand on the inner tire, put the brake on the other side and turn. This may take practice. No Miss Nice Girl, okay?"

The first time he pushed her she got her hand on the tire and the brake on, but her wheelchair didn't pivot fast enough.

"Take me out," he pushed.

She focused on Mr. Russel and the anger that she felt every time she thought about what he had done. She thought about Christopher. Each time she let a bit more of her anger and frustration go into the activity, but she was scared to let it all out as she didn't want to hurt Jon.

The third time, she placed her hand on the wheel, put on the brake and twisted the wheelchair with all her might. The foot parts struck Jon and he fell to the floor. Morocco came running over and licked his face.

"Thanks, girl." He smiled, petted her and looked at Elissa.

"You okay…?" Elissa reached him a hand.

"Like you could hurt me," he interrupted. He stood up and brushed himself off.

Morocco returned to the corner.

"Now put your arm under my arm pit and pull me forward. Get me on the floor, hang onto my arm, and run over my available limb." Jon stepped behind her and ran to push her.

She completed his instruction but instead of being passive she used every muscle to fight him. Elissa let all the anger and frustration that had been eating away at her go into her action. He got an armrest in the crotch before he let her pull him over to complete the technique. His face was red, he was breathing deep, and laying on the floor.

"Jon…I'm sorry." Elissa handed him his bottle of water and he sat on the mat for a minute.

"Great job," he panted. "I'm proud of you. Pretty brave girl, you are."

He sipped some water. Elissa looked down at the mat and then at him. In that moment she did not feel brave – rather, angry, scared, but at the least empowered. They worked through additional arm moves and the previous techniques until she could execute them easily and aggressively. Then they both sat for a moment and caught their breath.

"Better get you back before you're missed. Next cabin check, with heat sensors, is in half an hour." He got up and placed his laptop, supplies and mats in his bag.

Elissa gave Morocco a doggy treat.

"Jon, any details on how we will accomplish this mission?" Elissa looked to him.

Jon stopped what he was doing and sat down on the chair.

"I'm going to set up a meeting when the Ocean-Alias is docked. So it will probably be on Saturday after your team challenge in Los Angeles. I will let you know the details when I have them finalized. Can you get through the level of my game yet?" He rubbed his face.

"Almost. I'll work on it tonight and I'll get you in."

"I know you will," Jon said as he got up and walked over to the door to wait for her and Morocco.

Silence filled the hallways like an alarm lingering after it had stopped. It reminded Elissa how even in a ship with so many students, at times in her life, she was going to have to be alone. Tired from her workout, Elissa was quiet.

Jon dug out a small bag from the candy shop on Mercantile Avenue, back at the Car Wash, and handed it to her.

She opened up the bag to find four items and read the package descriptions:

    1. Package of square caramel candies - 'Get a Word in Edgewise' Chews
    a. Pink and green milky suckers - 'Lollipops to stick it to them'
    b. Plain green gum package – 'Knock them out with minty breath gum'
    c. Red shoestring licorice - 'All tied up licorice strings.'

"Cool," Elissa whispered.

As they waited for the elevator to reach the floor, he pulled out a red piece of the licorice. It was the consistency of a shoelace and he tied it around his arm to show her the strength.

Morocco sniffed his arm. Then she snorted, shook her head and turned away in disgust.

Elissa smiled and turned her attention back to Jon.

"Tough to eat, as it's not chewable."

There was also a metal tin of wrapped candies. On the bottom of the tin was a warning: *Causes dehydration, nausea and vomiting, unconsciousness, hives and itching.* She scowled as she read what each color corresponded to. Red: dehydration through nausea and vomiting. Blue: loss of consciousness. Green: hives and itching.

"You'll do great."

"We do make a good team." Elissa smiled at him. She felt confident that with Jon's help they could bring Christopher home. That hope filled her heart where all the anger and frustration had once resided.

By the cabin door, he bent down and petted Morocco. "Thanks girl." She licked him.

"Thanks for everything." Elissa reached out to give him a hug.

"I'll have more mission details tomorrow. Our mission will bring both you and Christopher home tomorrow," Jon said quietly. "Trust me."

Elissa entered the room quietly to find Katherine still sleeping. Jon walked through the suite, checking the windows and doors.

"Everything's secure. Get some rest. I'll see you tomorrow," he whispered.

Elissa picked up her note for Katherine and watched him close the door behind him. When climbing into bed she took off her shoe and something rattled around. She opened the secret door and remembered the nail file she had put in at home. She left it in her shoe in case she might need it tomorrow.

Twenty-Four

Waiting

Day Six

They all met for breakfast in the main dining room, excited to be docked in Los Angeles, but Elissa was ten minutes late as she slept in and had to rush to get ready. Elissa noticed Katherine staring at her, which made her feel self conscious. She wasn't into wearing make-up every day, but this morning, after only getting two hours of sleep, her eyes needed some magic to cover the black circles. Elissa smiled at Katherine, and she directed her attention to the dry-erase board, where Agent Larsson was explaining their mission.

"It'll be a challenge with such limited prep time," Kalan said.

Benjamin winked at Elissa. She smiled and her cheeks burned and flushed red. Elissa liked Benjamin, okay, liked him a lot, but the last thing she needed was him knowing how she felt. She wanted to keep her cool and keep her feelings to herself.

"Oh look, she's here." Malina sneered. Elissa met her gaze and enjoyed watching all the Guess outfits Malina had brought with her. It was like a fashion show as she always managed to bring her fashion sense to each outfit by using contrasting accessories.

"Malina, congratulations on making it this far," Elissa said.

Malina turned to face Elissa and for a moment she simply gazed at her.

"No problem – looking forward to kicking your team's butt in the next round." Her eyes twinkled.

"Oh, we so are," confirmed a girl whose clothes hung loosely off her bony elbows as she stepped in front of Malina and snapped her fingers. A preppy blonde boy joined in, too. Instead of Malina being cruel, she seemed to be a regular opponent going into a challenge with another rival. This time her comments didn't seem at all personal.

"May the best team win," Elissa said.

"We will," Malina shrugged. She flipped her long hair to the side and sauntered off, her team following her like pampered poodles.

"Welcome, students." Agent Larsson stood behind the podium. The crush of voices went silent as everyone sat down. "First, everyone open your computers. You will have twenty minutes to complete today's quizzes or tests for all of your classes. Then we can focus on the Academy Games and the second of the two challenges."

He walked back to the table. Everyone's faces indicated a hint of panic, except for Malina's, which seemed excited. She seemed to not only manage but excel at every class she took.

Elissa was on the side of everyone else, feeling the panic attempting to block her thoughts. She completed her flight test first and felt confident she did well. There was one test for the memory class, one for tech and none for their analysis class. She raced against time on the last two and hoped it would be enough.

Agent Larsson stood up at the podium. "Time's up. Your marks will be available momentarily."

With the tests and assignments finally finished, she could now focus on the team challenge ahead, and of course, the mission to bring Christopher home. She felt relief to have fewer distractions vying for her attention.

"Congratulations for getting to this round. Sabotage of any kind will disqualify your team. All team members must arrive together at the final spot. Today will be the last mission for this round. You have a maximum of six hours to complete the task, but time is of the essence, and you may use any supplies you have for your classes. A vehicle is waiting to transport you to the starting location. Remember all participants in this mission are actors and not real NERD-One operatives. Any questions?"

"Not everyone has a dog," Malina said loudly as she pointed to Morocco.

Katherine leaned over to Elissa and was about to say something when Agent Larsson spoke again.

"A dog will be no of advantage for any of the tasks. Any additional questions?" He surveyed the students but no hands were raised. Most of the students were slouching with worried expressions.

Rachel walked over to the table, sat down and handed each of them a leather portfolio.

"Workers in an office building in downtown L.A. are being held hostage by a new NERD-ONE cell. Your assignment is to rescue five hostages and use whatever means necessary to find out what the hostiles are plotting. The aggressors have security system access and they are monitoring communications, entrances and exits."

Rachel tipped the contents of an envelope onto the table. Out fell some of the same communicators that Elissa was already wearing in her ear. Benjamin handed one to each team member. She placed hers in the empty ear. Rachel stood up and held a pen and a button object.

"These are laser pens. You're allowed to shoot at the individuals holding the hostages. If you hit the target, your pen signals the small button receptors they are wearing which will light up to indicate they have been hit."

She aimed the pen at the button and the button changed from silver to red.

"That's considered a hit. They'll fall to the ground. However, your opponents also have these and you will each wear the button receptors."

When Elissa received the round circle that was the size of a compact disk, she attached and clipped it to the front of her vest. She only hoped she would not be taken out that way in the challenge. After all, she did not move as fast as everyone else.

"Good agents use their minds and bodies to take down opponents. Only use a weapon as a last resort. Until you've taken self-defense, these pens will even things up. Good luck." Rachel closed her portfolio, pushed in her chair and walked away.

"Let's figure out our game plan en route." Benjamin closed his computer and stood up.

Rows of vans and agents holding large cards with team numbers lined the parking lot. Elissa and her team went over to their agent. Elissa was happy to see a familiar face. While the task was going to be fun, she knew that afterward, Jon had planned to complete the mission to get him into NERD-One and get Christopher home. She only wished she had as many details about her and Jon's mission as the Academy had provided for their L.A. mission.

"Hello Sam." Elissa smiled as she headed to the van.

"Howdy, team 50."

Sam helped Elissa get settled near the seats that were arranged around a table and printer. Once she was secure, Sam got behind the wheel. "ETA is half an hour."

Benjamin assigned Elissa to find floor plans for the building, Jack and Katherine had to access the live camera feed and search the Madisyn database for the hostiles' profiles. Benjamin and Kalan searched the building's communication system. They all silently got to work, ignoring the bumpy ride.

Elissa found the floor plans, printed them and laid them out on the table. "Time for updates," Benjamin announced. Jack and Katherine read off the extensive profiles of each of the hostiles.

"They have a new state of the art communication and security system," Kalan said.

Elissa's news wasn't much better. It was enough to make her miss the fake kitchen rigged with heat sensors.

"Traveling to the third floor will require looping the real time videos from the elevator and stairwell. Once we choose the elevator we'll be using, I'll access the camera and record the loop."

For the rest of the team, this mission was real, but for Elissa it just seemed hard to get into. Maybe Elissa was just focused on the fact that after her real mission with Jon, her world would either be back to normal, well as normal as it could be after the past few months, or have a potentially worse ending.

"One hostile is posted in the stairwell and elevator area. The other two are guarding the hostages," Katherine said.

Kalan and Elissa couldn't access the plans for the sprinkler and security system behind a voice-activated computer firewall.

Benjamin checked his computer and was typing frantically as he was gathering information.

"Elissa, think we could improvise the voice dictation software?" Kalan asked. "We need to get the sprinkler system for a distraction,"

A smile spread on Elissa's face.

"Absolutely."

Elissa put together a few different voice profiles. When she hit the right one, the sprinkler and security system schematics appeared on her screen. She was glad to be able to be working as it made the time pass a bit faster. For just a moment, she sat back and watched the team working.

"Affirmative on monitoring," Benjamin said. "Who's going up?"

Jack, Katherine and Kalan raised their hands. Elissa knew that if there was any climbing Katherine, Jack and Kalan would rule the activity.

The people upstairs won't even know what's coming until it's too late, she thought. Looking at Benjamin deep in thought at his computer, her heart sank at the possibility of either of them leaving the Academy. Worse yet, what if she did not come back from the mission. She needed to ensure their team was in the top three so they would be accepted to the Ocean-Alias.

"Once the floor is secured, you two can join us," Jack said.

"I've opened an invisible back door into the computer systems security. Problem though – the entire floor is on one system," Elissa said.

"I'll disable the rest of the sprinklers and change control for us." Kalan typed on the keyboard and soon the other sprinklers were off.

Benjamin sat down next to Kalan, and Elissa and watched them work. His clothes smelled of Downy dryer sheets still from home, as they hadn't needed to have laundry done on the ship.

The aroma reminded her of her own home and Christopher's blanket they would huddle under during movie nights. Movie nights were something she was looking forward to having once again.

"Kalan, I'm sending the loop to your system," Elissa said.

"We're here," Sam announced.

"Okay, I know this sounds lame, but synchronize your watches," Benjamin said with a smile. Everyone smiled and set their watches.

The moment Sam opened the door, Morocco bolted out to find a tree. "Here is your key to your briefing room on the third floor." Sam said, handing it to Benjamin. "Good luck. I'll be here when y'all finish."

Elissa glanced around at all the Madisyn vans, parked along the sidewalks under the palm trees, and the pedestrians, all tanned and toned, briefcases in hand, who rushed to their destinations. Across the street was a van and the driver waved.

As she did a double take and waved back, she realized it was Jon and he gave her the thumbs up, which she knew meant their mission was a go. Now all she needed was to finish the mission at hand.

Twenty-Five

Practice

The team entered the pretentious-looking downtown building and proceeded to the banks of reflective elevator doors. As they rode up, Benjamin referred to the information sheet.

"Floor fourteen is our hostage area." Benjamin shook the envelope and pulled out the key card.

The elevator doors opened to many students rushing back and forth, weaving past water fountains resting on art deco tables. Elissa took a breath and prepared herself for the mission ahead. Benjamin pointed to a door at the end of the hallway.

"Our briefing room."

He unlocked the door and they all entered. In the room, there was a round executive table with leather chairs. Two large windows provided enough sunlight to eliminate the need for electricity. The downtown L.A. skyline in all its glory stretched as far as they could see. For a moment they stared out the window to absorb where they were. Elissa wondered where, in this massive city, NERD-One was holding Christopher and where Stephanie was. Laughter distracted her and she saw Katherine, Jack and Kalan in the corner of the room.

Elissa and Benjamin joined Katherine, Jack and Kalan. They were laughing and stumbling into their climbing harnesses. Benjamin reached out his hand, Elissa placed her hand underneath, then Katherine, Jack and Kalan did the same.

"Good luck, team," Benjamin said confidently.

Elissa nervously set up her gear at the table, all the time thinking she needed to not screw this up for the rest of her team. She flipped open her computer and hacked into the elevator cameras.

"Team, freight elevator three camera feed is up to the fourteenth floor. I've also added a feed in the hallway where one man is pacing. That'll allow us to get up to the floor and take out the man without them noticing anything different."

"Thanks," the climbers replied. With a wave, Katherine, Jack and Kalan left the room.

Benjamin pulled his chair up close to Elissa and turned on his computer. Elissa squirmed in her seat trying to get comfortable and trying to keep her face from blushing and the butterflies from appearing in her stomach when she thought about Benjamin being so close. She didn't need him to know how she was feeling.

"You okay?"

"It's just been a long week. As you know," Elissa said.

"Like she'd ever admit to being anything but good. That's what makes her a super agent," Katherine's voice whispered.

"We can hear you two," Kalan reminded them through their comm devices. Her heart sunk as she forgot that the team could hear everything they were saying. She was so relieved that there was no device to measure what she was thinking. Kalan, Jack and Katherine giggled quietly, and Elissa's cheeks turned several shades of red – almost as red as Benjamin's. They both looked at each other and exchanged a smile.

"We're in the elevator," Jack said.

Elissa prepared to set the sprinklers off.

"Now," Jack said.

Both Benjamin and Elissa watched the feed from the video camera in the elevator and hallway via their computers. Water sprayed down on the man waiting in the hallway. The elevator doors opened. The man charged but Jack aimed his laser pen. The combatant fell to the ground.

"You'll never get in there in time. We will win. We will be victorious." The man said as Kalan and Jack pulled him into the fourteenth floor board room they were assigned for storing captured prisoners. Jack and Kalan then went to the stairwell to get the other man and soon were dragging him into the boardroom as well. Katherine, alone in the elevator, gave the camera a thumbs-up signal and kept watch.

"The man was so anxious to share his predictions with us. Here's his voice profile." Kalan sent a file to Elissa as both he and Jack returned to the elevator.

"I'll filter his conversation and send the profile to the walkie-talkie," Elissa said as she went to her task knowing that this was something she could complete without a chance of failure.

"Sweet," Benjamin replied.

Kalan plugged his computer into the man's walkie-talkie and nodded at the camera. Elissa smiled and typed on her keyboard to send a miscommunication between the hostiles. With a click of the mouse, the restructured voice called, "We have intruders ... need help by the elevator."

The field team got into position and waited to ambush whoever came to help. When the second hostile entered, they hit him with the laser pen and tied him up next to his partner.

"Elissa, should we join them?" Benjamin asked. Elissa grabbed her computer and Morocco's leash while Benjamin grabbed his portfolio and bag and then opened the hallway access door. By now the hallway was deserted so getting to the elevator was quick. Morocco stayed close to Elissa's side.

"She likes you," Elissa told Benjamin.

Benjamin bent down and patted the dog's head. "Morocco is," he paused to look at Elissa, "special. Just like her owner." He straightened up and waited for the doors to open up.

In the elevator, Elissa put her head down to hide her beaming smile. It was nice to know that Benjamin liked hanging out with her as much as she enjoyed hanging out with him. The doors opened to a hallway identical to the one below.

"Let's finish this," Benjamin said.

Down the hall they saw Jack, Katherine and Kalan moving a table. "We're going to enter the room." Katherine said, as she grabbed a chair and set it on the table. Then she climbed on top of the chair, raised the ceiling tile and pushed it aside.

"You sure? We could try the door," Benjamin suggested.

"That'd take too long if it's booby-trapped."

Katherine prepared her climbing gear while Jack stepped onto the table. Katherine climbed into the suspended ceiling crawlspace. Elissa was glad that she was not in field ops as her body would not be as graceful as Katherine's.

Katherine hooked some carabineers into the ceiling framework to support their weight. Jack climbed up and Kalan followed.

"We'll keep our friend company," Benjamin said.

"Let us know when you're ready for our distraction," Elissa said.

"Will do," Kalan said into his comm device.

Elissa followed Benjamin into the elevator and to the fourteenth floor board room.

"Better be prepared," Benjamin pulled out his pen and so did Elissa, just in case they had gotten free. If this were anywhere else, in the real world they could be sure no one would be moving, but at the Academy, Elissa and

Benjamin had both been trained to think ahead. They each took a side of the door and Benjamin slowly opened it. Elissa held her pen aimed at the inside of the room and kept her hand on her joystick.

Benjamin and Elissa both peeked into the room and saw that one man was tied up and sitting on the floor in the corner, but the other was gone. The room was locked from the outside, so they knew he was inside.

Elissa saw him stand up from behind a bookcase, but he didn't notice her sitting in her wheelchair.

He was aiming his pen at Benjamin, who at that time wasn't looking in the man's direction.

She aimed her pen and shot a signal at the man while she grabbed her computer to block the signal from hitting Benjamin's receptor.

Benjamin saw her moving and the man dove out of the way. The actions seemed to go in slow motion and all Elissa could hear was the beating of her heart.

The man fell to the floor and his pen rolled onto the floor a distance away from him. His walkie talkie also landed on the floor.

Benjamin was on the floor in the hallway. He checked his receiver and it was not red. They both breathed a sigh of relief and smiled at each other.

A woman's voice carried out of the unconscious man's walkie talkie. "Markus, did you find Emile?"

Elissa rushed over to the table, in the middle of the room and used the voice profile Kalan sent her and transmitted an affirmative response.

"Thanks." Benjamin said as he tied up the man and set him next to the other one.

"You're welcome." Elissa said, beaming, as the reality that she could manage in this world and lifestyle, in the world of secret agents, reinforced her confidence.

"We're ready to drop in on our last hostile. Removing the tile," Katherine whispered through the comms.

"Go for distraction," Jack said.

Elissa typed on her keyboard. As her heart started to slow down, she enjoyed the temporary shot of adrenaline that had made her aching disappear.

Again via the security signals they were intercepting, Elissa and Benjamin watched as the fire alarm sounded across the floor. The female hostile searched the room, frantically typed on the keyboard, jumped and stared at the intruders, then fell over the computer monitor.

"Direct hit," Jack said.

Benjamin and Elissa watched the real time video as Katherine, Jack and Kalan rappelled into the room. All the hostages were sitting on the floor, arms and legs tied.

"We're secure," Katherine said.

"I'll make sure our friends are secure." Benjamin said as he checked the binding on the guards' arms.

Elissa and Morocco headed to the office door and waited for Benjamin. Then they went into the large office, past rows of cubicles. Katherine and Kalan were sitting motionless staring at the shot woman's computer monitor.

"We couldn't stop her. It's a Virus."

Katherine glanced up at Elissa and slid aside to reveal the screen. The monitor had the homepage for Sentinel national security web site and parts of the page were being corrupted and changing to black. The team watched the picture begin to dissolve. While they had an introduction to the Sentinel program in tech, the class had not been as informative as she had wanted.

"We have to stop the virus before it corrupts the Sentinel database," Elissa said as she pulled out her laptop and plugged it into the tower. Benjamin sat down at the tower and began typing. Elissa searched for the virus components. This virus was strong and malicious. While she realized this was just a Madisyn Academy challenge, in the back of her mind she was thinking how Ice Rose could crack the program and get into the Sentinel program. She swallowed and made herself focus on the task at hand.

Jack and Katherine escorted the hostages into the room. Kalan supervised to ensure all the hostages were indeed hostages and not undercover operatives. Katherine supported a terrified-looking middle aged woman on her shoulder, and helped the limping hostage to a chair.

"Wait a minute. The Gate Key, Elissa, but 3.0," Benjamin said as he leaned back in the desk chair, and revealed the virus components he found displayed on his monitor.

Relief washed over her as he found the codes and then they could potentially modify them to eliminate, or at the very least quarantine the virus. Shivers ran through her as the monitor began to display the codes of the Sentinel program as it accessed them and began creating a door to gain entry.

Benjamin and Elissa began typing codes into the corrupted system. Elissa referred to the information and continued to break into the security web site while the team gathered around the computer area just as the alarm stopped. It was just a bit different than the virus from class. Different screens flashed on the monitor and Elissa reloaded and refreshed the site, quarantined the virus and, a message came up on the screen:

Congratulations. You have successfully completed the task. Bring the hostages with you. Print out this page, take the completion card in the gold box next to the monitor, and proceed to the main floor to the card reader check out point. Remember, you're timed until the moment your card is scanned through the reader.

Benjamin printed out the information, and Jack got the completion card, while Kalan and Katherine got the hostages ready to move. Elissa unplugged her computer and enjoyed knowing that they had completed the task.

With all their stuff and the hostages, they went into the hallway and got into the elevator. The hostages were talking and making plans for their evening.

Elissa, for the past few minutes, had been engrossed in her task and happiness had filled her with hope. But, as the elevator got closer to the main floor, she thought about the evening ahead and was filled with a sense of dread.

Her mission would start right after this, and she could only hope it would have a good outcome. If all went according to plan, by tonight she would have Christopher home where he belonged with Stephanie and her. She couldn't allow herself to think of the worst-case scenarios. When the elevator opened, they saw a card reader in the middle of the floor. Stretched around the scanner was a gold finish tape.

"It's like a marathon," Katherine said.

Benjamin led the hostages to a roped-off area under the hostage deposit sign, where they smiled and joined the group.

Elissa counted two, four, six, eight, trying to figure out how many teams had completed the task but the hostage numbers were uneven so she was disappointed.

Benjamin ran back over to the team.

"Team, let's all finish together." Benjamin grabbed Katherine and Elissa's hands and they broke through the tape.

"Top five, please," Katherine said.

Elissa grinned.

"No matter how we rank, we made a great team."

They all agreed.

Benjamin ran their card through the reader. It beeped and a loud pop followed. Multi-colored confetti floated from the ceiling like snow on a wind free winter day. They all stood in the confetti for some time. Happiness and excitement radiated on Katherine, Jack, Kalan and most of all, on Benjamin's face. Elissa found herself swept up in the moment and was filled with that same joy. All of them had made it through the week, with all its challenges and as of now, their fate had been sealed.

"Why'd we get confetti?" Katherine asked.

"Time to party?" Benjamin asked.

"Always ready for a party," Katherine said. As they went out to the van, each member handed Benjamin their communication device. Elissa made sure to return the correct one.

"How'd you do?" Sam asked.

"Confetti," Katherine said.

Another black van pulled up to where they were standing. Jon got out and came directly to Sam, handing him a letter.

"I'm taking Elissa on a field trip."

Sam read it. "See you later, Miss Morris."

Katherine gave Elissa a hug and whispered, "Be careful."

Elissa smiled and pulled her left hand into her pocket. Maybe that would keep the truth, the fact that her fingers were turning white because she was nervous, a secret. She didn't need Jon to see her showing any kinds of stress or he might pull the mission.

"I'll see you guys back at the ship."

Twenty-Six

Cover

She followed Jon to the van. On the passenger seat was a black bulletproof vest. As she picked it up to move it, it felt squishy. She saw bullet holes and blood all over it.

"Sorry. That's Christopher's insurance. Gotta make the shooting look real so they believe."

Suddenly, she thought about the vest and the bullets and her heart sunk. The other van took off and Jon pulled away from the curb.

"Details, Jon. I need details. Who's going to shoot him?" Elissa looked at Jon and tears filled her eyes.

He stopped at a red light and returned her gaze.

"Elissa, they're going to want him dead. It will probably be my NERD-One initiation. When you are getting them into the program, I'll go get the vest on Christopher and explain how things need to go down. Do you trust me?"

"Of course I do! But things happen, Jon, they..." she broke off, unable to finish.

"Not this time. You're both going to leave alive," Jon assured her as they pulled away from the intersection.

"Where's the meeting?" Elissa tried to focus on the job ahead and rubbed her hands to get the circulation to return.

"We're going on a cruise to the Mexican Riviera for five days," Jon said.

"With no luggage? I'm too young to travel without a parent," Elissa said.

"Suitcases are in the back. Your signed permission slip that we need to appease the cruise staff, is in the glove compartment...well, one for Emmy Johnston. Paper work to confirm our identity, included." Jon opened the glove compartment and Elissa saw two cruise ship tickets. "Mr. Russel is going to meet us on the ship. Christopher is on the ship. Our mission and location information will be sent to Agent Larsson ninety minutes into our mission." Jon continued. "He'll know exactly where to find you and Christopher. He'll contact you."

Elissa took her candies and supplies and shoved them into her vest pockets. They pulled into the parking lot surrounded by large cruise ships.

"Any other questions?" Jon grabbed his bag and vest and turned to face Elissa. Her mind, which sometimes was swirling or racing, was just blank.

"Your first mission is to get Mr. Russel into the program so we can hack into the NERD-One network. Remember, to NERD-One, I'm one of their double agents."

"Got it." Elissa took a deep breath and petted Morocco. Morocco looked at her with big sad eyes and set her head on her lap.

"It'll be okay, right, girl?"

Morocco barked and licked her hand.

Elissa went over to the lift where Jon was waiting with an old manual wheelchair. Her heart flopped when she looked at it and thought how hard it was to push with her arms.

"We'll keep your custom wheelchair in a safe spot. They'll get it to you later. You sure you want to do this?" Jon asked.

"I want him back," Elissa said simply. "However that needs to happen." Elissa and Morocco maneuvered the lift to the ground. Jon grabed the suitcases and they headed for the ship.

She looked at the smiling passengers milling around. An elderly couple in straw hats and tacky beach wear were taking photographs of each other in front of the ship.

"Can I help you with that?" Jon asked.

"Thanks, deary." The woman stood next to her husband and they smiled. Jon snapped their photograph and then they all walked together toward the ship. At the boarding area, Jon looked at Elissa and smiled as he handed their identification over. Jon seemed to be tall and confident as he stood waiting for the attendant to clear them, while Elissa was trying to keep calm and remain cool.

A tall woman surveyed them up and down. Then she took their bags to the loading dock.

"Have a good trip," she said flatly, before moving on to the elderly couple behind them.

On the promenade deck, Jon led Elissa inside and past a bank of elevators.

Everyone was laughing, smiling and excited for the journey ahead.

Elissa's palms were now sweaty and she battled waves of nausea. *Almost as nice as the Madisyn Academy ship,* Elissa thought ruefully, looking around.

Jon led her to an Employee's Only door and into a freight elevator.

"We need her to stay here." Jon looked down at Elissa and held up a plastic disk. So far Elissa was doing a great job keeping her emotions in check, but that was something she wasn't ready for.

"She's trained to stay with me Jon. How am I supposed to get her to leave?" Elissa glared at him and then was mad at herself for being emotional.

Jon leaned down and met Elissa's gaze. "Mr. Russel will shoot Morocco without hesitation if she protects you. He dislikes her after your last encounter. I took care of that."

She looked at Morocco who was sitting on the floor and seemed tired.

"What did you do to her? Jon, how could you?" Elissa was angry with Jon for doing this to Morocco.

"Elissa calm down. It will last ten minutes and then she will be up and going again. She'll be fine. I promise."

Suddenly, it seemed as if Elissa didn't know Jon at all. The feelings she had felt about everyone keeping secrets flooded back, and her heart felt cold.

Jon gently picked up Morocco and walked into the hallway. He entered a room and set her on top of the bed. Then he closed the door while Elissa sat in the elevator trying to grasp what was going on. He walked over to her and knelt down.

"To be convincing, to be unconscious, I need you out of this crappy wheelchair. Sorry I didn't tell you in the van, but I needed your reaction full of emotion," he said.

She could feel the tears running down her face and wasn't sure if she was more angry at him or at herself. She never wanted to feel powerless again and here she was feeling exactly that way.

Jon wiped the tears off her face.

"This is too much. Do you want to quit?"

Elissa slapped his arms away from her, took a deep breath and met his gaze.

"Secrets and plans without my knowing are not acceptable. If you ever pull any crap like this again…"

Jon stood up and pressed a button to get the elevator to go to their destination.

"You need this anger towards me to be convincing. Use it. The entire mission depends on you being angry at me."

Hesitantly, she released her seatbelt.

Once the elevator was on the deck and the door was open, Jon pulled out his computer. He squatted down and hit a couple of buttons on his computer.

She leaned away from the back of the wheelchair and prepared to be picked up.

"Distractions." He looked at her and smiled.

He placed a mini bottle of water, chocolate bar, sunglasses and a flashlight in her vest pockets. Then he lifted her up, cradling her and exited the elevator.

The lights went out on the ship and an alarm blared and echoed through the dark hallway. Jon had his night vision shades on as he raced through the hallways and up and down several flights of stairs.

She tried to remember where he was going so she could make a quick exit. Her heart was racing, so she went through some of the breathing exercises she used to complete to calm herself before performing. Take in a deep breath for seven seconds, hold it for seven seconds, and let it go for seven seconds. Repeat. By the third time, she felt somewhat more relaxed.

"We're almost there. Remember, you're unconscious due to your struggling to come with me. I know you had a meeting with Mr. Russel, but he needs to think you're here on his and my request versus your own."

He grabbed her tighter and she let her body go limp. As he cradled her and carried her, she thought about Christopher and Stephanie and how she missed both of them. Then Jon was talking to someone, Mr. Russel she presumed. Her brain was telling her to open her eyes and identify the voice, but she needed to be convincing as being unconscious.

Elissa played unconscious as she orientated herself, by the sound of the echoes staying away and the lack of air flow, to the cabin Jon had set her in. She could hear whispering voices in the distance. She opened her eyes to see a small light and a laptop computer on a plain wooden table beside her. They were hooked up to a portable generator that provided the room's only light.

Under the table, were boxes and hidden behind, in the shadows, was a small wheel, which she figured was from a skateboard. The aroma of cigarettes, coffee and mold lingered in the windowless cabin and choked out the air. She wished she was back up on the deck breathing the fresh air and feeling the freedom of being able to drive away.

She felt the communication device in her ear and the immobile folding chair beneath her.

"Elissa, be careful." Jon rushed over to her and steadied her chair.

The fire alarm blared and made Elissa's ears ache. Vulnerable and immobile without her wheelchair, Elissa began to wonder if this was really the best plan of action. If something happened to Jon then she and Christopher would be in the hands of NERD-One for real. She pushed the doubts to the back of her mind as now was not the time to second guess herself or Jon.

"What do you want with me?" Elissa asked, scanning the cabin for Mr. Russel.

"Get to the end level in the game," Jon said as Mr. Russel stepped into the cabin and strolled over to where they were standing.

"What insurance do I have you'll let me go?" she asked as she glared at Jon and Mr. Russel.

"Absolutely none," Mr. Russel said. He leaned down and pressed a key on the laptop. A video came on the screen of Christopher, who was lying on a cot and not moving much. She stared in disbelief and watched for his chest to rise and fall to indicate he was breathing.

"Thought you might want to see that we have made good on our offer."

"This could be anywhere, on any ship. Prove it!" Elissa sat back in the chair.

Mr. Russel picked up his phone, clicked on the video icon and handed it to Jon.

"Show her where he is."

Jon left the room and held the phone camera so she could see him waving around corridors and through doors and stairs. His flashlight gave a view of his journey but it wasn't clear exactly how far away he was going. Then he stood next to a cabin door, W8, where a tall and muscular guard was waiting. He opened the door and Jon stepped inside.

Christopher lifted up his head and scowled at Jon.

"Your daughter wanted proof you were here." He shoved the camera close to Christopher.

"How could you bring her into this with that monster, Jon? I trusted you." Christopher's face was red with anger as he tried to get up off the cot, but he was being restrained by something that the camera pan didn't show.

"Lissy, get outta here. Don't help him or we're both…"

The tall muscular guard hit Christopher, and he fell back on the bed unconscious.

Elissa turned to face Mr. Russel, trying to keep the anger from rising in her chest. She wanted to pounce on him like he was a hunted animal, but she needed to keep her cool.

"Point taken on his location. Now call your goon off, please," Elissa crossed her arms and met his gaze but completed her activity with less energy than she would usually use, trying to ensure that the unconscious act was convincing.

"Jon, please escort Todd out of the room and join us," Mr. Russel said into his phone. Then he hit another key so the monitor returned to the main screen.

Fear and anger swirled in Elissa's mind and made thinking a challenge. She did her breathing trick as she studied the monitor. No email. No Internet. No outside world.

Mr. Russel stepped outside the cabin, and was talking to Jon but their voices were quiet enough so Elissa couldn't make out what they were saying.

She clicked onto the Ice Rose icon, which had Christopher's fingerprint and password entered and she set it to scan her finger and doddled to complete the scan as she had a few minutes before the virus made the laptop useless. Typing the sniffer and worm codes in another window, she popped back and hesitated on her completed fingerprint scan.

Jon entered the cabin, walked over to her and squatted down. Mr. Russel walked into the cabin and glanced at the laptop screen and at Jon.

"Christopher better be okay," Elissa said loudly, so Mr. Russel could hear her disapproval with Jon.

"Safe under Todd's care – as long as you get us in."

"You know loading the program on this system won't help? For maximum effect you should be on a network," Elissa said without thinking how Mr. Russel would react.

"Of course we know that!"

Mr. Russel frowned and his face turned several shades of red.

She thought he was going to have smoke come out of ears just like the cartoon characters, but knew that wasn't possible. She also knew he would never just let them walk away. Jon was relying on that certainty to get him into NERD-One.

"I give the orders!" He stormed over and leaned in toward her. Spit flew out of his mouth. After a deep breath he quietly and calmly said, "I promise we'll leave you here."

"They've figured out how to access emergency power. I've engaged the obstacle alarm and blocked communications. The ship's navigation will think it's about to hit a rock and order evacuation," Jon told Mr. Russel.

Elissa glanced at the clock on the computer and realized she should be celebrating with her friends instead of being in this situation – one that she had placed herself in. While her friends were celebrating and wondering if they got into the Ocean-Alias, she was trying to get both Christopher and herself out of this situation. The thought that she was actually being a secret agent right now made her smile. She entered her password.

"There you go." Elissa pointed to the Ice Rose icon.

"Tie her up. We have to take advantage of the distraction," Mr. Russel said as he picked up his satellite phone and watched Jon.

"You going to bring Christopher here?" Elissa asked futility as she all ready knew the answer, but was trying to play her part. She could not let Mr. Russel knew she trusted Jon. Everything was moving so fast but Elissa didn't feel powerless.

Jon approached her with a rope, and she kicked at him, trying feebly to put up a fight.

"Jon how could you betray us this way?"

He managed to tie her arms and legs loosely with thick rope. Mr. Russel left the room and dialed a number on his satellite phone.

"They'll come find you." Jon pushed her chair to the back corner of the cabin away from the door but so the skateboard was in her view. He took the light, computer, and generator then made a point of knocking over the skateboard and giving her a quick wink as he set it back under the table.

As soon as Jon left the room and closed the cabin door behind him, she untied the ropes around her hands. Squinting, she tried to see the door but the room was pitch black. She sat in the darkness listening to the alarm then she pulled out her sunglasses. With a switch, the glasses switched to night vision. When the alarm abruptly stopped, her ears echoed from the ringing.

"Help!" Her voice reverberated against the walls of the room. The lack of circulation made the air around her thin and hot. She wanted out of that room more than anything.

"Come on. You can do this." She lowered herself out of the chair and down to the cold floor. No amount of pressing seemed to make the communication device work.

On her stomach, she pulled herself toward the door.

Suddenly the lights switched on, but no one entered the room. The crew must have rebooted the electrical system. Elissa rolled onto her back and looked up at the ceiling. She knew she was not moving fast enough. If only she had her chair... Tears of frustration filled her eyes and she beat her fists against the floor. Then, under the table behind some boxes, she saw a skateboard and realized Jon left that for her as a replacement for her wheelchair. With one roll, she returned to her stomach and perched, trying to balance on the skateboard. Finally, she was able to pull herself to the chair.

In the distance she could hear Morocco barking. In this hopeless and frustrating place, hearing Morocco reminded her she wasn't alone and she could get out of here.

"Hey girl. I'm coming."

Once she'd dragged herself, and the chair, to the door, she pushed the chair against it and climbed up. The handle didn't budge. She reached for her lock pick kit, but it was not there. It must have fallen out in the hallway when she came in. She took off her shoe and pulled out the file. Then she placed it in the door and visualized the lock. With a turn it clicked open and she gulped in the fresh air.

Once back on the floor, she set the skateboard, and pushed the chair outside the room before climbing back on the skateboard. The hallway consisted of gray metal grid walkways with metal stairs on either end leading to stairwell doors that, along with all the ship doors on this deck, had floor and cabin numbers stenciled on the doors. The hall walls went all the way up to another grid hallway. Each door had rounded corners directly to the floor, to provide a seal should the water attempt to invade the ship.

"Morocco, where are you?" she whisper-yelled.

She heard muffled barking from above her that seemed to reverberate but not get free. She slid off the chair and dragged it down the hall towards the stairs. The metal grate was hard, cold and the bumps dug into her legs, but the small holes in the grid pattern gave her an area to place her fingers into to give her traction to pull. Sitting on the first step, she hung the chair on her arm, set the skateboard one step ahead, and used the railing to pull herself up toward the landing. Every movement made a small noise that she was hoping no one from NERD-One could hear. When she was two steps from the top, she sat down on the step, threw the chair up onto the landing with a crash, and rubbed her legs to soothe the burning ache. Her energy was fading and she fought to regenerate it. Morocco barked every few minutes and that sound was keeping Elissa's hope of getting to Morocco and Christopher alive.

On the landing she slid up to the door. Hope filled her as she reached for the handle but she couldn't reach the knob. Morocco barked and scratched at the door.

"I'm here," Elissa moaned. She used the last of her strength to climb onto the chair and turn the latch. When the door opened, Morocco bounded over. She tilted her head, dropped Elissa's lock pick kit in her lap, and then sat down a distance away. If Morocco had been a person, Elissa would have sworn she was mad at her for not telling her everything. Morocco tilted her head and barked.

"Jon did that to you, not me. But you can be mad at me. I deserve it. Morocco, we got Jon in and Dad should be safe now – if we can only find him." Morocco tilted her head as she listened. "I'm sorry. I'd be mad at me, too."

Elissa rubbed her sore arms and wished she was closer to Christopher's location. Morocco almost knocked her off the chair, licking her face, barking, and wagging her tail.

Elissa zipped her pick kit in her pocket, sat back in the chair and surveyed the area around her. There was no sign of rescue. The large, open room was filled with a maze of large machines and pipes. A hissing of steam was coming from an area in the far corner and dampness hung in the air. This one room she wanted to spend no more time in than she had to. There were two steep flights of steps leading up to the exits and one leading to a hallway with two doors, one of which, she was conviced, was where Jon had entered to find Christopher on the cot. Her arms were too tired to climb any more stairs. Elissa sighed heavily. At the far end of the hallway was a freight elevator but she wasn't sure if she could get the grate entrance, that opened up and down instead of left to right, open far enough for her to gain access.

Morocco barked and nudged Elissa. Elissa pulled herself to the elevator, making sure to drag the chair with her. Morocco walked with Elissa to the freight elevator, where Elissa was able to press the bottom grate down and lift the top grate enough so both she and Morocco could clear it and enter the elevator. Morocco walked her over to the buttons, and soon they were on their way up to Christopher's floor. On the floor, with Elissa's direction, Morocco proceeded to W8. Elissa used the skateboard to negotiate and kept the chair in tow.

"Dad," Elissa hissed. "Are you in there?"

Silence. Her heart sunk thinking maybe Jon's plan hadn't gone well, and he was injured.

The door was locked so Elissa pulled out her picks and fought her tired and heavy hands to pick it. When she heard the latch click, she took a deep breath. All she had wanted for the past few months could be behind this door. Her hand shook as she pushed it open.

All of a sudden static buzzed through Elissa's ear. "Cough if you can hear me," Agent Larsson said.

"Coast is clear."

"Elissa are you okay?"

"We're fine," Elissa said.

"We have your location. We'll be right down."

Morocco carefully stepped into the room and walked towards a cot. As she approached, Elissa blinked and tried to focus on the man's familiar features. Christopher was lying on a cot with one leg hanging awkwardly off the side and the other handcuffed to the bed frame. There was blood across his chest. Tears filled her eyes.

"Dad," she said in a small voice, hoping he would sit up, answer, anything. *But just be okay. Please!* She froze, not wanting to make a sound that might suffocate any noise he might make.

Morocco stepped close to the cot so Elissa was within range to touch him, but she was scared to deal with the possibility he wasn't okay. Christopher lifted up his head to see her.

"Lissy, girl."

"You're not really bleeding, are you?" She reached towards the two blood patches on his chest; he gently grabbed her hand and squeezed it. His hand was warm as she held on to it.

"Nope. That Jon. Little bugg… terminated…shot me." He smiled, referring to the vest. He sat up.

Morocco barked toward the door.

"Someone's coming." With Elissa on her back, Morocco tip-toed to the door. Elissa carefully slid off onto the floor. The big muscular man, Todd, she thought Jon had called him, was lumbering up the steps to their location carrying a black body bag and a gun.

"Uncuff me and I'll…"

"I got this." Elissa threw her lock pick at him, reached into her pockets. She pulled out her licorices, speckle chews, her Cat-napper, taser and her trusty roll of duct tape.

"Morocco, let's get his attention and then take him down." Elissa quietly opened the door a crack.

"Lissy I can't get it..." Christopher frantically attempted to open the cuffs. One of his arms had a blood spot that was growing. She knew that the gunshot in his shirt was real, and he was indeed bleeding real blood from one area.

On the floor to the left of the door, she opened the package of speckles chews and placed four pieces in her mouth. The gum tasted like campfire, and when it smoked she placed it in the door crack and blew the smoke toward the stairs and hallway. She needed the man to be temporarily distracted, to hide her and Morocco from his view. The gum smoke should provide that.

"Give this to Dad." Elissa handed Morocco her case with the taser. Morocco carried it to him and then returned to Elissa.

"Best I can do, weapon-wise. Only use it if I get into trouble, deal?" Elissa met his gaze, like he used to do whenever he wanted to make sure she was listening.

"We, um...deal," he said reluctantly.

Elissa could hear the man's footsteps approaching.

Morocco growled quietly as the man approached the door. Christopher lay back on the bed as the man stepped into the room, disorientated and sputtered in the smoke. Elissa watched, heart racing, for her moment to take this man down. He set down the black body bag on the empty chair in the far corner, turning his back to both Morocco and Elissa.

"Morocco attack," Elissa whispered.

Morocco raced out of the smoke and charged for the man. She bit his arm with the gun, and a shot pierced the wall across the room.

Elissa picked up her Cat-napper and shot the man's shoulder.

Morocco jerked his arm and the gun flew out of his hand. He dropped to his knees and fell limply to the ground. Morocco held onto his arm.

Elissa pulled herself towards him and Christopher sat up on the bed, frantically trying to reach the gun. Elissa carefully picked it up and handed it to him.

"Morocco, halt." Elissa pulled herself closer to the man. Morocco stood watching him.

"Where did you learn that?" Christopher asked.

"Jon." Elissa pulled out her licorice ropes and tied up his arms and legs. She petted Morocco. "Good Morocco."

Morocco crouched on the floor for Elissa to get back on and then carried her over to the cot. She slid off Morocco's back and onto the cot next to Christopher. He was right there in front of her and despite his weight loss, it still was him. Relief washed over her as she quickly unlocked the cuff at his ankle and hugged him tightly. Then she pulled some gauze out of a vest pocket and wrapped up his arm tightly.

"It's just a flesh wound. Jon had to for my cover."

If only that made her feel better. She knew the hospital would give a press conference and to add to the legitimacy of his injuries, a gunshot would be necessary as the hospital couldn't be given the truth or asked to give false statements. They could embelish the truth perhaps, but there needed to be some grain of truth to make the events that had transpired on the ship legitimate.

"Dad, this is Morocco. Morocco, this is dad," she said, sliding back onto the dog.

"It's nice to meet you, Morocco." Morocco licked his hand. Then she walked Elissa to the folding gray chair in the corner of the room where Elissa got settled.

"What if something had gone wrong?" Christopher demanded. "We agreed you weren't going to get into this."

Elissa took a miniature bottle of water and a chocolate bar out of her pocket and threw them onto the cot. He opened the water and took a sip.

"*We* didn't decide anything," Elissa corrected as she made herself look him straight in the eye. After all she had been through she was not about to let him intimidate her.

He scowled at her. He had a beard and moustache; his hair was matted with his blood and his clothes appeared to be from an older, larger brother he'd never had. He slowly stood up, bracing himself against the cot. Then he walked toward her. She just sat there and watched him coming. She was overwhelmed by excitement that he was alive, maybe skinnier and weaker but that could all be fixed in time.

"I just didn't want you getting hurt," he said.

Anger built in her stomach, leaving her in utter confusion as to how she could be so glad to have him back and so angry all at the same time.

"Not get hurt? You lied to me! Our whole lives were nothing but lies," she said. Morocco moved to Elissa's side.

"We were trying to protect you." He knelt down next to where she was sitting.

"You did a great job of that." Elissa rubbed her legs. "How could you do this to us?" Tears streamed down her face.

"I ... I didn't mean ..." He reached to hug her.

"Don't touch me." She lunged away and fell onto the metal grate. Morocco stepped back while Christopher squatted down and reached his arms around her. Elissa pulled away and hit his arms with her fists.

"It's okay." He tried to hug her again. She finally gave in and buried her face against his shoulder. His skinny arms wrapped around her.

"Oh, Lissy. I'm so sorry." Tears left clean streaks in the dust caked on his face.

"I know. I love you, too."

For a moment the world around them disappeared.

"Is this the end of it? Of this life?" Elissa asked, hoping with all her might for the answer she wanted to hear but knowing the answer in her heart.

"Lissy, there are others that need to be stopped. Mr. Russel wasn't alone." He rubbed her arm.

"But after all we've gone through, how can you keep this up? It seems like a high price to pay when you could actually just be the singer and songwriter everyone believes you are."

"So you'll be returning home with me?" he asked.

"Most definitely, but my Madisyn classes start again after our week break."

"You won't be going back there. That life is too dangerous." The vein in his neck bulged.

Elissa's mouth dropped.

"That's not fair."

The last few sentences that entered her brain were almost a dream, had to be. He was telling her this life was too dangerous after the past few months she had been through. All that time he was being held, she was recovering and trying to find a way to bring him back.

Morocco barked and ran to the door.

"We'll talk about this later," Christopher said.

"No, we'll talk about this now. You don't get to make this decision for me. You're not giving up this life. You weren't here when I lost my dancing – lost my dream – lost my life. You just got back and have no idea what's best for me." She pushed him and tried to make some distance between him and her.

"We're approaching your cabin," Agent Larsson said into her communication device.

Agent Larsson and Sam entered the room, Christopher stepped away from Elissa as she wiped her face.

"Excuse me. Where did you last see Agent Williams?" Sam asked.

Agent Larson joined him.

Elissa responded to the two of them. "He's inside. He's succeeded at infiltrating NERD-One."

Agent Larsson's face turned red. "Agent Williams put you in danger to ... He sent me details of this mission just a few minutes ago. I assure you, if I had known of such a dangerous mission, I never would have permitted such a thing."

"I had Morocco, my gear, and Jon, uh, Agent Williams. I was safe, thank you very much," Elissa retorted, cocking her head to the left.

Christopher smiled at Agent Larsson.

Agent Larsson chuckled.

"You certainly are a Morris."

"I wanted to ensure Agent Williams' safety. When NERD-One connects to the net and loads Dad's tracker, Ice Rose will send out a signal and initiate a sniffer and worm on their system. You can hack into their network if Jon doesn't disengage it."

Sam helped Christopher to the door then returned to carry Elissa to the uncomfortable wheelechair in the hallway. Agent Larsson emptied items from a bag, one she thought was a detonation box, and handed Christopher the remote.

"Christopher we'll get you out a back door and to the location where you will rejoin the world. Tomorrow your publicity team is having a press conference," Agent Larsson said.

"Right now all I want is to be with my girls."

Elissa smiled as she was so glad to hear him say his girls. Her dad was standing right in front of her. If her arms and legs hadn't been aching she would have had to pinch herself to make sure she wasn't dreaming.

Twenty-Seven

Invitation

Day Seven

After spending the night together, Elissa's family headed to the hotel in Beverly Hills for the press conference. Thankfully, Elissa had managed to avoid the topic of Madisyn Academy.

"Anything I need to know for the conference?" Elissa asked, as they entered their room.

"Yesterday never happened," Stephanie said, winking at her.

"Honey, we'll all meet back here after the conference."

Christopher's press team joined them to prep him on what to say and apply their make-up. Evelyn Dawn, her dad's publicist, wearing a black business suit just off the cover of Vogue magazine, ensured they were all prepared. They watched the news on a small TV while they waited for the conference to begin. An anchorwoman with short blonde hair and glossed lips read the headlines.

"According to Michael Connelly from the California Highway Patrol, singer Christopher Morris was found yesterday walking along the Pacific Coast Highway at 7:00 p.m. He was taken to Cedars-Sinai Medical Center in stable condition. Evelyn Dawn, from Sandstone records, had this to say about Mr. Morris's condition:

> 'Christopher has sustained gun shot wounds, weight loss, muscle deterioration and has missing pockets in his memory, but he is resting comfortably and will be released tomorrow.'

"This ends an extensive four-month search for the singer. On Monday, May 1, an explosion rocked Treble Time Studios. Christopher Morris was inside along with his wife and teenage daughter and a family friend whose name has yet to be released."

The anchor was handed a sheet of paper by an off-screen producer.

"We'll be joining a press conference about Christopher Morris soon."

Christopher squeezed Elissa and Stephanie's hands and they walked into the press room together. Bright flashes blinded them as they were escorted to their table. Elissa was not a fan of press conferences as their questions always kept her family on their toes.

Morocco turned and staggered sideways from the flashes.

"It's okay." Elissa petted her and she settled down on the floor. Stephanie sat next to Elissa and they listened as the reporters, one at a time, asked questions about Christopher's last few months. Elissa was blown away at the acting Christopher used to convince the reports he was kidnapped, held in a house but he didn't know where, or by whom, and left by the highway for dead. She wondered how he kept the two worlds straight depending on who he was talking to. This was going to be their life now and she needed to get used to leading a double life – a life that promised to be very interesting.

A tall female reporter stood and asked, "Elissa, how is it having your dad home again?"

"Until yesterday, it was like a black cloud has been following us around. Something's been missing. Now everything's whole again." She turned to face Christopher and smiled.

As the conference ended, Elissa drove into the hallway knowing she was half an hour late to meet her team, and clicked the wheelchair on high speed and headed toward the hotel lobby. Her team was waiting for her in the high backed armchairs.

"Your dad rocks." Katherine gave Elissa a hug.

"He sure does."

"Can you tell us your undercover assignment?" Jack asked.

"Making things right…and reuniting families," Katherine offered as she hit Jack and smiled at Elissa.

"Glad you're back." Benjamin gave her a shy smile.

That smile made everything in her world feel in place, just like the way it had before the accident.

The hotel lobby was decorated with floral fabric wicker chairs and couches. On one of the brown leather couches a father was bouncing his three-year-old daughter in his lap.

Elissa smiled, knowing that now she would have Christopher back to share more moments. There were open spaces between white pillars, and the potted trees stretched all the way up to the ceiling, giving children obstacles to run around.

Katherine handed Elissa an envelope with her name on it.

They all went into the elevator area. In the large wall mirror, Elissa saw Jack holding two fingers above Katherine's head. He spotted her looking and then they shared a smile. By then Katherine caught on and gave Jack a shove. Not expecting it, he lost his balance and fell against a side table. A vase wobbled. Benjamin leapt over and grabbed it just before it tumbled off the table.

Once they reached their floor, Katherine led the way down the hallway, which was decorated with abstract paintings and rich wooden tables. Of all the hotel rooms Elissa had been in, during all Christopher's world tours, this one had the most interesting art. The faces had long and short features, giving the appearance of looking in a mirror at a carnival.

"Adjoining rooms rock," Katherine declared.

Elissa left them in the hall and entered her room to find Stephanie sitting at a round table, with the sun shining in on her hair from the window. She was reading one of her large chemistry books and glanced up to greet Elissa. The simplicity of seeing Stephanie sitting and reading a book in the sunshine, actually having peace of mind and being relaxed, was a snapshot Elissa hadn't seen in a long time.

"There's a dress for you on the bed," Stephanie said as she referred to a garment bag.

"I'm gonna take a shower, Mom," Elissa announced, heading for the bathroom.

When Elissa returned to the main room, Morocco was sitting by the bed in a formal black satin vest with a white crystal and emerald trim. A strange woman was grooming her soft fur. Not that Elissa could be sure, but she thought Morocco was loving the pampering, maybe not the outfit, but definitely the attention.

Stephanie pointed to a medium height, slim woman with black and pink striped hair.

"This is Jane."

She pointed to a short woman, wearing a leather dress, with tightly braided hair. "And Dominique. They're here to give us some style."

Jane held Elissa's hair off her neck.

"I'm thinking an upsweep with curls."

"Sounds great," Elissa said as she was thrilled to have a stylist making her hair look the best it could.

She and Stephanie watched a TV talk show and critiqued some of the outfits the celebrities were wearing while the women styled their hair and applied their makeup.

"What do you think?" Jane asked as she held up a mirror to allow Elissa to view the back.

Elissa looked in the mirror at her long curly hair cascading down from a diamond clip.

"It's perfect," Elissa grinned thinking how she was going to blow Benjamin's mind. She had definite potential when she dressed up.

"You look so beautiful," Stephanie said beaming with pride. "Your father is going to be so proud."

"Thanks. I think." Stephanie brushed her hands down her dress and took one last glance in the mirror at her figure.

The two women finished up with some hair spray, packed up their cases and left.

"Where's Dad?" Elissa asked.

Stephanie lifted up her shoulders. "He had some loose ends to wrap up."

"Oh." Elissa scowled out the window at the smog hanging over the view. Stephanie strolled over and put her hand on Elissa's shoulder.

"Don't worry. He promised. Dad wouldn't miss your big day for anything in the world."

Elissa pulled the dress bag over to her lap. She unzipped it to find a floor length green organza dress with beading across the neck and a matching shawl. Her mom helped her to change into the dress.

"So, anyone special you want to dance with tonight?" Stephanie asked.

"Maybe. His name is Benjamin," Elissa admitted as she tried to stop a smile that was creeping across her face.

"Butterflies or drool?" Stephanie reached into the bag to get her shoes.

"Moooom. Drool? Yuk." Elissa laughed.

"I had both for your father."

Elissa scrunched up her face to erase the mental image. Suddenly there was a knock at the door, which made Elissa jump. Her nerves were still a bit raw from the past few days.

"I'll get it." Stephanie said. Morocco followed her to the door.

Katherine strutted into the room in a blue satin dress, hands on her hips. She turned like a super model and the sun beamed off the pearls in her hair. A tall woman, around Stephanie's age Elissa guessed, with flowers in her cinnamon hair, strolled into the room behind Katherine.

"This is my mom, Mrs. Hamari Bennison."

Both Elissa and Stephanie shook Mrs. Bennison's hand.

"Nice to meet you," Elissa said as she was so happy to watch Katherine with her mom. NERD-One had not managed to destroy another family despite everything they had tried to do.

"Miss Morris, thanks for helping get us out," Mrs. Bennison said.

"It was Jon," Elissa said as she didn't want to take credit for the work Jon had done.

She left the mothers and met Katherine at the window. "We look hot," Katherine said. Elissa giggled. Katherine was right. They *did* look hot.

"Let's go, ladies," Stephanie said.

Morocco stood next to Elissa as they followed the chattering mothers.

"Think the guys are wearing monkey suits?" Katherine asked as she strutted.

The ballroom was softly lit with chandeliers that reflected rainbow colors on the walls. Students were seated at round tables surrounding the dance floor. One large, long table sat at the top of the dance floor. The walls had silver stars on them, and a DJ was playing music. Only a few students were dancing so far. Elissa swallowed and was a bit nervous to enter the room. Her fate at attending the Ocean-Alias campus was all going to be revealed in a few minutes. She felt stupid for acting as if this was important to her, since after the past few months and trying to find Christopher, her priorities had changed. But for this space in time, for her future, now that Christopher was safe, she wanted more than anything to train on the Ocean-Alias.

"You hang with your team and we'll meet up after the ceremony," Stephanie said as she rubbed Elissa's arm and smiled.

"There they are." Katherine pointed to a table and bounced on her tip toes.

As the girls made their way to the table, the boys stood up to reveal the full effect of their clothing choices. Benjamin was wearing a black tuxedo with a blue bowtie and cummerbund.

"Hello ladies," Jack said.

"You both look..." Benjamin blinked twice. "Wow." He blushed as he moved a chair out for Elissa.

"Not bad yourselves," Katherine replied. The guys stuck out their chests and smiled.

"Dance with me." Jack grabbed Katherine's hand and pulled her towards the dance floor.

"I'm going to find my girl friend." Kalan headed towards a table at the far end of the room.

"So, do you think the big hero could dance with me?" Benjamin asked. His face turned red as he looked at her shoes.

Breathe, Elissa. She calmly answered, "I'd love to."

The beat of a fast song made the speakers vibrate. Benjamin and Elissa joined Katherine and Jack on the dance floor. It had been too long since Elissa felt herself give in to a beat. Dancing felt so natural, but in a totally different way than it used to. Katherine and Elissa exchanged smiles. After two upbeat songs, the music volume decreased.

"Guess that's our hint," Jack said, leading the group back to the table.

When everyone was seated, Agent Larsson began his presentation.

"Welcome students, staff, family members and alumni. Congratulations on all your achievements and for making it through the first week at Madisyn Academy. After the award presentation there will be dinner and dancing. Please let me say how very proud we are that all but one team succeeded at the last task. You all show great promise as agents. When your team is called, please come up and accept your award. Our third place prize goes to team thirteen from London Yard."

The team members went up and accepted their award. Elissa clapped and surveyed her parent's table. The chair next to Stephanie was still empty. Her heart sank into her chest to think Christopher was just back to them and already he was missing in her life.

"Congratulations to team thirteen and London Yard. Now team five from Sydney Arch, please come up."

The team raced up to the front of the room and Malina grabbed the award out of Agent Larsson's hand. The volume of the applause was decidedly lower than it was for the third place team. Elissa clapped loudly and was relieved to know Malina had a safe place to be. She knew Mr. Jenkins, a.k.a. Mr. Russel, was still out there somewhere and Malina would never be entirely safe in the regular world until he was put away.

"Congratulations team five and Sydney Arch. Now, with the best time of the Academy Games and a complete removal of the computer virus, let's all congratulate team fifty from Edmonton Ridge. Please come up and accept your award."

No way! Elissa smiled and fought the tears of excitement from entering her eyes. Elissa, Jack, Katherine, Benjamin and Kalan all looked at each other in amazement.

"Let's go," Katherine cried. Morocco followed the team up to the front of the room. Elissa glanced out at the students. Everyone was on their feet. For the first time since she could dance on her own two legs, she felt accepted in a world she used to walk through with grace.

She slowly turned her head towards her parents' table, dreading Christopher's absence. But he was standing and clapping. Tears filled her eyes.

"Would the other top teams join us at the front of the room?" Agent Larsson asked.

He picked up a stack of leather portfolios and walked towards the teams. He opened one of the portfolios and showed it to the audience.

"Each member of the top three teams will receive a certificate of acceptance for their first year at Madisyn Academy Ocean-Alias Campus."

Elissa stared at her certificate.

The bright flashes of all the photographers kneeling down on the floor reminded her of the red carpet at the Grammys and she knew how Christopher felt.

With flash spots in their eyes, the team returned to the table, high-fiving the whole way.

"Now I'll hand the floor over to Agent Wright to announce the students being accepted for our aviation program," Agent Larsson announced.

Agent Wright strolled up to the podium and took the mic. "Please come to the front of the room when I call your name." As she read the names, one by one, the accepted students beamed with pride. Elissa's heart sank a little bit as each new student walked to the front. If there was an activity she was meant to do, she was absolutely sure flying was it.

Then Agent Wright said, "Elissa Morris."

Christopher gave Elissa the thumbs up, whistled and clapped. As she stood in front of the room, the joy she felt was almost overwhelming. She had Christopher back and after months of trying to find a life beyond dancing, she had finally figured out where and what she was going to do. Soon Benjamin and Jack joined her among the future pilots.

When Agent Wright turned the floor over to Agent Sullivan, Katherine, Jack and Kalan were accepted into the field operative program.

Agent Larsson walked back to the podium. "Dinner will be served in half an hour. Feel free to mingle."

Benjamin sat in a chair next to Elissa.

"Elissa, there's something I've been wanting to ask you. I was wondering...well, would you..." He paused to swallow.

"Spit it out, Agent," Elissa teased.

He lifted his shoulders.

"Would you go to the welcome dance with me?"

Suddenly, the butterflies that had been twittering about in Elissa's stomach disappeared. "I'd love to, but are you sure? This will wreck your relationship with Miss Malina."

"That relationship is all in her mind. Totally not mutual," he assured her, taking her hand.

The butterflies rushed back, but not just to her stomach. Elissa's whole body tingled. When she'd heard her name announced for the aviation program, she couldn't wait to get back up in the air. But now, nothing could have made her move an inch.

Other Titles by Fireside Publications

- *THE FURAX CONNECTION* by Stephen L. Kanne
- *THE CLEANSING* by B.F. Eller, Ph.D
- *THE FIND* by James J. Valko
- *ESSAYS: On Living with Alzheimer's Disease* by Lois Wilmoth-Bennett, Ph.D.
- *18 DAYS IN SEPTEMBER* by Allen Hunt, Ph.D
- *THE COST OF JUSTICE* by Mike Gedgoudas
- *TEXAS JUSTICE* by Judith Groudine Finkel
- *LOVE TAG* by Peter Shianna
- *THE LONG NIGHT MOON* by Elizabeth Towles
- *INDEPENDENCE DAY PLAGUE* by Carla L. Suson
- *THE CRYSTAL ANGEL* by Olivia Claire High
- *BEYOND FOREVER: Experiences From Past Lives* by Taylor Shaye
- *ABOVE HONOR: Rachel's Story* by Donald Himelstein

For more information or to order any of the above books, please visit www.firesidepubs.com or contact:

Fireside Publications
1004 San Felipe Lane
Lady Lake, Florida 32159